HEA HEARTACHES

Wesley Parker

ADVANCED PRAISE FOR HEADPHONES
AND HEARTACHES

"Wesley Parker has a unique way of warming your
heart even as he breaks it. Headphones and
Heartaches is soulfully musical, painfully real, and
full of hope.

MARYANN TIPPETT, AUTHOR OF *PAIRS
WITH PINOT* AND *THE SHAPE OF US*

"Wesley Parker's sophomore title is a sucker punch to
the soul with its unyielding story, unflinching humor,
and a stellar cast of characters who linger with you
long after the books' conclusion. This story will rip
your heart out and put it back only to rip it out once
again."

LEIGHANN HART, AUTHOR OF *LOVING
ROSENFELD*

Headphones and Heartaches never misses a beat, its plot as carefully crafted as one of Percy's mixtapes. This incredible novel will make leave you breathless – with laughter, nostalgia, and, as the title promises, with heartache. But most of all, it will help you to see the world as Percy sees it: full of complicated people, deserving of kindness. If there was ever a must-read book, this is it.

SARAH NEOFIELD, AUTHOR OF NUMBER
EIGHT CRISPY CHICKEN

Wesley Parker invites you into the world of the foster care system and doesn't sugarcoat it one bit in this coming of age novel. Parker's accurate portrayal of the painful realities of growing up before your time gives you hope that we have the power to overcome the obstacles thrown at us in life.

MATTHEW HANOVER, AUTHOR OF *NOT FAMOUS* AND *NOT DRESSED*

For every child that was ever placed into foster care.

ONE

FIGHT OR FLIGHT

"Do you know why I'm here, Perseverance?" the social worker asks, momentarily distracting me from the reality of my situation. It's a stupid question, one adults are prone to asking as a way of reaffirming their positions of authority. We both know why he's here, and under different circumstances I'd say something slick in response. But hospitals aren't the place for one-liners, even the genius kind.

My eyes leave my mother's hospital bed and meet the social worker's. His badge is clipped onto his shirt, just left of the visitor sticker, introducing him as Alexander Parsons. He'd pass for any other run of the mill social worker, except he's wearing a flamingo-colored blazer that's louder than a Rolling Stones concert in the seventies. He seems nervous, which is odd considering that I'm gonna be the one dealing with whatever he comes up with. I ease the tension and my fear in one shot.

"Well, you're not one of her doctors, and I just happen to be a sixteen year old sitting alone next to his mother after a heroin overdose, so I'm guessing you're here on behalf of the

State of New Jersey." He smiles sadly and nods. "What client number am I in your case load?"

Alexander perks up at this. "You're actually my first client," he says, as if that's supposed to make me feel warm and fuzzy inside. "I got my license last week."

"Yay." I deadpan.

While he searches for a folder, I glance at Momma again, the machines doing the heavy work as she rests peacefully, oblivious to what's unfolding inches from her bedside. This wasn't the first time she overdosed—far from it—but seeing the one person that loved you unconditionally clinging to life by a thread is still as uncomfortable as the first time I sat by her bedside. While society will portray her as another statistic in the war on drugs, it's an offensive representation of who she is as a person, and on a more personal level, as a mother.

"We're poor, but we don't gotta go anywhere looking sorry," she'd say every morning before school when I'd dare to leave wherever we were staying with stained pants. She'd hide the stains by wrapping my sweatshirt around my waist, leaving me looking respectable enough to avoid being the butt of schoolyard jokes. After school I was required to spend time at the local library while she "worked." The internet login was timed by the hour, with a maximum of two sessions per day. She drilled in me that the first session would always be devoted to my studies because our circumstances weren't an acceptable excuse for failure. The second session I could use to engage in the two things I cared about as much as her, music, and writing.

The everyday struggle of trying to get by left little room for friendships, so I filled the void by discovering new music and writing my feelings out, figuring that spilling them on the page would hide them from my face. So I'd go on Pitchfork, find a new artist, then see if the library had their albums to check out. When I managed to get a couple dollars together, I'd go to the thrift store where the selection was better, the drawback being that sometimes a new album came at the expense of clothing. A worthy trade-off, in my opinion.

I can feel the lump swelling in my throat as it hits me that our run is over. But, like most of my life up to this point, the situation doesn't leave time for sentiments, and I refuse to give the State—especially a newbie with an atrocious looking sports coat—the satisfaction of telling a story over Thanksgiving dinner about how he "saved" a kid from the inner city. Nice as Alexander is, I'm not in the business of wasting his time.

"Look, you seem like your heart is in the right place, so I'll be upfront with you," I say.

He stops his search and eyes me suspiciously.

"Wherever you place me I'm just gonna run anyway...just figured I'd save you some time."

He doesn't even flinch, and that both surprises and intrigues me. I'd expect a brand new social worker to panic at the suggestion of losing their first client, but he just takes his glasses off and joins me next to Momma's bed. "Why?"

"The only person that's ever cared about me is touch and go right now; I don't have anybody else." I place my belongings in the reusable Walmart bag slowly and meticulously, giving me time to consider my next move. He showed up at the worst time, because dinner at the shelter is over by now and the beds aren't far behind.

"You have me," he says with conviction, his voice sounding like a booming speaker in the small confines of the hospital room.

"I don't even know you."

"That's fair, but I think we have more in common than you know."

I suck my teeth at him, his words sounding like every other adult that's come in and out of my life, each one rehashing the same lines as a way to build rapport with me, ignoring the fact that they're going home to a warm bed at the end of the night, while I'll be hoping to find a rock sharp enough to open a can of Campbells chicken broth. "You're really laying it on thick, Mr. Alexander. You should pace yourself and save those lines for a kid that's actually buying them."

He finds this funny. "Tough crowd...all right, lets try this. I'll make an attempt to guess what your plans are after you walk out of this room. If I'm wrong, then I'll take you out to eat at the restaurant of your choice and drop you off wherever you wanna go."

"Really? That easy huh?" I say, relief rushing through my body because I now only had to worry about my meal after the next one instead of both.

"But..."

Shit.

"...If I'm right, you agree to consider why I'm here, and just so you don't leave here empty handed, I'll introduce you to my favorite restaurant. What do you say?"

"You can introduce me to anyone except the person that sold you that jacket."

We share a laugh at this and the tension evaporates from the room. I've never had a real friend, but if I do find one, Mr. Alexander is the example of what I hope to find. We shake hands to seal the deal and I can almost taste the four course platter from the corner store.

"Okay," he says, taking his jacket off and checking the time. "It's currently four pm on a Saturday, which means Carlos is probably layering the macaroni and cheese with Kraft singles right about now."

My jaw couldn't drop any harder if you tied a forty pound dumbbell to my bottom lip. It's one thing to guess what a shelter is having on any given day. Hell, Momma always said even a broken clock is right twice a day. But to guess the name of the chef, and his lack of understanding in making proper macaroni and cheese? Odds like that are reserved for American orphans hoping to be adopted by Angelina Jolie. My reaction doesn't go unnoticed, and he continues.

"But seeing how late it is, you wouldn't make it there on time anyway. So, I was gonna say you were heading to..." he checks his file, "...four-fifty-eight Chelton Ave, Unit A."

I breathe a sigh of relief, because the address he has is one of the many places we've been evicted from, so technically he's wrong. And just like that, I can taste the sweetness of the fried plantain dipped in gravy from the chicken again. I might even get an orange soda to wash it down.

"However, I couldn't help but notice the particular care you took when gathering your shopping bag, and I wondered why a kid whose mother was rushed to the hospital would have time to gather so much stuff, especially when she overdosed down by Transition Park, commonly referred to as—"

"Tent City," I interject. The shift in mood is drastic as the feeling of triumph slowly gives way to dread. "Mr. Alexander—"

"Call me Alex."

"Okay...Alex. How did you know we were..." I trailed off. Being homeless was embarrassing enough without having to hear it from my own mouth. I'd gotten pretty good at keeping myself out and about during the day. It's harder to wallow in your circumstances when you're out amongst the general public. I even coined the term "residentially challenged" as a way to feel a little better about it.

Alex takes a seat on the floor next to me. "You know, the

worst thing about being poor isn't going without necessities," he said. "It's the world around you that makes you feel as if you're the only one going through it."

If there's one relevant skill I've learned from living on the streets, it's the ability to judge a persons' intentions and discern if they were genuine or not. Between the men that came in and out of my mother's life and the various residents of Tent City, I'd gotten pretty good at figuring people out. He didn't seem like the cookie cutter social workers I'd met before, the ones that spew lines straight out of a training manual.

Or maybe he just hasn't been in the game long enough to become jaded like most of them do. But I could tell he'd been through some trauma by how he spoke. Take the line about Carlos, the chef. On the surface it's a throwaway line, but to me its an invitation. When living in poverty, words are used as sparingly as our resources. You learn to say a lot with the minimum amount of words. Alex had just told me that he understood my life without having to use those words, and in turn it resonated with me on a deeper level. That and I lost the bet so now I have to listen to his pitch.

I go to Momma's bedside one more time to say goodbye. They said she had a chance of pulling through, but I donn't know the next time I'll be able to see her. I think she knew this day would come, and that our life together up until this point was her preparing me for navigating the world without her. But under the surface there was always resentment. With every place we got thrown out of, every bathroom or aban-doned home we shacked up in, the resentment blossomed inside of me. She held me to a higher standard with my grades, but didn't hold herself to the same ones as a mother. With a peck on her forehead, I table those feelings like I always do and shuffle to meet Alex at the door.

"Oh my God, are you hurt?" he asks, noticing my awkward gait.

"What?"

"You're limping. Should you see a doctor as well?"

I burst out laughing at this because its so common. I reach into my hooded sweatshirt and pull out my CD player. "I couldn't afford the one with anti-skip protection, so I walk like that so my music isn't interrupted."

"You're an interesting kid, Perseve—"

"Percy. People call me Percy."

"Wow," he says. "Was that a real revelation I just got out of you?"

I suck my teeth, mildly annoyed at this game everyone enjoys playing with me. "Let me give you some advice that I think will help you in this career path."

"Shoot."

"When you spend time trying to get a kid to open up, you shouldn't chastise them when they finally do."

"Noted."

We each grab our bags and I hold the door for him, sneaking one last peek at Momma, swearing that the lessons she taught me weren't in vain, before closing the door and heading for the elevators.

TWO

A DEAL IS A DEAL

If you're coming east over the bridge from Philadelphia, you'll see the sign welcoming you to Camden with the slogan 'Experience the Rebuild.' Well, I've been in this city my whole life and apparently the construction was delayed because it's only gotten worse. Being a resident of Camden is like being a fan of a small market sports team: you're constantly sold a vision of a brighter future, complete with 3D renderings and the pomp and circumstance that accompanies any politician. But the future never becomes the present, and by the time you realize you've been hoodwinked, the current mayor has either reached his term limit, or was fighting a federal indictment like three of our last seven mayors.

The city itself sits on the edge of New Jersey, with the towering skyscrapers of Center City Philadelphia visible from across the water feeling at times, like a promised land that was just out of my reach. I imagined the people in the towers would look down on us and describe the city like Mufasa described the 'shadowy place' to Simba in The Lion King.

While Philadelphia sits on one side of Camden, on the opposite side, directly to the East sits Cherry Hill. While geographically closer than Philadelphia, it somehow still felt further away. Both cities are housed under Camden County, but the day to day reality couldn't be more different. Cherry Hill was an affluent suburb, with residents that included Philadelphia sports figures and other well-off citizens with egos just as big as their athletic neighbors. After spending time reading about the other cities in Camden County, I came away feeling like we were living in a twisted science experiment, like the powers that be wanted to see how much shit someone could wallow in before they finally snap.

While there used to be a burgeoning steel industry, all that's left of the glory days are abandoned mills, and the businesses that did stay bleed the city dry in tax credits while finding people from outside the city to fill the decent paying positions. Tourism is non-existent, mainly because it doesn't account for the suburban kids that come in to cosplay the urban experience and sample the fentanyl-laced heroin before retreating back to their manicured lawns and well-funded neighborhoods.

But in spite of all that, Camden has a certain charm about it. It's a fairly close knit community of hardworking people that take pride in their city while making the best of what they got. Neighborhoods have block parties in the summer that go off without a hint of violence, an amphitheatre that's a prime time spot on most music tours during the summer—not that I could ever afford a concert, and one of the best hospitals in the region that's saved my mother's life more times than I can count.

The problem is the city is usually described by people too scared to actually visit, and revel in making the city sound like an American version of Fallujah. When Camden County residents try to explain the high property taxes, our city is often cited as the reason. I imagine that other impoverished areas are portrayed the same, but I haven't been outside the city long enough to find out.

However, there's one place that brings a positive light on Camden, and it just so happens to be Alex's favorite spot to eat at.

Donkey's Place has been on the same corner since 1943, serving cheesesteaks so good—at least I've heard—it allowed us to flip the bird at the folks across the bridge in Philadelphia. It's practically a landmark, the one business that didn't flee to Cherry Hill after the deindustrialization of the city, and in turn, it thrived through the years with a loyal clientele and word of mouth marketing that brought pride to a city that's been the Quasimodo of New Jersey for my whole life.

I walked slowly behind Alex, nodding at the patrons as if I were a regular, like I'd learned to do over the years. It's funny how a smile and a nod makes people feel like you belong. If it weren't for my bag, nothing would seem amiss. Alex mercifully left his jacket in the car—it wasn't thrown in a fire like it should have been—along with his badge which surprised me, but I was thankful for.

The setup is fairly simple: two tables with barstools to the left, a long bar leading to the back on the right, where there are tables with a more private feel. One deep breath and I understand the hype that validated this place being on my bucket list, and I haven't even tasted the food yet. The waitress asks for our drink orders and I instantly became nervous. I want a soda, but want to preserve my dignity in case he told me our deal was only for food.

Alex seems to sense this.

"Your cheesesteak is amazing on its own," he says to the waitress. "But the bottled cream soda takes it to another level. What do you say, Percy?"

I'm too busy breathing a sigh of relief to respond, so I just nod sheepishly.

She leaves us with the menus and goes to grab our drinks.

"I'll pay you back one day," I say.

He finds this funny. "It was part of our deal. Besides, I'm not really one to count favors." He studies the menu for a second, only because there isn't much of a menu. "I don't know what you've been through, but I need you to know you can let your guard down around me."

"It's gonna take more than a cheesesteak for that to happen."

"All right, what would make you comfortable?"

Its frustrating because I can't get a read on him. I'm used to adults with motives that are easy to deduce, coupled with a style of communication thats one dimensional enough that it makes me tune them out. At this point I figure he's either genuine, or an Academy Award winning actor and in the wrong career field—not to mention severely underpaid. What's undeniable is that he's making an effort, so I decide until I know for sure if he was full of it, I'd have to play the game a bit longer.

"Can we start with why you're here? I mean, that wasn't my mother's first overdose, and the other social workers were ecstatic to keep their caseloads light."

"Does the name Devontae Bell mean anything to you?"

I laugh before I can catch myself because it finally makes sense. "Any impoverished kid that reads the news knows that name. He's also part of the reason your presence unnerves me."

"They fucked that up," he says, the pain in his voice so real you would've thought Devontae Bell was his own son. It also was a check in the 'Alex is genuine' column.

While I laughed at his question, the name he spoke, and

ultimately what happened to him, sends chills down the spine of any kid with a home life bad enough to put them on the radar of Alex's department. Devontae Bell was a ten-year-old placed into the foster care system, like thousands of others each year. Nothing out of the ordinary.

He was dead before he turned eleven. Starved and tortured by his foster parents.

The headlines sent the state scrambling for cover. They found that on top of not making the required weekly visits, his social worker falsified reports of contact with him, when in reality she hadn't seen him in months. Officials from every government office in the State vowed to reform the system. However, the only thing worse than the government screwing up is them trying to fix it. Instead of taking the opportunity to make changes to the foundation of serving kids that have already drawn a shitty hand, they made that single worker the fall person and moved more money into the department's budget. It's like building a boat with a gaping hole in it, then firing the captain when it inevitably sinks and a passenger drowns. That case made me believe that even if my mother passed, I'd be better off living alone on the streets. Being homeless meant living with a lot of unknowns, and over time I'd learn to trust my senses and become comfortable with the unknown. My mother named me Perseverance for a reason.

"With all due respect, Alex," I start, "you're the sixth case worker I've had, and all of them ignored my situation because they didn't wanna do the paperwork. So excuse me if I'm not welcoming you as some long lost guardian angel."

"I'm not asking for that, Percy. I'm just asking you to let me help you."

"Taking me away from my mom and making me someone else's supplementary income isn't my definition of helping."

"I'm not like them, I'm...different."

"How so?"

"Because I've been you."

Right as he says this, our waitress returns with the sodas and takes our meal orders. We order cheesesteaks and fries with all the fixings, and after the waitress leaves we just stare at each other. I'm fuming inside, because after thinking he was legit, he pulls the 'I've been in your shoes' card that adults think is the all access pass into the VIP section of my mind. Unfortunately, I'm also starving and sitting in a place I've only dreamed of having a meal in, so I stay out of necessity. I say nothing, drinking my soda and enjoying the sensation in my stomach as it goes down.

Losing my Religion by R.E.M. played softly on the old speakers, just loud enough so I could know the tune, but not enough to know which verse was playing. I had a copy of that album, well, a burned copy of it anyway, but when we were kicked out of our last apartment—while I was at school no less —I arrived to find our stuff on the curb, pilfered through by the addicts. The stereo I left it in was worth enough at the pawn shop for an addict to sell for a fix, so my copy of Out of Time by R.E.M. became another casualty of the opioid epidemic. I pulled out my composition notebook and jotted a note to remind me to replace it.

"I was eight when they took me," Alex says suddenly. "October thirtieth, nineteen-ninety-six. They called me out of class, and the moment I saw Ms.Deidre..." He trails off.

"You remember the date?"

"My mom had saved a little bit of our check to make sure I had the ninja costume I wanted. Never got a chance to wear it though. Also, it was California, and I remember the weather had just started to change."

I'd like to jump in and tell him to stop wasting his breath, but Momma always told me to listen to understand instead of respond. So I do.

Unlike me he had a sibling, one sister in a wheelchair with cerebral palsy, and on nights his mother would pass out drunk without feeding them, he'd scrounge through parked cars for spare change, hoping to find enough for a platter from the corner store. What connects with me is how he speaks of his mom, never talking down about her, instead speaking with an empathy that touches the depths of my soul because I've finally met someone that understands my life, at least on the surface level, though I suspect it's deeper than that.

He stayed in foster care until he emancipated and went off to college. By that time his mother was clean and regained custody of his sister. He counted three foster homes, and spoke glowingly about them, reminding me of the first half of the movie Goodfellas when Scorsese made you think being a gangster was the best way to live.

"We're not the same," I say. "I get that our mothers struggled with addiction and poverty, but you're missing a pretty big difference."

"Do tell."

"You were eight, I'm almost sixteen," I explain, noticing the waitress gathering our order from the kitchen. "You were just a cute kid that was dealt a bad hand and needed a home. I look like a threat that needs a place to stay. So this idea that I'm going on some grand adventure is bullshit. Pardon my French."

He takes a long drink. "I'm not gonna let anything happen to you, Percy. I promise."

"I know you're not...because I'm not going. If that means you aren't gonna cover my meal anymore, let me know so I can bail before the food gets here."

"Dinner was on me, you're good." He finishes his soda.

"Let's table this conversation for now, but while we're eating think of one thing...it can be anything... that'll make you come with me."

I agree just as the waitress places our food on the table. Part of the allure in a Donkey's cheesesteak is the presentation: its served on a poppy seed bun, as opposed to a long roll anywhere else. Its cut in half, a small but significant detail because its tantalizing seeing the steak and cheese melted together like they were determined to take peanut butter and jelly's spot as the greatest food combination of all-time. The fries are the thick, steak cut fries that I love but rarely indulge in, with a sprinkling of seasoning, the specks glistening in the lights, though I may have just been so hungry it seemed that way. With one bite I understand immediately how they'd managed to stay in business so long. Soon after I start rocking, my eyes closed as I decide that losing the bet is now in the top five best things that ever happened to me. I pull out my composition book and make a note to visit again when I have the money.

"That's the second time you've pulled that out, you like writing?" Alex asks between bites.

"A little bit. Sometimes my mind moves so fast I forget things," I reply with a full mouth. "Writing helps me slow the world down and stay in the moment. It's too complicated to explain."

He thinks on this for a second, then hits me with something I wasn't expecting. "Well, this place doesn't close for another two hours, I'm all ears if you want."

Alex had told me his life story, and I had no intention of reciprocating because I'd lived it already. But this I could talk about.

"It's kind of a hodgepodge really," I say. "Some pages are ideas for mixtapes, other pages have places I've been, food I've enjoyed..." I look down at a page lamenting the loss of my stereo. "...things I've lost. I just feel like...I don't know...like, if I get my dreams and feelings down on paper the world can't take them away from me. It's like a North Star that keeps me fighting everyday. You ever have something like that?"

He nods. "Newspapers. I read them every morning, well, when I could get access to them. But here's the kicker, I only read the national and world sections." He laughs at my quizzical look. "There was a method to my madness. Part of the reason neighborhoods like ours stay the way they do is because the inner city makes you believe the world is only as big as your neighborhood. Think about it; think of all the neighbors you've known that have spent their entire lives here, they don't know anything else. When I read newspapers, specifically the sections that covered topics outside of my surroundings, I realized I had it all wrong."

"What do you mean?"

"The world actually begins when you leave your neighborhood."

"And let me guess. You're my savior that's come to rescue me from this place?"

He chuckles at this. "If I knew I could make a living being a savior, I'd have chosen a more lucrative career path. Besides, you could, as you so eloquently put it...run." He threw another french fry in his mouth. "I'm asking that you trust me and give it a—"

"I want a home," I say, firmly.

"A home?"

"Not one of those group homes where I'm herded like cattle in the back of a van from place to place. I want a place where someone will actually know my name. You give me that, I'll give you a year to get me back with my mom, assuming she lives."

"You want normalcy."

"Normal for me died the day my mother popped her first vein."

He nods at this, and I knew he understood. "I can't promise a reunion with your mom. A lot of that comes down to her, and at the end of the day I care about your well being. But I can promise you'll always have someone to talk to and that you're not gonna be alone."

It was a test, and he'd passed with flying colors. I knew he couldn't promise me that I would go back home, but most adults will promise you the world because they believe it gains them your trust. Alex had kept it real and I felt like I finally knew the kind of person he was. Having someone like him is the difference between feeling scared and feeling hopeful about the situation. I'd give him a year to get me back home, a fair amount of time that will allow me to save some money to go on the run in case it got weird. I agreed to his terms and he excused himself to make a phone call.

"Hey, Alex, one more thing," I say as he's walking away. "You guys don't just show up without someone reporting it. Do you know who made the call?"

"I have my suspicions," he says, not looking up from his phone. "But it's an anonymous hotline, so it could have been anybody. Probably a sympathetic nurse or something. Finish your food, I gotta find you a home."

He steps out and I wrap the rest of my sandwich and fries up in a plastic bag for later, unsure of the timing of my next meal. I hit play and was greeted with music by Joy Division, a band I discovered in the bargain bin at the thrift shop. The fast paced lyrics of 'Disorder' always spoke to me, but today, the lyrics about being normal just hit different.

At the end of the song I feel a hand on my shoulder. Alex is back, and I know its time to leave. He assures me that he's held up his end of the bargain, and that he'll fill me in as we drove. I gather my things while he pays, deciding once and for all that I'm all in, before I meet him at the register and follow him to the car. As we turn onto the highway I take one last look at the only home I've ever known. Bleak as it is, I miss it already, but I can feel the sense of excitement bubbling inside me, too. My stomach is full, and I have three whole bars left on my CD player batteries. With my leftover sandwich and my cd case, I feel like I could conquer the world.

It's what Momma would want.

THREE

8 YEARS BEFORE THE OVERDOSE

It's funny how you can remember the seminal moments in your life and the smallest details that accompany them. The first time I saw my mother shoot up qualifies as one such event. But life changing events don't come out of nowhere, and eight years later, I could kick myself for not recognizing the signs sooner. It was a Friday, which to a kindergartner was like a ticket to Willy Wonka's chocolate factory.

"Okay, class, make sure you have all your things and line up at the door," Mrs. Fales said. We didn't move at the speed she was hoping for. "Never thought I'd see the day where kindergarteners moved slower than me, on a Friday no less."

Friday was the magic word as we all picked up our pace, knowing the sooner we lined up, the sooner we could start our weekend. I threw my pencil case and folder in my Pokémon backpack and took my place at the end of the line, since I could never make it to school in enough time to beat the other kids who signed up for line leader. I double checked that everything was in its place and tightened the straps so tight I could hear the pencils rattling in the case.

"What are you doing this weekend, Percy?" a voice asked

from behind me. I turned to see Mikey, my table mate, sneering at me. It was the third time he'd asked me that day by my count, which I knew because we'd been working on counting numbers that day. He was going to the Eagles game, and was determined to drill it into my brain.

"I'm not going to an Eagles game, if that's what you're asking."

"Okay, then what are you doing?"

Truth is, I didn't know what I was doing. Momma worked odd hours, so I assumed I'd be sitting on the step until Mom's car came and picked her up. Momma had a lot of cars, and a lot of drivers, each driven by someone else. Some of the cars were nicer than others, and I realized that the nicer the car, the more dolled up Momma would get. It seemed like a great job; at least I thought it was, seeing how they gave her money every time they brought her back home. Maybe she'd take me for an ice cream and a platter at the corner store.

"I...uh," I stammered, unsure of what lie would sound believable. My shoddy clothing ruled out doing anything that sounded cool or expensive. "I'm gonna go and have a snowball fight at the park." Believable, and most importantly, free. I couldn't even afford to lie, and though I'm not certain, I think this was the moment I started jotting down things I couldn't afford to deal with.

Before he could say something smart, Mrs. Fales started moving the line into the hallway. We walked single file, the excitement for the weekend oozed out of everyone, even with the snow.

When we got outside, I noticed that Momma wasn't in her usual spot. One by one, I watched other kids get picked up, until it was just me sitting on the bench. Occasionally her work called for her during the day, but she always made sure to pick me up from school. But I'd made the walk home so many times I had it down pat.

While our house wasn't an unreasonable distance, the cold would make it almost unbearable. In addition, my jeans were so small they ended at my calves, and both of my shoes had holes in them, though I couldn't really complain because we got them secondhand two years earlier. I pulled an extra pair of socks out of my bag and put them on to add layers, pulling them as far up as I could to cover the shortfall of my jeans.

On the walk home, I passed the group of guys that Momma told me were the "doctors" of the neighborhood. They stood outside the corner stores, always on the lookout for new patients, and judging by the steady stream of people I saw approach them, there were more sick people in my neighborhood than I thought. They seemed to know her and would always say hello to me and ask how I was doing in school. Sometimes when Momma was working on the weekends they'd ask me to run to the corner store to get them something to eat, even let me get something for myself and keep the change. Another time they gave me money to stand on the corner and whistle if I saw a policeman coming. When Momma found out, she flipped, and that was the end of my career as a physician's assistant.

I once asked her why people would go to them instead of going to the clinic like I did.

"Their medicine is cheaper," she replied. Although I was six, I understood we didn't have a lot of money, and I asked if it would help us out if I started seeing them, and she got stern. "They're for grown folks, and your doctor suits you just fine."

The head doctor, Big Mike, saw me coming and greeted me with a pound. "How you doing, P-Man?" he asked. That was his nickname for me.

"Have you seen my mom? She didn't pick me up from school."

He suddenly couldn't make eye contact and told me he'd seen her about an hour before. He asked if I needed a ride home, which was tempting because it was freezing and he had a cool car with loud speakers that was so far off the ground I'd need a boost to get in. But Momma told me to never take rides from strangers.

"As she should, P." He bought me a hot chocolate for the walk and gave me a ten dollar bill from his roll of money and wished me well.

The hot chocolate made the walk more pleasant, and before I knew it, I had made it to our house. It was our third house since I turned five, and somehow worse than the last one. If the goal was to go up the ladder, we seemed to be going down, jumping rungs to get to the bottom faster. It was shaped weird, like someone made a mistake while designing the shape and just went with it. Square in shape, with the chimney protruding from the corner, almost like it grew there by accident.

We had two large windows in the front room, which Momma always told me to stay away from when the doctors in the neighborhood started playing with fireworks. It never dawned on her that kids like fireworks. From the outside it could've passed for two houses, because the lower part was a bright shade of blue with the paint chipping off by the day, while the upstairs had a brick facade with brown piping that I was told not to touch under any circumstances. The kids at school that knew where I lived said I lived in a 'trap house,' but the joke was on them because the rodents always seemed to get away from them.

Our yard was Momma's selling point to me.

It was vast, with the edges overtaken by grass, but with a

huge dirt field in the middle. I'd sit out there for hours, digging holes and burying treasure, or I'd go into the tall grass and pretend I was a Pokémon trainer in search of wild ones to catch. I'd found some red Christmas ornaments at a thrift store and scratched off the coating on half of them to make Poke balls. Momma would sit on the stoop by the backdoor, smoking her Newports and cheering me on before calling me in for Kid Cuisine frozen dinners, with the brownie in the middle.

I got to the second step before I realized I didn't have a key to the house, because Momma said I'd lose my head if it wasn't on my shoulders. But I knew by the bottom of the door gently while shaking the handle it would come open. I brought the mail in, sounding out the words on the envelope and getting excited because whomever sent it said it was 'important' and that we had 'collections' to take care of, which excited me because I liked collecting things.

She wasn't in the living room or kitchen, since I could see both from the doorway, so I ran upstairs and checked her room. I found her, sitting Indian style next to the window and gazing at the ceiling fan, holding her arm like she'd been bitten by a bug. Next to her on the floor was a needle that looked like the ones my doctor would give me shots with. Next to it was a spoon and little baggies like the ones she used to pack my sandwiches with, but much smaller.

"Momma," I said. She snapped out of whatever she was staring at and smiled warmly. "Momma, I made it home all by myself."

"I see that," she replied, in a slower tone than I was used to. "My big boy, growing up so fast." I leaned down and she kissed me on the forehead, the smell of her cigarettes and work perfume engulfing my senses. "I'm sorry, I lost track of time. My medicine makes me tired."

It didn't even matter to me that she missed pickup, I was happy to know she was alright. Hard as she worked, if anyone deserved a nap it was her.

"Momma, are you hungry?"

"Why do you ask that, baby?"

I pointed at the little sandwich bags. "A sandwich that small wouldn't fill me up, so I wondered if you were hungry. Big Mike gave me ten dollars and—"

"He did?" She seemed back to normal upon hearing this. "Let me hold it for you, I'll save it until we go to the toy store."

I pulled it out of my jeans and gave it to her.

She stood up, cleaned up the leftovers from her medicine, and told me she had to go to work. "There's a Kid Cuisine you like in the freezer, and the electricity is back on so you can cook it. I'll be back later." She collected herself, gave me a kiss, and was gone.

I hurried downstairs and put my food in the microwave, making sure to do it exactly as she had taught me. When it was done, I raced back upstairs with my hot chocolate and tray, heading to my room and putting the Titanic videotape in the VCR. There was supposed to be two tapes, but the thrift store only had one, and I wasn't going to miss out on half of a good thing. It starts playing at my favorite part, when Jack Dawson gave his speech to the people in the fancy suits about how he lived his life. I was only six, but I knew what he meant about taking life as it came, and how life can change for the better in a second. It hadn't for us, but I had a lot to be grateful for. And in that moment, coming off my successful trek home, with my Momma having money to get me a toy, my Kid Cuisine, and electricity so I could watch half of my favorite movie, I knew I hadn't wasted the day.

I had made it count.

FOUR

LET'S GO JOIN THE CIRCUS

One of the advantages of growing up in the worst neighborhood is that anything outside of it is considered a step up. Legally, the state is obligated to place me within Camden County so that visitations with my mother can be easily coordinated. As we weave through traffic, I bide my time daydreaming about the township I'm gonna be placed in. The rich areas like Haddonfield or East Cherry Hill are out of the question on principle alone, but I'm was hopeful of ending up somewhere that lacks the obvious signs of urban decay.

"Can you tell me anything about this home?" I ask.

He smiles. "You're actually going to be the first person ever placed with this woman." He holds his hand out for a high five, but I don't reciprocate.

"Even Jeffrey Dahmer had a first victim," I shoot back.

The sun isn't down enough to mask the neighborhoods as we exit the highway, and fear transforms to a nervous excitement, like I'm starting some grand adventure. We enter the township of Stratford and turn into the Laurel Mills section. I know two things immediately: any house I end up in will easily be the nicest I've ever lived in, and I'll stick out like a sore thumb just walking to the mailbox. There's a sense of security about the place, with bikes lying unoccupied in yards and garage doors left open without a resident in sight. Shit you'd never see in Camden.

We stop in front of a tan two story home with a well mani-cured yard and a white picket fence. It's the kind of house you'd picture when someone described 'The American Dream'. My mind is flush with the possibilities of what life could be like in a house like this, even if it is only temporary.

"I used to dream of living in a house like this," I say. "I just kinda wish Momma was here to greet me, ya know?"

"That's understandable. But from what I read, this woman has been waiting on a placement for awhile, and I can't help but wonder if that was because she was destined to care for you."

"How did you feel the first time you were placed?"

He whistles, followed by a long sigh. "Man, I just remember being thankful to have a place with a bed. You nervous?"

"A little bit. I just wonder in times like this why it had to be me. Like, why did I have to be the kid with a strung out Mom? Why couldn't she just be clean and take care of me instead of vice versa?"

"Did you ever talk to her about that?"

"A heart to heart isn't really important when there's no food in your stomach. Besides, I'm not any good at vocalizing my feelings, and even if I was they don't matter to anyone anyway." The tears well up in my eyes before I can stop them, and I'm mad because I can't control them. I've lived under bridges and in tents, kept warm in corner stores during the winter, all with a straight face, but at this moment I can't hold it in anymore. What have I done to deserve the life I've been given. It's not like I'm asking for much. One clean mother, that's it, not even two parents, just one mother and a stable housing situation.

"Look at me, Percy." I ignore his request, so he asks again with more bass in his voice. Our eyes meet and I can see that he's fighting back tears too. "Listen to me. Don't ever let anyone make you feel like you have no value. Do you understand me?"

I nod, wanting to believe that in spite of a lifetime of evidence to the contrary, that he's right..

"You've carried her burdens for too long, and it's time to let someone take care of you." He opens his glove box and gives me one of his cards. "This has my cell number. If you ever need me, I don't care what time it is, you call me, okay?"

I promised I would, and I meant it. Alex had held up his end of the bargain, and I swore to myself that no matter what, he'd get my best foot forward for the year.

Someone peeks through curtains, alerted to our presence, and out steps the woman that's taking me in. She's older, medium build with dark brown hair and a perfect smile that I can see from the car.

I pull a small bottle of Narcan from my sock and gave it to Alex. "I guess I wont be needing this anymore."

"Why did you have this?"

"This isn't my first time dealing with an overdose, and I've learned it's better to have that and not need it than vice versa."

After wiping my eyes I stepped out of the car with my belongings, feeling more at ease as she crosses the grass to greet us.

"Hi, Ms. Grace, good to finally meet you," he says.

"Likewise, its been a long time coming" she replies, before turning to me. "And you must be Percy."

I nod but stay silent.

"He didn't tell me you were a mute."

"Yes, ma'am...I mean, I'm not a mute."

We head inside and instantly I know the house is bigger than our tent and the last three apartments combined. The hardwood floors are pristine and I wonder how many hours I'lol spend waxing them as a chore. It's tastefully decorated, with quotes on the walls proclaiming it to be a house of love, and furniture that looks so comfortable it makes the thought of a nap enticing. My room is on the first floor, complete with a dresser and a queen size bed that's bigger than the tent I'd been staying in thirty six hours ago.

"I know there's not much in here, but if you stay for awhile eventually you'll make it your own," she says.

"This is more than okay, ma'am, thank you."

"Oh, we have manners. You and I are gonna get along just fine."

She mentions something about changing laundry over and leaves Alex and I in my new room. He looks around at my new digs, nodding his approval, with both of us understanding that he'd delivered beyond each of our expectations.

"You gonna be all right?" he asks.

"Yeah, I'll be fine. So, what happens next?"

"You'll have your first court date in the next week. Nothing crazy, just getting you in front of a judge, establishing your case on the record. We really can't do anything until we get some clarity on your moth..." He frowns and catches himself. "I'm sorry, I didn't mean for it to sound—"

"Don't worry about it, I know what you meant." He looks fidgety, and I can tell he's trying to find a way to make an exit. "You're good to go, Alex."

"Are you sure?"

"How is it that I'm the one that has to live here and you're more nervous than I am?"

"What makes you think I'm nervous?"

"Dude, I've lived around dope addicts for most of my life, I think I'm pretty good at knowing when someone is nervous. You held up your end, now it's my turn to do the same."

He promises to keep me updated about my mother once more, then he's gone. Sitting on the bed I notice there's a gift bag addressed to me on the nightstand next to the bed. The kind of bag you see in the stationary section at Walmart. Inside are T-shirts, underwear, a toothbrush and toothpaste, but what I noticed the most was a handwritten note.

Percy, I can't promise that I understand what you've been through, but I can promise to love you like my own and give you a place to feel safe. Grace :-)

"I meant every word, too," a voice says. I look up to find Ms. Grace holding a heavy comforter, her smile never wavering. "I didn't know what size you wore, so I just grabbed what I thought was an average size for a fifteen year old."

"It's perfect, thank you." I start unpacking my belongings, which doesn't take long seeing as it consists of two notebooks, a CD wallet, and one outfit.

"That's all you have?"

I nod, not wanting to explain my meager possessions..

"Well, that's not gonna work. In the morning we'll run out and get you some clothes."

"I don't really have the funds for that right now."

"What part of take you in as my own went over your head, boy?" She flips through my CD collection as I put my stuff away, my taste in music surprising her in a good way. Each page she flipped through elicits a response, a "ha" in the Classic Rock section, and a "okay, Percy, you go, boy" in the R&B section.

Grace is inquisitive, but in a genuine way, really wanting to know about my tastes in music and how I came to enjoy the music I did. She's really impressed when I tell her about digging through the bins at the thrift shop. "Thrift stores are great, aren't they? You never know what you're gonna find, and if you find something terrible, you didn't pay that much for it anyway."

"Yes," I exclaim, my reaction shocking her. "Sorry, I just love music."

"Never apologize for your passions, that's what sustains us as people."

That was some profound shit, I think to myself.

"So, Percy, you love music?"

"Yes."

"I guess my only question is...have you ever been to a record shop?"

"What's a record shop?"

She gives me a look like I had shit in my hand and eaten it. "How could someone that loves music like you have never been to a record shop?"

"Let's see: poverty, lack of transportation...shall I go on?"

She finds this hilarious. "I like you, Percy. All right, in the morning we'll hit the clothing stores to upgrade your wardrobe, have lunch, grab some groceries, and then I'll take you to Backside Records, how does that sound?"

"Clothes, food...and music? I'm game."

"And so it is noted..." she said in the tone of a court jester. "...Tomorrow young Perseverance shall be initiated into the world of record shops."

I can't understand why she's so happy to have me in her home, but I figure with time there's probably something I'll learn about her that will make it obvious. She tells me to get some sleep and starts to leave before remembering something.

"The state is paying me roughly eight-fifty a month, but the way I see it, people shouldn't be paid for doing something that should be done out of the kindness of your heart. I figure we can come up with an acceptable amount for you to play around with every month, subtract some of your normal expenses, and we can get you a bank account for the rest."

"Um, okay."

"Cool, now get some sleep, we got a long day tomorrow."

After she leaves, I wait until I hear her footsteps up the stairs before I finish off the rest of my sandwich discreetly and make myself a cot on the floor. Having a bed is foreign to me, and after sleeping on a mess of blankets in a tent for so long, laying on the floor makes me feel like I'm still connected to my mother. I worry about her, and how she will react if she pulls through and realize that I'm gone.

Alone with my thoughts, I can finally admit to myself that I'm overwhelmed by the changes, and all the new relationships that come with them. It's not anything against Grace or Alex, they were wonderful people that meant well, but they weren't my mother. For all her flaws, I knew she would never abandon me. Grace can wake up tomorrow morning and decide being a foster parent isn't for her and have me shipped out. I haven't spent one night in foster care and could sense the black cloud hanging over my head.

I feel like a traitor, knowing everything we'd been through and now I had left her alone in a hospital room on her deathbed. Here I am zooming off to this new life of luxury— relatively speaking anyway— and if she ever woke up, all the problems will still be there, except without me to share the burden with. It feels like we were a punk band that played for the love of music and I'm the lead singer that sold out and went pop. On the flip side, I'm excited at the prospect of what I can accomplish without any distractions, and that's what's keeping me awake staring at the ceiling.

My heart is with my mother, but my mind is looking forward to this new life. I'll be walking an emotional tightrope, with every move of the heart needing to be balanced with the mind as a way of keeping me sane and giving everyone that believed in me a return on their investment. This will all play out in public, from the docket of family court to the local high school I would attend.

I've always wanted to go to the circus, I just never thought I'd end up being the main attraction.

FIVE

EVERYTHING DOESN'T HAVE TO BE A SCIENCE PROJECT

The change had been so abrupt I expected to wake up in my tent to the sound of the winos arguing over missing whiskey, but when I opened my eyes there was the ceiling fan, humming silently as I tried to follow one of the wings around. I failed to keep up with it, but I was competitive enough to declare myself officially awake for the day.

After brushing my teeth, I head out in search of breakfast, following the music to find Grace in the kitchen, pulling cinnamon rolls out of the oven and grooving to the music playing from a Bluetooth speaker. The table is set with orange juice, eggs, bacon, and coffee. If I'd learned anything from the first night, it was that the temperature of the house wouldn't be an issue, and I'm excited to learn that food is also on that list. But old habits die hard, and I quickly grabbed two cups, filling one to the brim with ice from the refrigerator.

"Good morning, sleepyhead," she exclaims when she sees me. She has an energy that makes the worst days feel like they could be great. "For your first night in a stranger's home, you slept like you've been here for years."

One tends to do that when they aren't surrounded by

addicts looking to pawn their belongings for a fix. "I saw how hard you worked to make it feel like home, the least I could do is treat it like one."

This surprises her, and for a second I swear she's gonna shed a tear, but the moment passes and she tells me to help myself while she uses the restroom.

I fill my plate and she makes it back to the table just as I'm performing my patented double drink maneuver. You fill the cup of ice with the drink of your choice, and after you finish it, fill it up again because you still have drink left. Sure, it gets diluted, but it feels like you made the original cup last a little longer. Grace looks confused as I explain this to her.

"I've got a better way," she says. She gets up from the table and grab the bottle of orange juice from the fridge, refilling my cup and her own before leaving it on the table. "Since I know how much you like orange juice, I'll keep it stocked so breakfast doesn't have to be a science project every morning."

It's funny how you can tell the difference between someone cooking for a paycheck, and someone cooking with passion. This is definitely the latter. The warmth of her personality was baked into the rolls, and in turn it feels like she's feeding my soul. Its been awhile since I've had a meal like this, and even longer since I'd had the time to savor it since the shelter was about feeding as many as possible. Eating on the run had become the rule instead of the exception, and I'm as thankful for the time to enjoy the food as I am for the food itself.

"What's that?" She asks, pointing out the four cinnamon rolls on a napkin to the side of my plate.

I'm scared of insulting her by telling the truth, but I don't want our relationship to get off on a bad foot with me lying about something so simple. She cocks her head to the side, as if she knows what's going on in my head. "I...I was just saving them for later," I say.

"So...there's this wonderful invention you might've heard of called a refrigerator," she said, taking my stash from the napkin and putting them on her own plate. She'd wrapped her hair up and thrown on a sweatshirt from The Who's 50th anniversary tour. "This is your home too, and you're welcome to eat as much as you like. I also know our introduction was a bit rushed last night, so let me lay down some ground rules."

"Okay."

She pours herself another glass of orange juice. "First, don't lie to me. You might not like my response, but I assure you it's preferable to the alternative. In the last sixty seconds you seem to have passed that test."

"Noted."

"Second, don't steal from me. As a waitress, I have enough to worry about with people skipping out on their tabs; I refuse to worry about the same thing in my own home."

"I'd go without before I'd steal from someone."

"Good to hear. Now, I'm off for the next couple of days to get you acclimated, but I usually work nights, with my off days being Sunday and Monday. Once school starts, I expect you to let me know when you leave in the morning, and if you can't make it home before I leave for work, a phone call is mandatory."

"Um, I don't have a cell phone."

"Well, it's your lucky day because I was gonna upgrade mine, so in a few hours time that won't be an issue."

Did I hear her right? I'm gonna join the twenty-first century with my own cell phone. "You're serious?"

"It was gonna be a surprise, but I'm getting the vibe that surprises aren't really your thing."

I'm not sure where she got that idea, but she isn't wrong.

In my experience I'd found it was better to take shit directly to the face instead of from the side. "I don't know how I can repay you."

"I'm deducting it as a monthly expense. It's a forty dollar line fee, and you're gonna pay that to learn about budgeting your money."

"That's fair."

"Then we're in agreement. Now, is there anything I should know about you?"

The question catches me off guard. "What do you mean?"

She munches on her cinnamon roll and thinks up a response. "I mean, even if I am your guardian, you're still a human being with pet peeves of your own."

Nobody had ever asked me that, not even my own mother. I was always expected to reshape myself into whatever someone else needed me to be for their own security. For my mother, I had to be the doting son that ignored her addiction and follow her blindly, and for the rest of the world I had to treat people as if I were lucky to have them. This was the first time someone had asked me what got under my skin, in essence allowing me the ability to fortify the defenses around my psyche as I saw fit.

"Are you gonna get rid of me at the first sign of trouble? Not saying that I cause trouble, because I don't. But I've spent most of my life looking over my shoulder, and last night was the first time I let my guard down. I just need to know you aren't gonna wake up and decide I'm not worth caring about anymore."

"I think you're smart enough to know what the line is, but you don't seem like the type of kid to go near it. As long as you follow the rules I told you about, I'd like you to stay as long as possible. Is there anything else I should know?"

"Why are you doing this?"

"You mean for you, or in general?"

"For me."

She starts clearing the table and lets my question hang for so long I assume she's gonna ignore it. "Because, you don't know it yet, but this is the last time in your life when everything is pure. Relationships, friendships, everything that lays the foundation for who you become as an adult starts in your teenage years."

"I've never thought of it that way." My life had been about making it to the next day, meal, or government subsidized handout. In fact, I found questions from teachers about where I saw myself in ten years to be a joke, if not outright annoying. Thinking of life on a week to week basis was a struggle, let alone pondering the great unknown of a time when I was legally an adult. My existence was so tied up in Momma's addiction, that it didn't leave time for me to consider what my dreams even were.

Grace seems to sense that the conversation is headed to a dark place so she changes the subject. "What are you most looking forward to at the record shop?"

Now *this* I can talk about. "Everything. Just the fact that my selection will be based on my preference instead of hoping someone donated a hidden gem to Goodwill."

"I think you'll love this place. I'm friends with the owner, an old soul like us. Why do you enjoy music so much?"

"I've never had friends, so music is my way of..." I trail off, unsure of how to explain it, even though its vivid in my mind. "It's like a vast library of strangers that could understand how I was feeling and walk me through it. Sometimes I wish I was born in another decade so I could experience albums like nineteen-ninety-nine for the first time like everyone else."

"Oh, so you're a Prince fan?"

"Huge." That is an understatement. Prince Rogers is the

single greatest musician that ever lived. One time, I checked out his entire discography from the library and went through each record in order, marveling at the consistency in quality while constantly reinventing himself.

"I'm so happy you're here. Prince is my guy; hold on a sec, I'll show you something cool." She dashes out the kitchen and comes back with an old photo album. Finding the page she's looking for, I marvel at what I see. It's a ticket stub from the 1999 tour at the old Spectrum arena in Philadelphia.

"Dude. You have to tell me about this."

And she does.

"Okay, so he comes out and there's this bed on stage that he laid in and serenades the crowd. I tell you, his falsetto just does something to you as a woman. But when the band kicked in, it went to another level. He knew what songs to play in what order, with him holding the love songs until the end. I ended up making out with this guy that was two rows behind me, not that I recommend that, but it was a Prince concert."

"Wow," I say, genuinely amazed. "I like to listen to live albums in the dark, it's my way of feeling like I'm there, especially comedy albums. Is that weird?"

"Hell no, Percy. That's living."

"Have you ever listened to a comedy album in the dark?"

"I grew up on comedy albums, but nobody appreciates them anymore. Everyone wants to watch the specials now, but it's not the same."

She's right. Sometimes the library would be low on music, but the comedy albums were always untouched, like peppermints in a trick or treat basket. But comedy albums were the most precious of all. You could hear little things that you couldn't see on a broadcast, like the person who found the punchline funnier than everyone else and laughs for that extra second, or the hush that comes after everyone has laughed, when they're waiting for the next punchline. If you listened close enough you could hear the cocktail waitresses taking the glasses off the table. The first one I ever checked out was *No Respect* by Rodney Dangerfield. Other than liking the title for obvious reasons, the cover is what hooked me. It's just Dangerfield staring into the camera, sweating with a towel, clearly sick of everyone's shit. He seemed like one of us that was lucky enough to make it out, a working class guy with a gift that elevated him out of the slums.

The album itself was forty two minutes of self depre-cating humor, and it changed my life. I'd mutter 'no respect' to myself whenever I felt slighted, and eventually I came to see the world as an inside joke that only Rodney and I were in on. Later on, I discovered the greats that were criminally over-rated. Guys like Redd Foxx, Patrice O'Neal, and Paul Mooney, who was so good at making the audience examine race issues that people would walk out of his shows. Comedy albums told the history of the world and society in a way that made me question everything they were teaching me in history class. These were artists traveling the world and living it in real time, unapologetically speaking the truth as they went along.

We chat about music for a while longer before she realizes we'd better get on the road if we wanted to make the record shop before it closed. As she leaves a question comes to mind.

"What's that?" I ask, pointing to the circular device on the counter playing music.

For a second she looks confused before it hits her. "That's an Amazon Alexa," she replies. "You can ask it pretty much anything and it'll give you the answer."

"What about music?" I ask. "Can it play anything I think of?"

She smiles at this. "Absolutely. Let's try this, I'm gonna go get dressed, and while I'm gone you play around with it and tell me what you think when I get back."

I rub my hands together after she leaves, wondering just what song I think will stump this little box. After careful consideration, I make my move.

"Alexa," I say. The top of the device turns blue indicating that it's listening. "Play '*London Calling*' by The Clash."

The blue light spins a ring around the top, taking long enough to convince me that I've won. But before I can gloat, the ring stops spinning. "Now playing, *London Calling* album by The Clash," it spits out, followed by the familiar guitar opening of one of the greatest albums ever produced.

"Is that supposed to impress me?" I ask. "Its their most popular album, you're supposed to know that." It doesn't respond, instead letting the album speak for itself. I begrudgingly nod my head to the music while trying to come up with another song. Halfway through track three I come up with a song so random and obsolete that I know it will stump Alexa.

In the mid-eighties when Eddie Murphy was at his peak, someone convinced him to record a R&B album, even getting Rick James onboard to produce the lead single. The album became a success but was quickly forgotten my the masses, which is how I was able to find it in the bargain bin of the thrift store. There's no way Alexa would know a mediocre Pop record from the eighties.

"Alexa." I say. The volume lowers and the blue ring that's currently the bane of my existence reappears. "Play 'Party All The Time' by Eddie Murphy."

The circle spins for a bit longer than it did at my last request, and I pour myself another glass of orange juice in anticipation of victory. But just as I take a celebratory sip, Alexa decides it her turn to speak.

"Now playing, 'Party All The Time' by Eddie Murphy."

The synths come blazing in behind it's voice as I concede that technology has entered a realm I'm not familiar with. Though, in my defense, I haven't exactly had the type of living arrangements that would allow me to keep up with such changes.

I spend the next fifteen minutes trying to decide if I like this machine or not, asking it random questions about famous records and celebrity birthdays, each one more random than the last. Grace returns to the kitchen just as I'm conceding that Jeff Bezos is now the ruler of planet earth.

"What do you think?" Grace asks.

I look at the Alexa then back at her. "Its...interesting."

"Don't feel bad, I wanted to throw the damn thing out the window my first day with it." She checks her watch. "We gotta get going if we're gonna hit everything today."

I clear the table and put my dishes in the dishwasher before following Grace to the door.

Grace is like the cool Auntie that lives life to the fullest, sneaking you beer under the table and reassuring you that engaging your creativity was more important than math class. I've always believed that people who need each other will find a way to cross paths. She needed someone to love and impart her special kind of wisdom upon, and I needed someone to remind me that the fun in life is the journey we take to our destination.

We're like the Hall and Oates of the foster care system.

SIX

A SHOT OF JADE FOR THE JADED

One would assume that impoverished people constantly hope to win the lottery and escape their circumstances. While the sudden influx of cash is always welcome, the truth is our wishes are more simple in nature than you would think. We wish not for money, but for experiences within society. Maybe it's ordering a value meal instead of off the dollar menu, or buying a movie ticket on opening night to take in the movie with everyone else instead of waiting for a matinee ticket.

For me, it was being able to shop at Costco. Hell, I'd even settle for being able to walk in the place, let alone buy anything,

It doesn't sound like something to waste my days dreaming about, but dammit if it didn't sound and look amazing. Classmates would brag to each other about buying food in bulk, while Momma tried to make single portions filling enough for two. They'd also talk about their takeout deli, with huge portions at ridiculously low prices. Now that I think about it, I usually heard these snippets at lunchtime on days when I saved my school lunch to have as dinner, so I'm probably a bit biased, but the sentiment is still the same.

Luckily for me, Grace has a membership and prefers to upgrade her phone at the kiosk inside the store. I can barely contain my excitement walking inside. Grace picks up on this and tells me to look around while she handles her business.

I oblige.

The store itself is huge, and I start in the section dearest to my heart, the music section. If I made a list of life essentials, headphones would place top three with clothes and food, and rank higher than clothes if I lived in a society where being nude was accepted. Their selection of headphones is bittersweet, because while it is up to date with the latest wireless headphones, it's another signal that my favorite headphones—wired ones—are becoming a thing of the past.

But there's something I find comforting in wired headphones. Take mine for example. Sure, it helps that they're only twenty bucks, but it goes deeper than that. I put these on and become a walking 'Do Not Disturb' sign, a wallflower that's present in this world physically, but in another one mentally. The 3.5mm jack connects my favorite artists right into my soul like an IV, securing my hopes and dreams that wither under the assault of everyday life. They've been there on the nights when the heat wasn't, at the dinner table when the food wasn't, reminding me that better times would come, even if they couldn't give me an estimated arrival date.

But most of all, wired headphones are incredibly loyal. When the cord would inevitably short, they kept the music going, well, halfway anyway. But they held on long enough for me to scrounge up another twenty bucks to keep that light on in my soul. Of course, that didn't stop me from trying on as many as I could.

And then I heard the song.

It started with a simple bass line before the piano keys came in suddenly, as if they'd been dropped off by a stork.

The instrumentation alone was great, but it was the lyrics I was stuck on, the kind that feel as if the singer had a conversation with you on a park bench then went to the studio and wrote a song about your feelings. There's certain songs that are so good they defy the confines of a genre. So good that they discombobulate you, making the hairs on your body stand up. It might speak to your life circumstances, or just be a masterclass of musical precision. This was both. The lyrics aren't the most complex, but to connect with the soul they don't have to be. All it takes is the right message, and this song, with its message of running away and starting over, is exactly what I need to hear at this time in my life.

Simple words that sum up my most complicated feelings. That's the beauty of music for me. In the span of ten seconds the first verse and chorus articulate everything I'm feeling, the catch-22 of feeling hopeless about my circumstances with the excitement about new experiences. I can feel the yearning in the hook, as the singer longs for someone to hold, which is more impactful than saying he wants to have sex with her. He's singing about more than sex; this was about the connection that's unexplainable between two people, the moment when you know that someone just...understands. I imagine that hook kills in concert, and after learning the band name I vow to one day see them in concert and experience it myself. Since I don't have my notebook to jot down the band's name, Muse, I repeat it to myself over and over in case the record shop we go to has their music.

I take in the rest of the store, noticing how differently people move in this store compared to the corner stores I'd spent most of my life in. The customers move almost at a snail's pace, going over each piece of produce, asking for specific cuts of beef in the meat department, and, most shocking of all, grabbing the first gallon of milk off the shelf.

Shocking because I'd learned to go through the milk section like a fine tooth comb looking for the furthest date so it would last longer.

And in what I see, there's the contrast.

These people lived in a different world that I'm now a part of. They didn't check milk dates because they knew they'd be back to buy more. We weren't sure we'd have enough money to be back. Ordering specific cuts wasn't an issue because they know it's an option. In my neighborhood, we took what was on the shelves, not because we didn't want anything better, but because you knew that if you didn't take it the next person would, and they probably needed it more than you. It was a world in which we operated on empathy for the next person, with an unspoken honor system of making sure that everyone had at least the minimum. We didn't ask for anything better because we didn't know any better. I lived to survive and these people lived to sustain, and that slight difference of mindset creates a gulf so wide I feel like I've moved to another country.

"Would you like to try a sample?" a voice says, snapping me out of my daze. The woman, maybe in her late twenties, is holding a tray of popcorn shrimp, and seems happy to be there. I can always tell a real smile from a fake one.

"Um, I don't really have any money, but when I find my guardian maybe she'll help me out."

She contorts her face in confusion before snapping back into being friendly. "Oh, no. It's free."

"Free like I sign up for something or..."

"Free like you take as many as you want and you're good to go."

This seems like a setup. I couldn't even convince the Chinese food place to fill up a platter I paid for back home, but I'm supposed to believe popcorn shrimp is free at Costco.

I hesitate but eventually take two, figuring if they try to arrest me for shoplifting I could explain that it was a misunderstanding. "Thank you."

Grace catches up to me in the frozen food section, sampling orange chicken made in some device called an air fryer. Between discovering Muse and eating approximately ten dollars in chicken and seafood, I consider the trip worth it.

"This is for you, Percy," she says, handing me her old cell phone. "It's only a year old, but I think it's perfect for you."

"Wow," I say.

"A couple of rules. No porn, and no calling anybody in another country."

"I don't even like talking to the people around me, so we're good there."

"Perfect."

We hit the deli after grabbing a few things and sit at the tables, eating cheap pizza as I tell her about discovering Muse and all the samples I'd eaten, which she found hilarious.

"You really thought they were gonna bust you for shoplifting?"

"Yes."

She laughs again. "Can I ask you something?"

The question makes my stomach churn. "Sure."

"You have Spiderman on your notebooks, but when I asked if you wanted the Marvel macaroni and cheese you chose the store brand. Why?"

"I'll be sixteen in two weeks, can't still be eating superheroes with my dinner, right?"

"What was rule number one?"

She knows I'm not telling the truth, and I don't want her to think any less of me. "Okay, the store brand has more servings."

She stops chewing when I say this. After wiping her

mouth, she takes both my hands and looks me right in the eyes. "You will never have to worry about having enough to eat in my home. Do you understand me?"

I nod.

"Until the courts say otherwise, you are one of my flock, and even if they say otherwise you're on my phone plan, so you're still part of me. Never be afraid to ask me for something."

"I don't want anything."

"Good, because I only look like money. I'm not made of it."

* * *

I WONDER if the first day in the Witness Protection Program is like this.

This is the only thought running through my head as we pull into the strip mall where the record store is. If it wasn't for the side mirrors on Grace's car and the brand new Chuck Taylor sneakers squeezing the living hell out of my feet, I'd swear I'm not the same person. In the last hour, we'd set up a checking account—a student one, so Grace could monitor it— and purchased my approximate weight in denim from Walmart. I'd lost count of the number of times I would reach for something and freeze like a public Wi-Fi network. I was stuck in this weird purgatory, one in which I was trying to enjoy life instead of surviving it, and I could feel myself becoming someone else every time Grace swiped her debit card.

Everything I did was so foreign to her it required an expla-nation, followed by assurances from her that whatever I had done to get by would no longer be an issue. She seemed deter-mined to rebuild my psyche from the ground up, which confused me because I thought my mindset prepared me to live through anything.

"You know how to survive," Grace said, after she had to reassure me about something for the millionth time. "But now you must learn to live."

Well, I have learned more than enough for one day, shit, even school was over by 3:00, because they knew students could only take so much. I just wanna find some good music in this shop, go home, and lock myself in my room to recharge my batteries.

Backside Records is at the end of the strip mall, about three blocks from our house based on the Rite Aid I remember from this morning.

"The owner's name is Randy, and he's good people," Grace says as we approach the door. She says this as if the strip mall isn't in disrepair. Half of it is taken up by an abandoned grocery store with the rest occupied by Backside, a nail salon, and a pizza place that looks like one of the other million ones that populate Jersey.

I hold the door open for Grace and realize two things in quick succession upon entering. One is that I will be spending a decent amount of my money here, and two, that paled in comparison to the amount of time I would spend here. The place is massive, at least relative to the rest of the storefronts. Each section is clearly labeled, with sub genres inside of them. For example, by the door is the Rock section, but within it are individual labels for classic rock, alternative rock, even something called industrial rock, which sounded like some shit done by union steel workers on their lunch break. It feels like a time machine, where people who connect with music on a deeper level could come and indulge in their passion.

Behind the counter sits the good stuff, boxsets like The Beatles complete Apple recordings, and a Springsteen anniversary box set for Darkness on the Edge of Town nestled on a shelf, well out of the reach of potential thieves. The place also sells clothing, band shirts organized just under the box sets. Grace only let me pick two Spiderman shirts from Walmart, and I suspect it's because she knew we were coming here.

Randy comes out of the back to greet us, the Wu-Tang logo on his shirt making him look like a retired superhero. My guess is he's about the same age as Grace, with a quick smile and kind demeanor. His hairline is starting to show signs of receding, but not far enough back yet to declare it a lost cause.

I take it he and Grace are close, since they actually hug before introductions are made. I'm nervous about this because she hasn't introduced me to anyone yet, and this will give me an idea of how heavy the stigma I carry will be.

"Randy, this is Percy..." We lock eyes. "...my son."

Wow. She really went for it. But I'm more shocked that I'm okay with it. Part of my apprehension to this whole arrangement was not wanting to feel like someone else's burden, even if they were compensated. This goes beyond the money she spent today, anybody could do that, and in my experience it's been done to make themselves feel better. But Grace wasn't content with telling me I was one of her own; she took pride in showing me that she meant it. Maybe I'll wake up tomorrow and feel like she's overstepping her bounds, but after seeing her put herself out there, laying down the gauntlet and declaring she's all in, I doubt it.

We shake hands and I notice The Rolling Stones tattoo on his forearm.

"Nice set of headphones," he says. "Sony's?"

"Yeah. Good set of eyes."

"Best twenty bucks you could spend, aside from the music itself."

Even better taste. "This place is amazing," I say, still astonished that such a place exists.

"I can tell by your headphones that you're a music guy, and you're living with the right person to talk music with. What are you into?"

The song from Costco pops into my head. "Do you have any Muse?"

He smiles at this and points to a section near the back that's occupied by the only other person in the store. "I'm impressed. Most people your age only want DJ Khalid and Justin Bieber. It's good to know some of the youth still appreciate musicianship."

"He's also a huge Prince fan," Grace says, and we spend the next few minutes debating his greatest album, with Dirty Mind being the only one we could get close to agreeing on.

I leave them to talk and find the section Muse is in. Discovering a band well into their career is one of life's treasures. There's a history you can track, seeing their growth from one album to the next. If you're lucky, you'll find an artist like Kanye, who's never sold the same album twice. If you stripped the lyrics from his albums and only listened to the production, you'd swear each one is by a different artist.

When I get to the section it dawns on me that I only know lyrics from the song and the name of the band. Thankfully, I now have a cellphone with access to the internet, and after a quick search I learn the album I'm looking for is called Black Holes and Revelations. I grab the copy that's in stock and examine the rest, unsure of which ones I want. Grace put $150 in my bank account to get it started but was clear about me needing to be smart with how I spent it. Therefore she put a limit of twenty five dollars on this little trip, and when calculated with Randy's prices, I had enough for three CD's if she showed me mercy and covered the taxes.

"All right, Muse, talk to me, where do I start?" I say to nobody in particular.

"Anything after Absolution is prime Muse," a voice says. It's a sweet voice, but with a passion about the band that I would have when answering the same question about Prince. "Their early stuff is good, too, but Absolution and later is the height of their powers."

I turn to thank her and my mind goes blank so fast you'd swear she was a member of the Men in Black holding the memory wiping device. Her eyes are dark green, bordering on brown, and I'd be willing to complete a meticulous study to come to a conclusion on them. She's wearing ripped jeans, but in a way that was planned by the company, not the 'we don't have enough money for more pants' edition that I wore while with my mother, with a gray Blink-182 hoodie that looked amazing. Not that I could speak.

"Are you okay?" she asks.

"Yeah...um, pizza from Costco," I say. "At a dollar a slice someone's bound to get sick every now and then, right?"

She finds this funny, even taps me on the shoulder for good measure, so naturally I won't be washing this shirt this century. "I'm Jade."

"Percy."

"I've never seen you around school; did you just move here?"

"Yeah, from Camden. I'm heading into my junior year."

"So we are in the same grade. You don't seem like the typical Camden kid."

"I'm definitely more Kendrick Lamar than YG," I say, and she laughs again, even harder than the first time. I'd spent so much time alone I wasn't sure if people would get the metaphors I saw in the world everyday. But like prime Ryan Howard sitting on a 3-0 pitch, she crushed that shit.

"Stop it," she says. "That was a good one. Well, I gotta get going, but stick to that era of Muse and you'll be all right. Maybe I'll see you at school. Nice to meet you, Percy."

I turn quickly because I have this weird thing about watching people leave. It feels like they never come back, so I just stopped watching them go, like that would curry favor with the gods. Old habits die hard, I guess.

I head up to the counter with the three albums she recommended.

"These are good choices," Randy says, examining my haul. "So, I was talking to your mother and she mentioned how much you love music and that you're a trustworthy kid. I could use some help around the store a couple of hours a day once school starts."

I look at Grace and she's smiling, a bit too excited in my opinion, but I couldn't figure out why. "Seriously?"

"As long as you keep your grades up, I don't have a problem with it," Grace chimes in.

If I work this job I could conceivably save a decent amount of money. Honestly, I'd do it for free just to access all this music, but at two-hundred a week plus unlimited CD's, I can't say no. "All right, I accept."

"Brilliant," he says, before high fiving Grace. "You can start the first day of school."

SEVEN

THE MERRY BAND THAT NOBODY WANTED

The county van that comes to pick me up for court is so plain you'd think I was being smuggled out of the country. Alex said it's customary to be taken to court by the county for the first appearance, so Grace was sitting this one out. Of course, he left out that electronics weren't allowed—something about the state not being liable if they were stolen. It's honestly a wonder they manage to keep on top of everyone else while they're always covering their own ass. So, I'm alone in the van with a driver that doesn't talk and Top 40 radio that's barely comprehensible because of a bad signal.

I've always enjoyed people watching, but watching them through the tinted windows of the van feels more authentic. When people are unaware of your gaze, they act more natural, as opposed to how they *think* they should act if you're within their radius. You see them stare into space, almost like they're rethinking their choices in life that led to this point, and it's that look that scares me. I never noticed the difference until I moved in with Grace. She has a contagious zest for life, creating happiness out of thin air. She didn't make much at the diner, but possesses a richness in spirit you can't put a dollar amount on.

In the week since I arrived, we've spent many nights getting to know each other. This has mostly consisted of doing chores together with music blasting, impromptu dance parties while cooking dinner, and evening strolls through the neighborhood just as the sun was starting to set. What I loved the most was she didn't ask too many questions about my life before I was placed with her. Not that she doesn't care, I'm sure she does, but she's content with letting me open up when I feel comfortable doing so.

But I can't.

To do so would mean being honest about my mother's shortcomings, and I don't feel like that's fair to her. The feelings I had that first night were starting to manifest at an alarming rate. I missed my mother dearly, but for every meal or conversation I enjoyed with Grace came a burning resentment for my mother. To compensate, I'd shut down with Grace, figuring I couldn't allow her to have the upper hand over the woman that birthed me. If this affected Grace, she never showed it, and sometimes I wished she'd have me sent away because I could feel myself loving her more and more each day. Not because of the money she had spent, but because of her time.

Living with her for me felt like renting an awesome movie from Redbox. It was better than anything I had in my own collection, but I couldn't really enjoy it because I knew it would have to be returned. At some point I will return to my old life and she'd be nothing more than a bright spot in my miserable existence. Late at night, when she was sleeping and I stared at the ceiling fan; I secretly wished she was my real mother, and I'd cry myself to sleep, because I know how much Momma loved me and I felt like an ungrateful child.

The longer I spent in her home, the harder it would be to leave, and I'd rather break the small piece of my heart she's holding than to have her take it over and watch it all break at once.

* * *

THEY PUT all foster kids on one floor of the courthouse. It's nicer than I expected it to be, with the floors freshly waxed and furniture that looks fairly new. If it wasn't for the picture of the Governor on the wall, you wouldn't know it was a state building. I never understood why he was on the wall of every state facility. He'd been on the wall of the local welfare office when Momma would get her card reloaded, a subtle reminder that this handout was only due to his generosity.

The ego of this fucker is astounding, and I'm surprised they managed to get his head into one picture frame.

Every elevator in the place operates by keycard—state covering their ass again, and upon entry I'm given a name tag with my courtroom number and designated section. To get to where the teenagers are stationed, I have to walk through the little kids section, and I'm astounded by how many kids are here. While being in an actual foster home is a secluded experience, seeing a group of them in one place was comforting for me, because it reassured me that I'm not the only kid with screwed up parents. Some played outside, others did arts and crafts, all of them having a great time feeling a sense of normalcy for a moment. We're all members of an exclusive club, just a band of misfits that nobody wanted.

The section for my age group was less boisterous, all of us stripped of our cellphones and staring at one another like apes in a zoo enclosure. I head to the computer room and search around on Google for a while. I'd been obsessed with Muse since I bought their records, and was delighted to find that they were releasing a new album in a couple of months and had a tour date in Philadelphia scheduled for January. It was sold out, which means I'll have to pay above face value to go, but I figured I'd be living back on the streets next year anyway, so I'd figure out a way to go.

"I hoped to see you at school, but I never thought you'd stalk me at the courthouse," a female voice says from behind. I turn around and my heart skips a beat. The Blink-182 sweatshirt has been replaced with a Led Zeppelin one, and she's wearing glasses this time around, but thankfully those beautiful eyes are still visible. "Percy, right?"

I nod. "Jade?" I ask, knowing damn well she'd been running through my mind like a Kenyan distance runner since I met her at the record shop. Did she say she hoped to see me? I say a silent prayer of thanks that Grace made me wear a sweater or she'd see me sweating through my shirt. She takes a seat next to me and it hits me that if she's here that means her family life is complicated, too.

"So you took my advice," she says after looking at my screen. "What did you think?"

"They've taken a spot in my top three bands of all time."

"What's your favorite album?"

Now we're speaking my language. "As a whole I'm gonna go with The Resistance. I feel like it flows better overall, and I kinda got a thing for big orchestra sections. But they're all great."

"I like your style Percy, hold on." She runs her fingertips over the top of my head and I damn near melt. She removes a piece of lint and flicks it away. "Can't have you looking all crazy in front of the judge, we got our parents for that."

We laugh together at this, because it's a great joke, and if you're not laughing at life, you're doing it wrong.

"So why are you here?" I ask.

"What do you mean?"

"Jade, I don't know if you've realized it, but we're not exactly at Disneyland."

Another laugh, and I make it my mission to see her smile as often as I can.

"Long story short, my parents love their pills more than they love their responsibilities, or each other for that matter. But Mom finally cleaned up enough and this trial period with her has gone well enough that they're letting me stay."

"So you're staying in Stratford?"

"You trying to get rid of me, Percy?"

"Of course not. I actually want you to stay for as long as possible."

She cocks her head to the side. "You have a crush on me."

"What? No," I say, giving myself away.

"That's really flattering, but I have a boyfriend." The only thing missing was a studio audience moaning. "You'll meet him; he's the quarterback of the school football team."

Wonderful.

"I've told you mine," she says. "Why are you here?"

"My mom overdosed last week, so now I'm living in a foster home."

There's something about knowing a person understands your situation that makes it easy to open up to. She didn't give me a look of pity, just a sad smile conveying that we both got the short end of the stick in the family department. A voice boomed over the sound system declaring it was time for her to leave. We exchange phone numbers and she starts to leave.

"Hey Jade," I call out. "Not that it matters, but I'm not sad you have a boyfriend. I'm happy just to have you in my life."

She smiles at this. "Me, too, Percy." Then she was gone.

I meant what I said. If there's one thing I'd learned from

having a mother on drugs, it was keeping people in some capacity was better than not having them at all. I had pulled the lever on the friend slot machine and hit the jackpot.

Even if I had to split the winnings with the school quarterback, my share was more than enough.

* * *

ALEX IS the first person I see as I'm being escorted into the courtroom, but before I can greet him, he smiles and points to one of the tables closest to the judge's bench.

"Momma," I shriek, causing a slight panic as I rush to give her a hug. I've never been so happy to smell stale cigarettes in my life. She isn't moving as quick, and I can tell by her sweats that she's detoxing, but I'm happy to know that she's was alive.

"My baby," she says. "I missed you so much." She examines me from top to bottom. "Are those new shoes? My baby boy looking all handsome."

Alex comes over and greets me with a fist pound. "Surprise. I figured seeing her was better than me telling you."

"Good call."

I'm led to my table that's opposite Momma's, like we are adversaries instead of in this together, and before I can object, we're all standing for Judge Carolyn Martinez to enter the room. I make sure to be quiet, remembering the scene from Liar Liar when Jim Carrey mocked the honorable tag and it was picked up by the stenographer.

After all the legal jargon, it's clear that I'm staying with Grace at least through the holidays, and that Momma would be entering a treatment program. After confirming I would get a visit with Momma after court, Judge Martinez orders a regular visitation schedule to be overseen by Alex and adjourns us.

I've had drive thru orders take longer.

EIGHT

PRESCRIPTION FOR THE FRACTURED FAMILY

Momma is pacing when I enter the visitation room. My chaperone tells me she'll be outside if I need her before she closes the door.

I wouldn't wanna sit in on these visits either.

"Jolly Rancher?" Momma offers. She knows it's my favorite and I oblige.

We sit in silence for a while, because, well, really our situation is pretty cut and dry.

"I'm sorry," she finally says.

"I know, Momma." Throughout my life the one thing we never did was play the blame game. I didn't want her to spiral so I shared it with her equally, even though we both knew where it laid. As much as I want to yell at her, I don't see the good in it. She's a shell of herself, and I know that in this stage of her recovery being kicked by the only person she loved would push her over the edge. "I finally ate a Donkey's cheesesteak."

"Did you?"

"Yeah. My social worker took me the night he picked me up from the hospital."

"Damn nurses couldn't mind their own business," she says, as if we were living the high life and the nurses ruined it.

I run my hand over the sofa, wondering how many kids had sat in this same seat, having the same stilted conversations with parents determined to question everyone else but themselves. How long did it take them to realize they weren't going home anytime soon? Did their parents show any contrition?

I don't know what to talk about with Momma, because everything leads back to her failure to keep her addiction under control. Every triumph is an indictment of her, from my clothes to my new job. These are milestones she should be a part of instead of outside looking in.

"They treating you okay?" she asks. I wanna lie and tell her I'm in a terrible home; maybe that would force her to get her shit straight, knowing I was going through hell. But if it were that easy, she would've cleaned up the first time I found her lying in vomit, or after we got evicted for the umpteenth time.

"I'm in a great home, Mom." As much as I'd like to give her that motivation, I can't bear to portray Grace as anything other than wonderful. "I got my own room, I mean, sleeping in a bed took a little getting used to, but I'm doing all right."

She smiles sadly. "I'm going to get you back, Percy. I promise you I'm gonna bring you back home."

I can feel the lump forming in my throat and the tears aren't far behind. Truth is, I'm not sure I wanna go back home, because with Momma home is a state of mind, a mere feeling. Home with her is knowing she was around with nothing to show for it. With Grace it was tangible, somewhere I can walk into and lay my head, a warm meal prepared with love, or a hot shower that didn't run on a timer.

Momma pulls me into a long hug and rocks me gently, like she did on the winter nights when the heat got turned off. Life was so simple when she was in the hospital, because I could pretend she'd stay there, but having to look her in the eye and see how broken she is, I can't abandon her now. A knock at the door tells us our time is coming to an end.

"I know your birthday is next week, but I'm not sure I'll be able to see you, so you can have your gift now." She digs in her purse and pulls out something wrapped in a newspaper. I can tell by the shape it's a CD case. "I know you loved that album."

It's a copy of Out of Time by R.E.M., just like the one I made a note to replace. "Wow," I say.

The chaperone enters to end the visit and Momma gives me one more hug. "Please don't give up on me, Percy. I'm gonna make it right." She gives me a number to the treatment house she's living in and slips out of the room.

Most guys would love to be caught between two women, but I'm learning that this shit isn't all it's cracked up to be.

NINE

TRAINS, WINGS AND 16 YEAR OLD THINGS

Grace's fingernails tap on my door three times before she enters. "Happy birthday to you. Happy birthday to you. Happy birthday, precious Percy. Happy Birthday to you." She ended the 'you' with an impressive falsetto, honed over years of cooking delicious meals from the comfort of her kitchen. "This is for you," she says, handing me a birthday bag and taking a seat at the end of my bed.

"Wow, you didn't have to do this." My birthdays have been depressing for most of my life, so I'm kinda shocked she even thought to do something for me. I've also been a prick since my court date last week, so I wouldn't have blamed her if she ignored it.

"Open your gifts, I wanna see your reaction."

There's three gifts in the bag and I choose the smallest one first. It's a new phone case, but my excitement increases when I see that it's a custom phone case. On the back is the Muse logo, just under a swinging Spiderman and a picture of Jack Dawson from the dinner scene in Titanic. "You really put some thought into this."

"Keep going," she says, and who am I to argue.

The second package is significantly bigger, and I let out a yelp when I see that its brand new headphones. Not just any headphones, but top-of-the-line Sony ones. I'll never miss an obscure synth line or snare drum again.

"So you got headphones, what else could you possibly need," she says, relishing the moment.

I open the last gift and I'm speechless. It's a Sony CD Walkman...with anti-skip protection.

"No more limping around here like you're older than me, here's to walking like someone your age."

We share a long hug, and I apologize for being so moody lately.

"You're a teenager. I'd have you committed if you weren't." She pecks me on the forehead and all is well in our house again. "I was thinking, you start school and your new job on Tuesday, so what would you say about getting a hotel and spending the weekend in New York City?"

"Are you serious?"

She frowns. "No, I enjoy getting your hopes up and crushing them. Of course I'm serious. You in or you out?"

"Oh, I'm in."

The drive to the train station is a fun one, filled with songs and laughs, she even let me steer while she mimed the bass on Prince's D.M.S.R. I can't help but think she's enjoying this more than me. Grace didn't seem to have many friends, at least none that I had met, and though it was none of my business, I wondered if having me in her home was her way of staving off the loneliness. We never talked about her past; I wasn't exactly forthcoming in that department either, but it was driving me crazy that someone so full of life had nobody.

Maybe we were destined to meet, two jagged halves of a broken heart that could only mend with each other. I decide to love her as she loves me, and hope that when it's time for me to leave, it's worth enough that she'll want to stay in my life.

My phone beeps as we step onto the train and my heart jumps when I see that it's Jade.

What you up 2?

I text back telling her about my birthday trip and her response makes me wanna go back home.

Aww, Happy birthday dude. Was seeing if you wanted to hit the record shop and hang out. Well, enjoy your birthday and I'll see you at school. I'm happy that we met.

Do I really have to go to New York City? Excited as I am at the prospect, hanging out with Jade is just as good. But Grace was having a good time and I'd be incredibly ungrateful to ditch her to hang out with a girl.

But the idea of junior year sounds infinitely more pleasant than it did five minutes ago.

* * *

IT TAKES me less than a minute to fall in love with New York City.

I'm standing just outside Madison Square Garden, the Madison Square Garden, a place where every one of my favorite artists has made a name for themselves. The people move at a frenzied pace, averting eye contact and walking with a singular focus on getting where they need to go. It's overwhelming, but only for a second, because I realize that in this city, who I am and what I've been through only matters to me.

In neighborhoods like the one I come from and the one I'm currently living in, everything stands out. From your walk, to the brand of your clothes and sneakers, everything is fair game for questioning. But here, I can truly be myself. There's a guy walking around in a Deadpool costume, almost two months before Halloween, and nobody cares. Grace watches me intently, taking in the wonder on my face as I realize just how big the world really is.

"It's crazy isn't it?" she says.

"It's amazing." Somehow, I feel like I'm selling it short.

Grace grabs my hand and we head into the mass of people, all of the chaos around us still feeling organized. After walking for three blocks, I realize we are in Times Square, and the feeling I got standing outside comes rushing back again. The billboards advertise everything from clothes to music, rotating every few seconds, as if they knew we'd get bored with them. I manage to stay in the moment, thinking of all the times I spent my fun hour at the library looking at the very spot I was standing in. A trip like this was one of those things I'd promise myself I would take one day, even if I didn't believe it in my heart.

"It's amazing, isn't it?" Grace asks. "I've lost count how many times I've been here, and I still get that feeling I got the first time. Back in high school my friends and I used to sneak up here, fill up Gatorade bottles with vodka, and walk these streets for hours."

"Are you from here?"

"North Jersey, Elizabeth, actually. Four stops on the same train we took to get here."

"Did you ever take family trips here?"

This question makes her sad, and I regret asking it. "My

mom left me with her sister when I was four, not that my aunt was any more qualified to raise a child."

I have so many questions, but I had learned that if you are quiet, the questions sometimes answer themselves.

She takes a sip of her water and continues. "My aunt was a party girl, out every weekend like it was her job. I guess I shouldn't say I snuck up here because she wouldn't have cared anyway. But I fell into that life, drinking on the weekends and working twice as hard during the week to afford the next weekend."

"Is that why you don't have any children?"

She rubs my face. "Yes and no. I never thought I'd be stable enough to care for a child properly, and I refused to put a child through the same things I went through. By the time I convinced myself I could care for a child, life reminded me that it required a relationship, which to me felt like another ten years of soul searching and therapy. So, I decided it wasn't gonna happen for me and made peace with it."

I grip her hand in mine. "If you made peace with it, where do I fit into the equation?"

She smiles. "I thought you'd ask that. Not sure if you're a math kid, but you're the part of the equation that makes it the correct answer." She squeezes my hand, and even though I'm not a math kid, I understand we need each other. "Okay, now that you've heard my story, it's your turn to talk."

Words are failing me, because I'm not sure what she wants me to say. I've never had a conversation like this with anybody, and you would think that years spent alone, writing my feelings and giving monologues in the mirror to imaginary friends, would prepare me for this moment. But even I know this was too important of a moment to let slip away, so I opt for the truth.

"I wanted to hate you," I say. I can feel her gaze bearing

down on me, so I focus on the taxi stand. "I guess I thought...I don't know, maybe I thought it would make being a foster kid easier. Or that you were going to make me forget about my mother. But then I wondered...I wondered if having two moms was even a bad thing, and I've come to adore you." My heart is racing, but my thoughts are clear as I mentally mark things off my emotional checklist. "But as much as I want to love you, I'm scared, because one day I'll have to leave your home and you're gonna move on, you'll forget about me while I'll always remember you."

"Oh Percy, you don't have to—"

"That's not all."

"All right. Let it out, kid."

"I don't wanna go back home, back to having no food and no friends. But if I don't go back, or even give the hint of it, my mom will spiral and I'll never forgive myself for abandoning her."

My eyes finally meet hers and I can see that she's fighting back tears. "Let me ask you something: do you really think I'd forget about you?"

Hearing her pose the question made me realize how crazy the idea was, but I was too entrenched in my position to switch sides. "Maybe not right away, but eventually someone will come along and take my place."

"There is no other someone, Percy. It's you, and it'll only be you. The only time I wanna see you leave my home is when you're heading off to college." She smiles and wipes away her tears. "Who else can I count on to make sure the ice maker on the refrigerator is running properly." We both laugh at this. "You will always have a place in both my home and my heart, and if you want to stay, I will fight for you. And I promise that I'll be a part of your life for as long as you want me to be."

She leads me to the top of the TKTS stairs, and luckily we find a spot at the corner. "Let's take a picture." She pulls out her phone and opens the camera. "On three, okay?"

We both smile when she snaps the picture, and it immediately becomes my favorite picture ever. Our smiles are genuine, and for the first time in my life I feel a sense of normalcy I'd thought was impossible. Nobody on these steps with us knows who we are, or the separate roads we traveled to get here. For all they know we're another mother and son enjoying the last days before school starts.

She didn't want to replace my mother, but even if I allowed her that it would be selling her short. Grace is her own entity, carving out a special place in my heart by the second.

A place that even my mother couldn't access.

TEN

6 YEARS BEFORE THE OVERDOSE

I had badgered Momma for weeks to take me to Jake's Place, a park in Cherry Hill that was built to be all inclusive so those that were disabled had a place to play. Looking at our situation, I could only hope that applied to the financially disabled as well. It took a train and two buses to get there, but once I saw all the different jungle gyms, I knew it was worth the travel.

In Camden, the parks were equipped with bare minimum equipment. A slide, maybe some monkey bars, and if the city had recently elected a new mayor, that park would likely be upgraded with a fireman pole. Every park should've come with a tetanus shot voucher since upkeep wasn't in the budget.

But this park? This was different. I counted three slides before we entered the gates, and once we got closer, a four way seesaw, a bridge that teetered when kids ran across it, and a boat that rocked back and forth as you tried to keep your balance. What excited me most was the amount of kids at the park, with the odds in my favor that I'd actually have a friend to play with. At home it was just me and Momma, and while she tried, her medicine didn't make her the most willing play date. We found a bench under an awning to put our things and Momma reminded me that we didn't have too long because we had to make the food bank before they closed for the week. On top of that, the clouds were rolling in for the daily South Jersey thunderstorm.

"Go out there and make some friends," she said. "I'm gonna go take my medicine and I'll be right back." She grabbed her small handbag that held her medicine and headed to the bathroom.

I headed to the nearest group of kids, joining their game of tag on the sly, as if I had gotten lost. It was a game I would play at every playground, seeing how long I could join another family's game before they realized there was an imposter among their ranks. I'd wait until they were in a group, see who was 'it,' then break with the group of kids that were looking for cover. When they were done counting, they couldn't differentiate me from the other kids and I'd always let myself be caught. This was key, me giving myself up, because no kid ever wanted to be the one chasing everyone else. I'd always volunteer to do what the other kids didn't want to, figuring that little peace offering would make them like me. It worked most of the time, and when it didn't, I'd retreat to the jungle gym and wait for another group of willing kids to come along.

That day at Jake's place it worked, and we played spirited games of hide and seek for so long I really felt like I was part of their family. There was one kid, Ernest, that I got along well with, and we separated from the group to play on the parts of the playground that were more fun with two people.

"You jump high," he'd say, impressed with my ability to reach the monkey bars on my own. I'd spent so much time by myself that I didn't have anybody to help me up. Then he'd call his dad over to lift him up, but he could only make it halfway across.

A Mister Softee truck pulled up and it was like time stood still. Every kid ran to their parents, pleading for ice cream money, and all of them acquiesced, taking their hands and walking them to the truck. I knew it wasn't an option for me, and it's not like I could ask, because Momma was asleep on the bench next to our backpack. She'd packed ketchup and mustard sandwiches for us, and I ate mine while I waited for the other kids to finish their ice cream. She always loaded up on the ketchup so it was more sweet than tangy, and I could pretend it was a treat.

Once Ernest was finished, he waved me over and we continued playing, this time with his Pokémon figures."I only brought ten of them," he said, almost apologetically.

I noticed that his mother was hanging around us, never taking her eyes off of me whenever I would pick up a figure to play with. She could see I had no toys of my own to play with, and she'd eye me suspiciously whenever Ernest and I would run off in our battle.

A drizzle started coming down and his mom told him that it was time to leave.

"Mommy, can my friend, Percy, come over and play sometime?" he pleaded.

She took one look at me, in my stained shirt and scruffy shoes, then looked at Momma. I've never forgotten the look on her face, a mixture of disdain and pity. She was frustrated that 'street people' like us had not only infiltrated her neighborhood, but took it a step further in befriending her son. You'd have thought I'd asked to live with her, or that Momma had woken up and asked for bus money or a ride.

"I don't think that's a good idea," she said. "Maybe they'll be here next time we come back." Clearly she hoped to never see us again, and that Ernest would find better playmates next time. We high fived goodbye and I noticed his mother wipe his hand with a sanitizing wipe as they walked away.

The rain started to come down harder and Momma didn't move when I returned to the bench.

"Momma," I said. "Momma, all the kids left now." She didn't move an inch, sitting there drooling on her coat and oblivious to what was going on. I'd been here before, and I knew that all I could do was wait until her medicine wore off, and hopefully we'd be able to make the food bank, though I still had two sandwiches left just in case we didn't.

Looking back, that was the day I realized how rewarding, and ultimately fleeting, friendships could be. Those games with the other kids, and later Ernest, were a break for me. For once I didn't have to think about how poor I was, how little I had. But it had only brought disappointment, and I had enough of that on my own. My only friendship was over as quickly as it began, a reminder that any happiness I would experience would be temporary. While the park was an amazing experience, it also served as a reminder that I didn't belong, and I've carried that feeling with me everyday since.

As I sat on that bench with Momma, I vowed not to put myself out like that again, because with every passing day I was learning I couldn't depend on anybody to protect me. My dignity was the only tangible thing I had of value, and I would protect it with every fiber of my being.

ELEVEN

LIFE IS WAITING TO BEGIN

No matter your circumstances in life, the first day of school always inspires hope. I imagine it's how Cleveland Browns fans feel before kickoff of week one every year. They know they're in for the same misery, but that moment right before kickoff, when the fighter jets fly over the stadium and the players are locked in arms for the National Anthem, it carries infinite possibilities.

The walk to school takes fifteen minutes, with the large group of students resembling a cult walking through the neighborhood. I scan the crowd for Jade, but she's nowhere to be found, and just like that, my day loses some of its luster.

There's a stereotype that people from the inner city don't care about their education. While this may be true for some, I think it's a bit overblown. School for me has always been the one thing in my life that brought a sense of calm amidst the chaos of my home life. When I put my headphones on and walked the halls, I could pretend that I was someone else. Nobody knew that my mother was strung out, or that we were on the verge of being evicted again. At most they could guess my clothes were second hand, but judging by

Kanye's burgeoning fashion line that seemed to be the thing. I could pretend Momma was a homemaker, and that my father was on a business trip in Europe, and my fellow students wouldn't suspect a thing. As long as I kept to myself, snuffing out potential friendships with a sarcastic demeanor, this little world I had built in my head could thrive.

But my love of school goes deeper than my imagination. The classroom always leveled the playing field for me. The car your parents dropped you off in couldn't help you, neither could your parents gross annual income. It was about brain power, and my hours in the public library devouring knowledge made me feel confident enough to match wits with anyone, and that could get me where I needed to go. I'm honest about myself, so I can admit I lack the athletic requirements that would get me a scholarship, and while I enjoy writing, I'm not spitting hot sixteens that would bring record labels into my orbit. My mind will be my ticket out of this hell hole, hopefully into a nice college, but I'd settle for a place where nobody knows who I am.

The first indication that this school is different from my old one is the absence of metal detectors at the door. Administrators trust us, or at least trust that our home lives are stable enough to keep us from going crazy. The second indication is more mental. I enter this school with new clothes, a good paying job waiting for me after school, and the guarantee of a hot meal at the end of the day, but I still can't shake the feeling that I'm inferior to everyone else. Old habits die hard I guess, but every step I take into this building is a step out of a world I was comfortable in, and I vow not to let these new surroundings change who I am.

My first class is U.S. History, and I arrive before the teacher, but seemingly after everyone else. All eyes are on me when I enter, and I quickly spot the cliques gathered in every section of the room.

The intellectuals cover the front of the class, speaking in hushed tones with their heads on a swivel for the arrival of our instructor. They tap their fingers when they talk, just itching to raise their hands to assert their intellectual superiority. Behind them, tucked in the back corner of the classroom, are the goths. Some people are freaked out by them, but I've always thought they were kinda cool. They rarely spoke, and as an introvert myself, I can only appreciate their commitment to solitude. Across from them, occupying the entire other side as if it were a protest are the popular kids. A vast mix of Ugg boots and frappuccinos for the girls, and letterman jackets and Gatorade for the guys, with a collective IQ that topped out in the double digits even if you rounded to the nearest hundred. Unfortunately, the only open seat is in this section, so my arrival pushes the cumulative IQ points above the hundred threshold. My good deed for the day is done.

"Looks like someone is benefiting from donations to the Salvation Army," one of the guys says. He's the king of the jocks; I can tell by his seat in the middle. He's got a scar on his forehead, and I can only hope it's because someone slapped the shit out of him.

"And it looks like you benefitted from your parents failed coat hanger experiment," I reply, running my finger across my forehead.

This gets laughter from the other side of the class, and just like that, I'm champion of the underclass.

"What does that mean?"

"Look, dude, I don't have the time, or the required amount of crayons, to explain it to you."

He shoots out of his seat, making a beeline for me and validating my suspicions of his intelligence.

"So, you can see where he got his clothes from, but couldn't see the triple coverage you threw into on that pick six at the scrimmage?" a voice asks from behind me.

The whole class turns to see our teacher has arrived. I knew the teachers would be different, but I didn't think they'd be this cool. His sense of style is sharp, walking the delicate line between professional and leisure with the skill of a trapeze artist. The outfit he's wearing was good enough to teach in, with the dark brown cargo pants pairing nicely with the white button up; but the Chuck Taylors, denim jacket, and Pharrell Williams style hat made it just as acceptable at a cigar lounge. He's a good looking guy, and I'd be willing to bet my first paycheck that he gets more attendance from fathers at his parent teacher conferences, and it ain't to know how their kids are interpreting the invasion of Pearl Harbor.

Wait a minute, did he just say this blockhead threw an interception? That means he's a quarterback, which would make him Jade's boyfriend. I'd spent many hours listening to Muse and cursing this guy's existence, wishing I had met her first. It feels nice to put a face to the hate.

"Take your seats, gentlemen," the teacher says. "We'll study our fair share of wars in this class, no need to reenact them." He sits his bag on the desk, and once we are back in our seats, introduces himself. "My name is Mr. Jones, and while your class schedules say I'm your history teacher, it means nothing. The only difference between us is that I've experienced a little bit more life than you."

He writes the word history on the board, lets it sit for a few seconds, then crosses out the first two letters. "That's what this class is, one long ass story after another."

A hand shoots up from the intellectual section. "If it's just telling a story, then why are we here?" the girl asks.

He strokes his goatee. "That's a fair question, and thankfully, I have an answer, because if I didn't...well, I'm pretty sure I'd be unemployed." This gets laughs from all of us. "My job isn't to rehash what happened before, there's whole libraries for that. My job is to teach you to think for yourself. Look around the world we live in. Everything, from the news to our smartphones, is trying to sway you. Everyday your psyche is under attack, and it would be easy to find an argument you're comfortable with and hold onto it."

He takes a sip of his coffee, and it's so quiet I can hear the sneakers squeaking outside the door of kids that were late. "The problem with that...lies in the fact that as a society we equate easy with being right. It's easy to believe poor people wanna be on welfare, because studying the issue is too hard and might reveal truths that make us uncomfortable. It's easy to believe that anyone who leans to the right politically is a racist, because we've been trained to view conversations about conflicting ideologies as an effective method of burning bridges with those close to us. So, looking at it through those lenses, my job isn't to teach you history, it's about teaching you empathy for your fellow person."

I always thought English would be my favorite class, given the ability to articulate my thoughts and compare my feelings to authors past and present. Physical Education was a bore. Math was easy because being poor my whole life taught me how to deal with numbers, and science, well, I'd held a lighter underneath a spoon enough times while my mother was dope sick that I can make an argument for letting me transfer in science credits. History has always been a toss up, but I can admit that this will be my favorite class, and it's not even a close contest.

"Now, before you run home and tell your parents about the radical history teacher, understand that I'll never try to sway you. This class is about human interaction as much as it is history. We'll have debates, maybe a couple of laughs, but when you leave this class, you'll be able to communicate effectively, or at least well enough to avoid ending up on the news."

* * *

IF THE CLASSROOM was God's way of leveling the playing field, then lunchtime was his way of restoring the world of high school to its proper pecking order. The jocks and the popular kids took all the prime real estate under the shade, with school security mingling so close to them they looked like their private security force. Everyone else is forced to find relief from the sweltering heat in their own ways, which leads to some of the most creative uses of a backpack that I've ever seen.

Back home, school lunch for me meant I was guaranteed at least one meal a day, two if I woke up early enough to make it before they stopped serving breakfast. Most days I'd be so hungry that I didn't care what they cooked. If you were poor enough, you were entitled to free meals. Before the school year, they'd send you a book of lunch tickets, organized by month with a ticket for breakfast and lunch each day. It was poverty's version of an advent calendar, and instead of chocolate everyday, we were greeted with food containing sodium levels that were higher than our parents on the first of the month. School lunches taught me more about Socialism than my government classes ever did. Sometimes I could scrounge up enough money for a slice of pizza, because even Cinderella got to live the good life for a bit before the carriage turned into a pumpkin.

At this school I get to live the best of both worlds. Since I'm a ward of the state, free lunch was included—what a deal. And because I have a loving foster mother that views me as more than extra income, I have money for lunch. On the menu today is Salisbury steak, and since my bowels have been working just fine, I opt to buy lunch instead. Unfortunately, they run out of pizza two people ahead of me.

"Sorry, guys, all I got left are tacos," the lunch lady says. Everyone groans and a majority of students leave the line, kinda like the home crowd at a basketball game after the visiting team hits a three to put the game away.

"If you wanted to keep the bigger slices for yourself, just say that," says the kid in front of me. "I only have enough money for pizza, don't do me like this on Salisbury steak day."

They argue back and forth long enough for a couple of minutes before I can't take it anymore. "I'll take two orders of tacos, ma'am," I interject. "One for me and one for him." I pay for our food and we head out in search of a table.

"I appreciate it," he says. "But by doing that you let the powers that be win."

"What the hell are you talking about?" I reply. "We're two students arguing over tacos prepared by underpaid cafeteria workers, not Che Guevara and Fidel Castro overthrowing the Cuban government."

He takes a bite of a taco and considers this. "You're right. it's just first day jitters and Megan's law. I'm Eric, by the way."

"Percy—wait, what did you say?"

"I said first day jitters—"

"I got that part, you said Megan's Law?"

"Yeah...you know, the rule about anything can go wrong will go wrong."

"Um, I think you mean Murphy's Law...pretty sure Megan's Law is for registered sex offenders."

"No way. Are you sure?" He stares into the sky as he thinks about it. I can see his mind working like a pinball machine, with my nugget of truth bouncing around the corners of his brain before settling. Suddenly, his face turns to amazement. "Oh shit, *that's* why people look at me like that when I say it."

"You're funny as hell." I look around for a place to sit, and Eric can sense my despair.

"Dude, lets go sit at one of the shaded tables."

"I'm not sure if you realize it, Eric, but that's not exactly our section."

He twists his face up. "The hell it's not, our parents pay property taxes just like theirs. We have a right to sit anywhere we damn well please."

I don't think Momma has ever paid taxes, but that's beside the point. We find a table, and it gives me the same feeling I had the first time Grace took me to Costco. The popular kids know we don't belong, and within a minute they're on us, led by our illustrious quarterback. He's got his letterman jacket on now, proclaiming him to be Casey, and I'm smiling before he even opens his mouth.

"Now you two know damn well this isn't where you should be eating," he says.

His fellow players laugh in a way that makes me feel small, which is quite a feat considering just two months ago I was eating out of a garbage can. Eric decides to take point for us.

"Coach Fitz knows damn well you aren't leading us anywhere either, but hey, we all make our choices right?"

Okay, so negotiating isn't his strong suit. Noted.

The players move closer to us as their girlfriends step to the side, and apparently our friendship is about to be solidified by getting our asses kicked together. We're outnumbered by at least 8-1, possibly more because I only counted the letterman jackets. It's like the scene in Mulan, when they fired all their rockets and the Huns came storming down the mountain.

Casey removes his jacket and the rest follow suit, relishing the chance to flex their muscles early in the school year and make an example for anyone that dared to stray from the pecking order.

Before we can formulate a strategy, someone grabs both of my arms, lifting me in the air, and before Eric can help, he's in the same position. The bloodthirsty crowd roars with approval, while school security is oblivious to what's going on. Casey gets in my face, close enough that I can count the acne on his face, sitting like snow capped Rockies on his cheeks.

"Mr. Jones can't save you this time, Salvation Army," he sneers before driving his fist into my stomach.

Eric tries to kick out but is greeted with the same treatment. We both cough, trying to recapture the wind that was knocked out of us.

"Hey, Percy," he says between labored breaths. "Next time lunch is on me."

Through the pain I manage a laugh, before deciding to join in on the fun. "Actually, lunch is on Coach Fitz, since that punch is the most accurate thing he'll throw all year."

Now Eric is drooling with laughter, and we get a few giggles from the crowd. I'm pretty sure I've found my best friend, the Andy Richter to my Conan O'Brien, because if someone can crack jokes with you while being held up like a piñata, they're good people.

Unfortunately, Casey doesn't find our jokes funny and winds up to hit me square in the face when someone grabs his arm.

It's Jade.

I've known Casey for about thirty minutes, wondering what she saw in this guy that seemed her polar opposite in every way, but seeing them next to each other was still striking. She's refined in all the right ways, destined to forever be the girl of my dreams, while he seemed like the type to eat his cereal with a fork if left on his own. Life is so unfair sometimes.

"Casey, what are you doing?" she asks, horrified.

He looks at her, then back at us before nodding to his minions who release us. "These guys are nobodies, babe," he says. "We had to put them in their place."

"Get out of here before you get suspended; we'll talk later."

They leave just as the bell rings and the crowd disappears.

She stays, looking at us with pity in her eyes. "Nice way to introduce yourself at a new school," she says to me. "Are you all right?"

I consider the question, and while on the surface I'd just gotten my ass kicked, I'd found a new friend in Eric and finally found her. Not a bad first day. "Never been better. Eric, meet Jade."

He nods and she smiles back innocently, as if her boyfriend didn't just try to break the record for quickest trip to the nurses office on the first day of school.

"Thanks for saving me. I didn't wanna have to explain to Randy that I couldn't work my first day on the job because my face was being put back together."

"You got a job at Backside?"

"Yeah, my foster mother wanted me to learn life skills."

Eric looks puzzled by this information, and I shoot him a look letting him know I'll explain later. We were fending off the invasion of the idiots before we could get to know each other. "I hate to break this up," he says. "But we better get to class before we end up on the truant list."

As luck would have it, Eric and I have math together,

while Jade officially becomes my classmate during last period English. Now I'll have something to look forward to at the end of every day. A group of girls that are way outta our league tell Jade it's time for class, and she smiles at us before running off.

I'm not sure where my friendship with Jade will go from here. We have each other's phone number, and share similarities that few others could match, but she was part of the 'it' crowd, a group I wanted no part of. It makes me sad, because if I had met her under different circumstances we'd be perfect for each other. But for now I have to be happy with the occasional text, or the cursory glance in the hallway when we lock eyes, and amidst the chaos of high school, know that there was someone else out there that just...understands.

"You two have something going on?" Eric asks.

"I'm only good enough for girls like that in my dreams."

"That's some profound shit, but if we don't make it to Algebra in the next five minutes, we'll be writing our own Shakespearean tragedy."

TWELVE

FIGHTING THE GOOD FIGHT

I'm in a funk when I make it to Backside Records for my first day of work. I thought having Jade in a class would be a great idea, but I knew from where she chose to sit that it wasn't gonna play out like I thought. She took a seat with the popular kids, and for the duration of class pretended that I didn't exist. When I stuttered while introducing myself, she laughed with the rest of them, the laugh that I fell for in the record store and at court cutting deeper than the others because I could single it out amongst the others. But I knew it wasn't her, because when nobody was looking I'd catch a stolen glance, a subtle reminder that she was just playing her part to get through the day. That made it hurt a little less, but still threw my day off.

I know that when you're feeling your worst, that's when others seem to be the happiest, so I'm not surprised that Randy is practically bursting at the seams with positivity the minute I walk in.

"Walking in for his first day of work," he yells like a PA announcer. "Grace's newest son, and the de facto employee of the month for the foreseeable future, Percy—"

"I get the point, Randy," I say.

He works quickly to get me up to speed. A steady stream of customers allows me to learn the register system, while he explains how I would be responsible for doing inventory every other shift. I'm doing said inventory when he calls me over to the register. "This," he says, pointing to a large stereo next to the register, "is one of the most important aspects of the operation."

"What is it?"

"It's the stereo that controls the sound system in the store. Before a customer even sees you, what they hear coming in the door is what ultimately determines if they stay or not. If you play some bullshit, they're gonna leave. So, the key to this is knowing what to play, and when to play it."

"And how do I do that?"

"Well, thankfully I've got years in this business and have it down to a science."

He explains it eloquently, but when I take off the employee goggles, I admit to myself that its really just customer traffic patterns with a hint of age discrimination. Hip-Hop can only be played on weekends, since we are most likely to have a younger demographic. The majority of the time rock from the 80's and 90's would be playing, catering to the middle age customer that makes up most of our business. Once the store is closed, I'm free to play whatever I want—except for Nickelback.

"Can I ask you something, Randy?"

"Shoot."

"Everything is digital now; what keeps us in business?"

If we weren't in his store, I'm sure he would've spit on the floor at the mention of digital downloads. "Middle age folks can barely work their phones, so I can count on them to go with what's familiar. I don't count on your age group too much, because for every one of you there's ten other kids that use Spotify."

"Do you ever feel like giving up?"

He ponders this. "This place cost me my marriage, so I guess we're past the point of no return. But I grew up playing music, and it kills me that people have forgotten the concept of an album. The beauty of taking a piece of work in as a whole, seeing an artist's vision and finding how it relates to your everyday life, ya know?"

"It's like if someone showed you half of the Mona Lisa, you wouldn't see it as the masterpiece that it is."

"Exactly. Music is art, and should be treated as such. If an artist wanted you to listen only to certain songs, they'd put it out as a single or an EP. So as long as I have money, Backside Records will be here to guide the willing souls and reclaim the ones lost in the digital matrix."

Hearing Randy describe the store like this makes me feel like I'm serving a bigger purpose. I would've taken any job, but I've been blessed enough to find one I'll actually enjoy.

Grace walks in with two Tupperware dishes, dressed for her shift at the diner. She gives him a hug and kisses me on the forehead, a gesture I've come to look forward to.

"So what do you think, Randy?" she asks.

"I think this is the beginning of a beautiful relationship."

"Good to hear." She hands each of us a bowl. "Spaghetti and meatballs, courtesy of yours truly."

"You're truly an angel, Grace," he says.

"Don't I know it." They exchange smiles that make me feel weird, but I convince myself to think nothing of it. "Percy, can I see you outside?"

We head outside to her car, passing customers coming into the store. "I'm off to work, but I wanted to let you know that there's extras in the fridge if you're still hungry when you get home."

"Thanks. I wanted to run something by you."

"Let's hear it."

"Well, it looks like I'll make enough here to cover any extra activities I might do. Do you think you can just put my state checks straight into my savings account?"

"You're really taking this money thing seriously."

"It's the first time I've ever had it."

"I hear that." She checks her watch. "Oh, can't be late. I wanted to let you know I'm covering an extra couple of hours so I'll be home later than usual. Also, I gave Alex your phone number, so he'll be calling to set up our visit schedule and coordinate visits with your Mom."

In the midst of everything going on I'd forgotten about her. I also was disappointed with how our visit had gone after court. But with her brought back to the forefront I realize how much I miss her. Grace kisses me on the cheek and drives off to her job.

The customers are leaving as I get back into the store, and I find Randy reorganizing the box sets. I notice the Beatles Apple set has been sold, and I vow to not let it slip through my hands again.

"You sold the set?" I ask.

"Yup." He notices my tone. "You sound disappointed."

"I was hoping to buy that one day."

"We get those in all the time, your day will come. I couldn't help but notice your notebook next to the register. You like making playlists?"

"I prefer the term mixtape." I explain to him the differ-ence. Playlist sounds too modern, like it's thrown together with no regard for the listener's emotions. A playlist is a role of the dice, a grouping of random tracks created by people that enjoy elevator music. A mixtape is different, more personal, almost like a love letter. It's more like playing darts, with the listener being the dart board. The bullseye is the heart of the person you make it for, slowly seducing them with a mix of songs that are both familiar and foreign, organized in a way that they'd never know the difference. Simply put, playlists are for the mood, mixtapes are for the moment.

"You ever made one for anybody?" he asks.

"No. Never really had the means or the special person to make one for. But when the time comes, I'll be ready."

"I feel like you could do the same thing with an album."

"Albums are great, I'm not knocking them. But your message can get lost when they hear the same voice over and over. Think of it as telling someone you love them with fifteen different voices. Right when they get tired of Prince, boom, David Ruffin and the Temptations come in to take the baton."

"I like the way you think. Who knows, maybe I'll need your expertise in that area soon." He checks his watch. "I gotta order some inventory. Hold the fort down up here and give me a shout if you need help."

I keep myself busy by getting a head start on my homework. An hour later the store phone rings. My first shot at telling the world I'm an employee.

"Thank you for calling Backside Records," I say, figuring it's a telemarketer.

"Percy," my mother says. "How are you doing?"

I don't know how to feel about this. On one hand I'm happy to hear her voice, but on the other she knows where I work, which means she knows I have income coming in. "How did you know I was here?"

"Your social worker told me you worked in a record shop. I wanted to see how your first day of school went."

"Oh." My mind flashes to Casey driving his fist into my stomach. "It went really well. How are you doing?"

"I'm good. Listen, I don't have time to talk, but I want you to know that I've been clean since I left the hospital and I'm going to get you back."

I'm not really in the mood to play the game of placating her right now, so I keep the focus on her. "Where are you staying?"

"Back at the shelter, but just until I get back on my feet."

I've been alive for sixteen years, and I've never seen her gain her balance, let alone stand stable on her feet. "Look, Mom. I don't think I can take personal calls here at work." I make a rash decision to avoid conflict. "I'll give you my cell phone number so you can call me directly, just don't tell my foster mother or Alex."

She agrees, and against my better judgement, I give her my number. She promises again to 'make everything like it was' and hangs up.

Make everything how it was?

What exactly did she mean by that? Because 'how it was' is what got us in this situation, and now that I know what it means to have a stable home life, going back to that isn't an option. But what if she's really changed? That's the question that'll keep me up tonight. In spite of everything I owe her the chance to make it right. But I also know that she's an addict, and their chemically warped existence is predicated on manipulating loved ones into getting what they want. So the question is: does she really want me back, or does she just want the confines of my unconditional love that enables her to live how she pleases?

The answer is both, and in that is the evidence of how devastating addiction is. I carry her addiction as if it were my own. It's funny that I was foolish enough to believe that being in foster care would allow someone else to carry that burden for a change, allowing me to focus on myself at this critical juncture in my life. But the truth is, it weighs on me heavier than it did when I was home. Back then I could protect her, knowing that I had Narcan in my sock in case she overdosed, or by taking the license plate numbers on the cars of the Johns that picked her up in case she went missing. Heck, even coming back to our tent and finding her nodding off was comforting because I knew where she was.

But now I'm out of the picture, transforming from an enabler of her self destruction to a spectator of it. I don't know where she is, or who she's with, what their intentions are, and the unknown scares me.

I used to think watching her struggle up close was hard, but I can say watching it from afar is worse. When I was with her, I could tell myself the next needle was the last one, or pretend that while I was at school, she was in an outpatient clinic getting the help we both knew she needed. Giving her my cell phone number is my way of staying close to her, because from afar I'm forced to take her promises of sobriety at face value and rely on something that's been avoiding me since I first learned how to walk.

Hope.

THIRTEEN

A SIXTH SENSE FOR DESPAIR

The pizza place Alex takes me to looks like every other pizza place in New Jersey. Huge pies sit behind the glass, ready to be consumed at a moment's notice. Since we're having our visit around my work schedule he picked me up from school, with a promise that we'd eat at a place that's far enough away that I wouldn't risk being seen by any classmates. I should've got assurances he wouldn't wear something hideous, with his white puffy coat making him resemble the Michelin Man.

We order two plain slices each and take a seat in a booth.

"So," he says while dumping heaps of Parmesan cheese on his pizza. "What's life been like this first month?"

"It's been...interesting." I take a bite of my pizza. "I guess I had all these emotions lined up in my head, but what I'm actually experiencing isn't matching up."

"From what Grace tells me you're doing well. Got yourself a job, and she says you've learned how to budget your money. I'm proud of you."

The last part stops me in the middle of a bite. Nobody has ever told me they were proud of me. We're long past lip service in our relationship, so I know he means it. It's a weird feeling hearing it, though, having a person congratulate you for surviving day to day life. Maybe when I was back in Camden living hand to mouth, but with the situation I'm in now I would be a fool to screw it up.

"Thanks, Alex, but it's really not that hard to do well when you're given the tools to succeed."

"There are people that live their whole lives without figuring out what you just said." He finishes his first slice and loads up the second one with cheese. "What did you mean about things not adding up?"

"It's hard to explain, but I guess the simplest way to put it was I expected to hate it. Grace, my situation...everything. But it's been cool to see what I can accomplish with a level playing field, even if I have to go back one day."

"Do you wanna go back home?"

"I love my mom."

"That's not what I asked you."

I push my plate away and take a sip of my drink. "I wanna go back, but I know in my heart it's not for the right reasons. I have friends here, Alex, real friends that I can pick up the phone and call right now. When we hang out, I feel like I'm an equal, just any other kid trying to get to graduation. I've even started looking up scholarships for college."

"Oh yeah? Any school in particular?"

"I wanna go to NYU. Grace took me up there for a weekend trip before school started and I fell in love with the place."

He nods as listens to this. "It sounds like you wanna stay with Grace."

My stomach turns at the suggestion and I run my palms over my thighs. "It's not that simple for me."

"Yes, it is."

"It's not," I say, slamming my palms on the table.

He's not startled in the least, like he expected that reaction.

"If I stay, then I can't protect her, and she's worth more to me than anything. Did you ever deal with anything like that?"

He raises both eyebrows and cocks his head as if to say he experienced something similar. "Yes and no, but a lot of it comes down to me being much younger when I was placed in a foster home. It's been you and her your entire life, same as me, the difference is I didn't know any better at my age so my upbringing felt normal."

"That doesn't make any sense."

"It makes perfect sense. You don't want it to make sense because it'll make you question everything about your life. But you trying to rationalize going back to where you came from tells me you know this is where you want to be."

"I have to be there to help her."

"Help her how?" he asks. "By sitting by and watching her inject poison into her body? That's enabling her, even if she'd like you to think you're helping. Now, you can go back to how things were, and I have no doubt that one day you'll make it out and be successful. But you know what the roughest lesson I learned in foster care was?"

"That social workers are assholes."

He chuckles at this. "That's a good one...but no. The hardest lesson was learning to separate my mother's burdens from my own. We live with these people for so long that we take their addictions and life failures as our own, when it's not ours to carry. Separating yourself doesn't mean you love her any less."

"I just feel like I'm losing part of myself."

"What do you mean?"

"Everything I'm experiencing now is so different than what I was used to. Every meal leaves me feeling guilty instead of full, even wiping my ass with toilet paper makes me feel sad because I feel like I left her behind while I'm living the good life."

"That's an interesting way to put it."

"But it's the truth. Everyday I feel like I'm losing appreciation for the simple things in life, like I'm becoming one of the kids I used to envy. I guess...I guess I just feel the life I'm living now is meant for somebody else."

He gives me a half smile, almost as if he can see himself in my plight. But I sense that he's not sounding the alarm because what I'm feeling is natural, and there are times when I tell myself to snap out of it.

"I used to feel that way," he says. "But with time I've come to appreciate the experience because it allowed me to view the world with empathy. Of course, I didn't always see it that way, but over time I've come to believe that everything happens for a reason."

"I see Parmesan cheese isn't the only thing you lay on thick."

"You might think that, but consider this. Why did I end up being your social worker? Of all the people in my office, I was the one on call the weekend your mother overdosed. The one person from the same neighborhood as you. And of all the foster parents in this county, why was Grace the one you were placed with?"

I don't have an answer for him, and if he gave me a whole month I still wouldn't have an answer, because I've felt it everyday. "When I'm dancing with Grace in the kitchen, or hanging out with Eric, that's when it all makes sense."

"That's because you're experiencing love in its healthiest form. Your mother loves you, so don't take this the wrong way, but it was toxic. Having you be her pseudo guardian is toxic. Love comes in many forms, and hers was toxic. You not wanting to go back to how you were living is tough love."

"Do you think she can get me back?"

His entire mood changes with that question. Now he's rubbing his hands together nervously, and if it weren't dealing with my living situation, I'd find it hilarious. "If she can get clean and stay that way, it's a possibility." This makes me nibble on my thumb as I consider this. "But if you want to stay I can make it clear to the judge that you're comfortable where you are."

I appreciate his candor, but my mouth still goes dry at the reality of the situation. Assuming she stays sober it's going to come down to what I wanna do. I'd always enjoyed making decisions for myself, but this time I wish someone else could share this burden.

Or at least the consequences of it.

FOURTEEN

SO THIS IS HOW FRIENDSHIPS WORK?

My first couple weeks of work pass by with little fanfare. The money has been great, and now that I've proven myself to be reliable, Randy leaves me to run the shop on Sundays and Mondays. Other than his weird rules for the playlist, I hold the fort down pretty well, bringing in steady sales through my conversations with customers. Friday through Sunday are the busiest days, bringing in a diverse clientele, from high schoolers looking for the newest releases, to adults looking for a way to relive their youth over the weekend. The other days I spend staying ahead of my homework load, with Momma's old 'study hour' rule guiding me to perfect grades in these first few weeks.

Working here has brought me out of my shell, and I've come to enjoy the back and forth with the customers, especially the older ones. They tell the best stories, letting me in on which bands are worth seeing live, what albums I should skip while going through a discography, and my personal favorite, debating the merits of current musicians versus older ones. Retail work itself is about studying the customers and devising strategies that keep them coming back.

For me, this job is deeper than that. It's taught me to interact with other people while viewing myself as an equal. Growing up, I never thought of myself as having anything of value to offer in a conversation—or life in general—so when I'd find myself in conversation with someone it was always one-sided. People love to talk about themselves, so I'd ask enough questions to keep them talking, all the while divulging as little as possible about myself. I'd found so much comfort in being alone and keeping things to myself that the arrangement was a win-win for me and whomever I was talking to. They got to boast of their accomplishments, and I got to believe they liked me because I was willing to listen to their stories. I was starting to understand that I'm on equal footing as a human being with everyone, and now I was setting the tone in conversations instead of following someone else's lead. This extended to my interactions with Randy.

You can learn a lot about people by watching them shop for music. Whether it's in the choices they make, or if they're reluctant to try new genres, every move they make in the store gives a little insight into what makes them tick. Realizing this, I suggested to Randy that we use the stereo near the register to allow customers to skim through the used CDs they were considering. My argument catered to his belief that we should be engaging customers, with my idea being that if they didn't like what they heard, I could engage them and hopefully convince them to keep searching, ultimately ending in a sale. I also let slip that iTunes allowed customers to sample songs before they buy them, and after a ten minute rant about how digital downloads were killing the music industry he agreed to let me run with it. It had been a success, with our sales up enough that Randy gave me a cash bonus of $250.

With the more talkative customers, I made a game of asking them one question while ringing out their purchase.

"If I never see you again," I'd say, "give me one album I have to listen to before I die."

I didn't mean it in a morbid way, that's just how I phrased it. Every customer I'd asked got excited about the question, giddily giving me their favorite albums, like they'd been sitting on a secret and they were happy to let it out. And that is the beauty of this place. We offer music, sure, but what we really do is sell people a vacation from their daily lives. Seeing the excitement on a customer's face when I confirmed that we had their favorite records in stock is an example of this.

"Oh, man," a customer would say after I handed him a copy of Weezer's debut album. "This is my childhood right here, man."He bought the record, along with a few others, and promised to stop back in. Sure enough, three days later he was back, swapping recommendations with me before buying another five albums.

I'm happy that work has been going well, because my personal life is a train wreck. Since my visit with Alex, it's been a struggle to reconcile that I'll be walking away from all this. My mother is my mother, and if she was doing enough to turn her life around and get me back, then I owed my loyalty to her. Even though I know it's months away it's affecting me now, with me avoiding the same things I was ecstatic about weeks ago. In my mind I had to distance myself from these things, figuring if there was no emotional connection, it would be easy to live without them.

My friendship with Eric has suffered the most. While we still ate lunch together everyday, thankfully without having it come with a side of whoop ass, I was resistant to his overtures of having me come over and hang out with his family. I'd claim I was working on days I was off, or blame Grace and non-existent chores when that was convenient, when I was actually just sitting in my room marinating in my sorrows like a pot roast. Even though I knew he had both parents at home, there was something about him that let me know he understood what I was going through. What I enjoy the most about our friendship is how we communicate at times without using words. When he would cover lunch, or an after school trip to 7-11, he'd wave off my money.

"Just get me next time," he'd say, a subtle acknowledgment that he was committed to our friendship over the long haul. Which makes me even sadder because he doesn't know that one day there won't be a next time. He knows I'm living with Grace, but he doesn't know why, and if I give him that, it means I'm giving him a piece of myself, and I can't afford to have that kind of attachment be ripped away.

He must know I'm thinking this because a call from him is coming through on my phone. I let out a sigh and debate which lie I'm gonna use to get out of the inevitable invitation. "What up, E?"

"My right hand man," he exclaims. "What would you say if I told you that in spite of your distant personality lately, I've lined up the greatest Halloween of your life?"

The tone of his voice makes me nervous. "I'd say you're full of shit. But I'm working that night anyway."

He smacks his lips. "I thought you'd say that, but I called the store and apparently you guys are closing early on Halloween, you know, since customers are out trick or treating."

If he's anything, it's persistent. I don't have a reason to say no and we both know it. Instead of acknowledging it I study the back of Oasis's second album and wonder why the opener starts with the chords from *Wonderwall*. Eric, sensing that I'm trapped, decides to help me out.

"All right, look," he says, with a more serious tone. "Maria agreed to go trick or treating with me. But since we're meeting at my house she needs to be sure I'm not a serial killer." He waits for me to finish laughing before he moves on. "So she's bringing a friend with her, but how the hell can I make a move with mother hen watching what's going on?"

"I'm not sure I'm the best person for this role?"

"You kidding me? You've got that mysterious way about you that girls find appealing, and you haven't asked what she looks like, so I know that you're not shallow enough to blow this. Plus, we got beat up together, why not have our first date together?"

I can't help but laugh at his logic, and my cackle makes him seethe through the phone. "I kinda wanna see if, you know, maybe there's something there with Jade."

Now it's his turn to laugh, and he takes full advantage, laughing so hard he chokes on his own spit. After catching his breath and being sure I understood how crazy I sounded, he replies, "Yeah, and maybe the Rays outbid the Yankees for the top outfielder on the market."

I laugh with him because it keeps me from crying. Truth is, since the first day of school my friendship with Jade has been non-existent. She smiles at me in the hallway, grabbing my hand as she passes my locker, but it's clear we live in two different stratospheres. We're two kids from screwed up situations that have chosen to handle them differently. I've chosen to keep my connections to a minimum, waiting for the day when this carriage I'm riding in turns back into a pumpkin. She's opted for the opposite, jumping into friendships and relationships that don't make any sense to me. I'm still reconciling how the girl I met in that record shop, the one that touched my shoulder and laughed at my jokes, could roll with people like that. To her I'm an interlude, thrown in every now and then to pass the time before the next song on an album.

"I hear what you're saying, Eric, but I've never been on a

date before. I wouldn't know the first thing about being out with a girl."

"That's what you're worried about? Dude, it's simple. If she looks at you, give her a smile. If she tells a joke, you laugh, even if it's horrible. And if by God's grace her hand ends up in your pants, think about organizing your CD collection so you last long enough to not embarrass yourself."

"We're not getting laid," I say, angry at the 'we' part.

"Not with that attitude we aren't." His mother calls for him, so he decides to close the deal. "In all seriousness, I need you on Saturday. I really like this girl, and I think meeting a girl will be good for you. Plus, you get to meet my family, my Dad is cooking, and you go home with a plate and a big bag of candy. I'm asking as a friend."

I let him hang for a second, not because I'm considering it, my mind is made up, but more to be an asshole and take in the feeling of being needed. I'm used to needing others, but hearing the sincerity in his voice makes me feel bad that I've been so distant with him. "All right, I'll be there."

"Sweet. I promise, it'll be one of the best nights of your life."

After he hangs up, I consider what just happened. A smile slowly creeps across my face as I realize what it means. I wouldn't call it a date, since we're being thrown together like two cereals that don't have enough left in the box for a bowl on its own. But there's a weird excitement.

Because for the first time, I feel like a real teenager.

FIFTEEN

COSTUMES AREN'T ONLY FOR HALLOWEEN

I haven't been this nervous in my entire life.

Unfortunately, this was one emotion I'll be carrying on my own since everyone else in my life is acting like this is the greatest thing in the world.

Eric has forgotten everything else that matters in life since I agreed to come on this little adventure. Every moment we've spent together has been about tonight. He planned the night out entirely, accounting for any potential mishaps with contingency plans for each. I'm to walk no further than eight feet behind him and Maria, while coming no closer than six feet. Just enough distance to stay out of earshot, but not far enough to freak her out. When we go trick or treating, I am to hang back at every house and keep the friend, codename 'warden,' occupied long enough for him to get uninterrupted conversation. Seriously, if JFK had put this much thought into the Bay of Pigs, Castro would've been out a long time ago.

Grace reacted like I'd won the World Series when I told her of my plans. Taking the situation out of the equation, it felt good to see how proud she was of me. My progress report had me on pace for a perfect GPA, so her investment in me was paying huge dividends. She took me to the mall for an outfit, the first sign to me of how significant this was.

"It's so good to see you out meeting people," she said. "My little guy is growing up right before my eyes. Pretty soon you'll be getting ready for homecoming."

"I'm not going to homecoming."

"You have to go; it's where all teenagers...never mind, we'll cross that bridge when we get to it. This might be a weird question, but are you strapped up?"

I laughed right in her face. "It's illegal, and besides, I don't need a gun for a date."

She gave me a quizzical look, smiled, then sent me off to try on a sports coat. When I told Randy of her reaction later he laughed, explained how I got it wrong, then upped the awkwardness by giving me a condom from a box in his back-pack. I couldn't help but notice that the box was already open, but I'd had a great lunch that day and wanted to keep it down, so I chose not to dwell on why he had an open box of condoms.

Alex, my affable and fashion challenged social worker, had the reaction that aligned closest with my own.

"Not bad for a kid that swore he was gonna run away the first time I met him," he said. Little did he know that it was definitely an option if I embarrassed myself.

So all of that brings me to Eric's doorstep with sixty bucks in my pocket, a sports coat that's itchy around the collar, and a condom that'll only be used if an impromptu water balloon fight breaks out. I'm early because I misjudged how long it would take to walk two blocks, and I consider leaving and coming back but the door swings open.

Eric greets me with a devilish grin. His usually wild hair is tamed into a bowl cut, and if I squinted he could pass for a fifth Beatle. Unfortunately his membership in the Fab Four is suspended by the rest of his ensemble. He's got a powder blue dress shirt, unbuttoned at the top, exposing his chest hair and some sort of religious pendant. Dark jeans and dress shoes complete his outfit and I'm not sure if we're gonna double date or negotiate cocaine prices. If he and Alex died today, Ross and Marshalls would file for bankruptcy tomorrow.

"Please tell me that's your Halloween costume," I say.

"Says the guy dressed like a recently divorced single dad."

I look down at my own outfit, the 76ers 'trust the process' tee shirt showing through my jacket, and offer a shrug. I never had a dad, so the idea that I know what a divorced one dresses like is hilarious to me.

"Sorry I'm early. If you need me to, I can walk the block until you guys are ready."

He waves me off. "That's ridiculous, it gives us more time to plan."

"Eisenhower didn't put this much thought into storming the beaches of Normandy, I think we'll be all right."

"Suit yourself."

His house is spacious for a single story, with beautiful hardwood floors throughout. Like every other house in Stratford, there's an addition at the back of it, and at this point I'm starting to think that whoever built all these houses ignored the fact that people might actually procreate and raise a family. The walls are decorated with pictures of Eric and his brother, Danny. By all accounts it looks like they've had the perfect childhood, with the pictures showcasing them doing things I'd only dreamed about like snowboarding. I do notice that there's more pictures of Danny than there are of Eric, particularly when they're older. Whatever is cooking smells delicious and thankfully he leads me in that direction. His mother is cutting coupons out of the newspaper while his father works the stove.

"Mom, Dad, this is Percy," he says.

His mother stands and shakes my hand, with a heavy accent from a European country I can't place. I'm not an expert on social cues, but she seems suspicious of me, her gaze giving me the same feeling I had at Jake's Place when I was a kid.

His dad wipes his hand with a towel and greets me like a lost member of his tribe. "It's so nice to finally meet you. Eric has told us so much about you. I'm Louis," he says, his voice gravely and making me want to clear my throat. "Rumor has it you can take a punch with a smile."

Eric winks at me, as if to say relax.

"If you're not laughing at life, you're doing it wrong," I say. He digs my philosophy and I can feel myself relaxing a little bit. "Whatever you're cooking smells amazing."

"Pork chops, Spanish rice, with potato salad and plantains. I hope you're hungry."

Am I ever. Danny comes out of his room and we all do our part in setting the table. His mother aside, I'm treated like I'm part of the family, with every inside joke explained to me so I don't feel left out. When I ask if I should set plates for the girls, Eric tells me that they went out to eat on their own and are coming over after. I'm more than okay with this because that means more food for me. I learn that his brother figure skates, which explains why he's dressed up like a cat in one of the pictures. Because of the schedule he's home schooled, with their mother staying home to make sure he makes every practice and tournament.

"Tell us a little about yourself," his dad says.

The request makes me stop chewing. This is exactly why making friends is a bad idea. Everything about me, from my current situation to where I come from only invites pity and more questions that I'm not comfortable answering. I haven't told Eric much about my home life, and he senses how uncomfortable I am.

"He just moved here from Camden, Dad."

"Really? My first network job was at the hospital in Camden. Have you ever been to Donkey's?"

What makes me feel at ease isn't the question, but more in his response as a whole. Living in a house and neighborhood this nice I'd expect some lame joke about the drug markets, or the urban decay that people love to laugh about so much. But he seems genuinely interested, and I'm happy that Eric talked me into this double date. It's been worth it for the food and conversation with his dad alone.

"I went for the first time a month ago, sir—"

"Please, call me Louis."

"Done. But yeah, people talk about the cheesesteaks, but it's the fries that really make the place special."

"Don't I know it. If you and Eric get your hearts broken tonight, we should commiserate with a guys visit over there. Nothing mends a broken heart like a clogged artery." The table explodes with laughter.

Holy shit. Was that an invitation to be part of something? Pretty sure that's what it was. Not bad for a foster kid meeting his friend's family for the first time. I finish my plate and sit nervously. The food is out of this world but I'm not sure if I'm allowed a second plate. So, I sit and listen to stories about Danny competing in ice skating, remembering that Grace left me dinner in the fridge for later on tonight. Comfortable as I am in their home, I can't shake this feeling like I'm intruding. I start to reach for more food, but panic and play it off well by picking up my glass of water instead. My eyes meet his dad's, and I can tell he knows what's going on. But he does something that makes me thankful Eric and I crossed paths.

"I cooked all this food, and you're only gonna eat one plate?" he asks.

I smile sheepishly and refill my plate while the conversation returns to Danny. It dawns on me how quiet Eric is. None of the conversation has been about his adventures, only his brother's. Whenever the conversation got away from that he'd perk up, only to quiet down again when his mother brought up a new trick Danny had mastered on the ice. Adding that to the ratio of pictures between him and his brother, I'm getting the sense that I'm not the only one with a complicated home life. My phone buzzes and my heart flutters when I notice its' a text from Jade.

Got any Halloween plans?

I swear she's got a knack for trying to plan things at the wrong time. Eric sees the message and before I can reply he snatches the phone and replies that I'm going on a date, hitting send before I can stop him.

"She's gonna learn you have a life that doesn't revolve around her pity dates," he says. While I appreciate him sticking up for me, Jade could show up at my funeral asking me to hang out and I'd jump out of the casket.

A date? Well don't let me disturb you. I know I haven't been the best friend to you and I wanna make it right. There's gonna be a huge party next Friday night. You should come thru.

My mind goes blank and I reply yes before she can change her mind. She replies with a smiling emoji just as the headlights of a car shine through the driveway. Our dates are here, though I'm ready to go home and listen to The Smiths and daydream about walking into a party and sharing a dance with Jade.

There's a knock at the door and Eric returns to his usual self, albeit a bit more jittery.

His dad opens the door and after welcoming them in he ushers them to the dining room.

Eric rises from his seat slowly, and I feel bad for not having a paper bag because he looks ready to pass out. At the very least the night will be entertaining.

Maria is pretty, and I understand why he is on edge. Not that he's an ugly guy, because he's not, but in the high school hierarchy she's way out of his league. In fact, if you added my league to his there wouldn't be enough between us to deserve the night we're about to experience. Maria is beautiful, smiling in a way that I wonder if she's ever had a bad day in her life.

My date, Christina, is pretty as well, but doesn't seem to have the same warmth about her as Maria. Not that I blame her. Lord knows what the hell Maria had said to convince her to come along. I think she's in one of my classes, but she hasn't been an asshole to me which seems to be how I'm distinguishing folks at this new school. They're wearing matching sweatsuits from the school dance team, instantly rendering us overdressed for the occasion.

"You look great," Maria says.

Okay, so they share a terrible sense for fashion, which is the bedrock of any relationship.

"Hi, I'm Percy," I say to Christina.

She gives Maria a quick glance that tells me we weren't the only ones with a game plan for how the night should go. Maria gives her a look that says 'be nice' and she reciprocates.

Great, I'm on the first date of my life, and my companion has the emotional range of an overnight convenience store clerk. I could kick Eric's ass for dragging me into this. Forget a water balloon fight, I like to blow the condom up and float away from this whole situation like an urban progressive version of Mary Poppins.

"You guys ready to trick or treat?" Eric asks.

Maria perks up. "Oh my God, yes." A look of panic comes across her face. "We don't have anything to put the candy in."

"Don't worry, I'll grab us some pillowcases. Join me, will you, Percy?" he says, tilting his head to signal that it was time to strategize. We excuse ourselves and head down the hallway toward the linen closet.

"Yeah, Eric, I don't think I'm gonna last," I say.

"What are you talking about? I think it's going great."

"That's because your date is smiling at you. Mine looks at me like I ran her dog over and then took a shit on its carcass."

"She's actually allergic to dogs."

"Really?"

"Yeah...well, I don't know. But you gotta loosen up."

"I can't go through with this."

"So you're just gonna abandon your boy?" he asks, sounding as pitiful as my mother when the rent was due.

"I've been abandoned before; it only hurts for a little while, and it builds character."

We stare at each other, both of us knowing I'm not gonna leave. He grabs four pillow cases, and tries to break the stalemate. "Look, just help me get through this. You'll be home beating your meat to Jade's text messages in no time."

"Beating my meat?"

"Jerking your...you've never..." He gives me a look of amazement, like I'd just done the greatest magic trick he's ever seen. "You've never masturbated," he exclaims.

Sadly, he says this a bit too loud and we hear his mother

drop her spoon on the plate, followed by a long and uncomfortable silence.

"This really isn't the best time for this conversation," I
whisper.

"It's nothing to be ashamed about; we'll fix that."

I snatch one of the pillow cases from him. "That isn't
really a 'we' type of moment."

"I didn't mean literally...never mind, we can talk about
that later. Let's just go out there and have the time of our
lives."

We head back to the dining room, where the amount of
people that know I've never masturbated has multiplied by
six. Eric is content with acting like nothing happened."You
guys ready to go?" he asks, and they can't move quick enough.
He gives them their pillowcases and we start for the door.

"Excuse me, where are you going with that?" his mother
says. We all turn, wondering what she's talking about, and to
my surprise, she's glaring at me. "You can't use that pillowcase, those are my good ones. What gives you the right?"

"Um, I'm sorry. I didn't know...I just took the one..." I look
at the others to confirm that I had the same one as them. She
starts toward me but Eric steps between us.

"Mom, he's got the same pillowcase as the rest of us. What
are freaking you out for?"

"I just wanna know why *he* has to use that one."

The way she said 'he' makes me feel incredibly small. In a
life of embarrassment this moment is climbing to the top of
the list by the second. "It's all right, Eric, I can use a plastic
bag or something."

He looks at me like I'm an idiot. "The fuck you can—"

"Language, Eric," she says.

"Mom, he's not some street kid, he has as much a right to
use that as they do. Dad, a little help here?"

"Babe, it's really not that big of a deal," Louis says. He puts an arm over her shoulder and they turn towards the kitchen.

At the same time Eric uses the distraction to shove me out the door with the girls following behind. I have a feeling this isn't the first time he and his dad have pulled a fast one on her.

But I'm also thankful because my lack of masturbating is now the second most awkward thing to happen tonight.

Life really is about the little victories.

SIXTEEN

SO WHERE'S THE EMERGENCY EXIT?

While I've always enjoyed Halloween like any other kid, my approach to it couldn't have been more different. Halloween for me has always been the Super Bowl for exercising my survival instincts. Since food was a struggle to come by, I always treated Halloween like a bear preparing for hibernation. I needed to stock up for the inevitably lean months ahead. My planning was thorough; it made Eric's scheming look like an improv comedy sketch.

I'd head out earlier than the other kids, taking careful inventory on what was put in my bag, carrying a second mask so I could hit the good houses again before the night was over. It was a well crafted operation, tweaked and perfected over time, but now irrelevant because food is no longer an issue and my attention is required to ensure my best friend gets the girl of his dreams. That should punch my ticket into heaven alone.

The date is turning into a living exercise of yin and yang. Eric, free from the burdens of awkward family dynamics, is thriving with Maria. They're even holding hands, laughing at each other's jokes, and ignoring the fact that we're missing the good houses. Christina and I on the other hand, are coexisting like two death row inmates wondering which one is going to the chair first. If we were indoors I'd pull a fire alarm and run home. After about ten houses I try to break the awkwardness.

"Do you like music, Christina?" I ask, hoping to find something in common that'll pierce the silence.

She shrugs her shoulders and the stalemate continues. A breeze starts to pick up and I notice her shivering. You'd think with a personality as cold as hers she'd be right in her element, and watching her shiver like Boss Nass in Star Wars: The Phantom Menace is rightfully hilarious. But I wasn't raised to mock the suffering of others and I know what it's like to be cold, so I make an executive decision. Since the sound of my voice will only make her shivers worse, I remove my coat and put it around her shoulders without saying a word. Eric sees this and gives me a nod and a smile, which I return by flipping him the bird. My gesture of chivalry seems to warm her more than her body.

"It's not you, Percy," she says. "I just have feelings for someone else and I'm not sure what your expectations are for tonight."

I didn't expect to meet Satan's mute daughter, that's for sure. "Well there's something we have in common; my head is with someone else, too."

She smiles at this and the awkwardness is forgiven.

I extend my hand. "I'm Percy, your friendly and one hundred percent platonic friend date for the evening."

She reciprocates. "Thank you for not making it awkward."

"I figured you didn't wanna be here anymore than I do. Besides, it's not like they need our help," I say. We look over and the hand holding has graduated to her head on his shoulder.

"I know, right? You have no idea how many times I told

her that if she liked him so much, what was the point of drag-ging me along."

I find her funny, and not because that was the rule that Eric laid out. We walk past a few more houses, stopping to get candy and comparing our respective hauls.

"So," she says between houses. "You gonna tell me about your girl, or do you wanna hear about my guy first?"

If anyone in the universe had my first date being a double therapy session about our respective crushes on their bingo card, please come forward and claim your prize.

"Ladies first," I say, using chivalry to mask my nervousness.

I don't know if she takes it that way, but she obliges.

His name is Ashton, and listening to her describe their situation makes me feel a kinship with her. He's in the same social circle as Melody and Casey, and since she doesn't fit the mold, hasn't been able to crack the code that would allow her to pursue him. She even joined the dance team in hopes of making herself one of the cool kids. On the surface it seemed like another case of wanting something far fetched, until she reveals that his family rented a shore house next door to theirs over the summer. They spent every day together, and outside the confines of high school politics became close, even making out on nights when they'd sneak down to the beach together. When they got back to town, she thought they'd turned a corner in their relationship, but he won't even look at her on most days.

I start to reach for her hand and hesitate, unsure for a second because I don't know how she'll take it, before I decide it's worth the risk. Her hands are soft, and though she tenses up for a second, she starts to run her finger over my knuckles.

"It sucks, doesn't it?" I ask.

"What?"

"The heartache of knowing that even at your best, you'll never be enough for that one person."

Instead of responding, she places her head softly on my shoulder, where we stand swaying for what feels like an eternity. I've missed these moments, where you understand the person next to you without having to say a word. They've been few and far between, but when they happen, it makes the pain and disappointment of my life worth it.

We take a seat on a curb in the parking lot of a Rite Aid, with the rules Eric set about distance long forgotten. We can't see where they are, but Maria hasn't screamed, so we leave them be. She opens a pack of Whoppers and offers me one, along with the most sincere smile she's given so far. "You've heard my sad love story." She pops two of them in her mouth. "Now it's your turn."

I exhale loudly, because I don't even know where to begin. "She came out of nowhere, like...finding a new band while digging through your parents records." I'm staring at the pavement but my mind is replaying the moment we met. "She just gets..." I struggle to find the word. "...me."

She hands me another piece of candy. "You ever thought about telling her this?"

I shoot her a look and she smiles, knowing how improbable that is. "Some days she walks by me like I don't even exist, and it hurts so much, seeing her everyday and knowing that I'll never be good enough for her. I'm sorry...I didn't mean to turn this into a comparison of our suffering."

"I'm actually enjoying this, in a sick way. It's fun knowing that someone else is dealing with the same thing."

"Not sure I'd go with fun, but point taken."

She finishes off the Whoppers and lets the wrapper fall on the concrete, and we watch the wind carry it across the parking lot. "You ever thought about just staying away from her?"

"I tried, then her boyfriend kicked my ass on the first day of school."

"Your crush is Jade Stevenson?"

"Guilty."

"Why, dude? No offense, but you're so far out of her league."

"I didn't know dyslexia carried over to speech."

It takes her a second, and when it clicks I hear her laugh for the first time. It starts with a high pitched yelp, followed by several small ones. It's genuine though, and a part of me is sad when she stops. "I mean it, Percy. There's something about you that's just...different. You're comfortable in your own skin at a school wherever everyone is living to be the fantasy of the next person. People should be fawning over you, not the other way around."

"Not sure I'll ever see it that way, but I appreciate your encouragement."

The chocolate leaves me with a dry mouth so we head inside the Rite Aid for something to drink. There's only one register open and the clerk is arguing with a woman. She has a child with her, a boy that I guess is no more than six, and he's standing with his head down staring at the Snickers bars while his mother pleads her case. On the counter is two gallons of milk, a loaf of bread, and a jar of peanut butter. The sight of that combination makes me recall the darkest times, even if peanut butter sandwiches taste great. The argument is over her benefits card, which keeps getting declined. This isn't surprising to me, since ours seemed to do the same at least three times a month. We were already on public assistance, couldn't they give us the dignity of loading our card on time?

The cashier sees us and decides to use us as an excuse to

get rid of her, arguing that he has other customers and inviting her to call the number on the back of her card, which is even more insulting. Government workers don't like doing their jobs during normal business hours, does this asshole really think they're paying overtime to make sure we had a place to call, when they didn't wanna give us money in the first place? The thought makes my blood boil.

"You have everything you want?" I ask Christina. She nods and hands me her bottle of water. "Excuse me for one second." I place our drinks on the counter next to her items, along with a pack of gum and the last three Snickers bars from the box. "Just ring it all up, sir."

"You don't have to do that," the mother protests. "I swear I have the money on my card."

"I don't doubt you, ma'am. But trust me, I know firsthand how fickle these cards can be." The total is just under twenty dollars, which I gladly pay before stuffing the other forty in her palm. "Take this. It's not a pity thing, I promise."

She shuffles the cash in her hand, like she's in disbelief that it's there. "Why are you doing this?"

I'm not sure how to answer the question. "Because...I understand."

Her free palm finds my cheek and she smiles at me. "Thank you, and God bless you." She shuffles off and I slap hands with her son as he passes by.

Back outside the store, Christina is in awe. "What made you do that?"

I'm still not quite comfortable sharing my story, but I also feel like we've told each other enough that lying would feel wrong. "Not too long ago, I was that kid."

She smiles at me and I can't describe the feeling that roars through my chest. "You're one of the good ones, Percy. I hope one day your girl sees that."

"Ditto."

"Do you like bookstores?" she asks.

"Love them, why?"

"Maria and I normally walk through Downtown Haddon-field on the weekend, but I have a feeling both of our week-ends are about to get lonelier. What do you say?"

Two hours ago I was ready to pull a fire alarm to get away from this girl, now I'm excited about hanging out with her again. "I'm in." I check my phone and realize how late it is. "Let's go get those two lovebirds before her parents issue an A.M.B.E.R. Alert."

SEVENTEEN

THE CIRCUS ACT WITH NO RINGMASTER

Since Eric is taking Maria to the movies tonight, and Christina is on the agenda for tomorrow, I'll be riding solo to my first high school house party. Funny enough, I'm not as nervous as I thought I'd be, even though I haven't a clue what to expect. Yes, I'm excited that Jade invited me, but like going to Costco, I'm more intrigued by the idea of what a party is like. Hall and Oates is pumping through the speakers, and the track that's currently playing—'I Can't Go For That'— seems fitting for every outfit I try on in the mirror.

Grace sneaks in the room, phone in hand to get a picture.

"Please don't," I say.

"Why not? One day you're gonna look back and realize these are the best days of your life."

I'm living in a foster home while my mother is getting treatment for a heroin addiction. If these are the best days, maybe I should just give up now. "I'm sorry, I just don't know what to wear."

She looks me up and down for a second, hand on hip, with an intense focus like she's trying a new food and can't decide if she likes it or not. "What are you trying to portray with your outfit?"

Jade, please leave that idiot and go out with someone that actually appreciates you. "I don't know. How about, give me a chance? I'm not that bad of a guy."

Her face goes stern. "Is that why you wanna go to this party? To be liked?" I suddenly find the carpet to be interesting. "Don't lie to me."

"No. I mean...it's complicated."

"Complicated applies to a relationship status on Facebook. Try again."

Lying to her doesn't feel right. "Well...can I be honest with you about something?"

"Anything."

"I just like the feeling of being a part of something. You know...feeling like I fit in somewhere. I've been an outcast for most of my life, so...I just want that feeling of being like everyone else." I'm not sure if it's the answer she's looking for, but it's the honest one.

She doesn't say anything, and I'm wondering if she's gonna tell me I can't go because it's for the wrong reasons, but instead she calmly walks over to my closet, removes a black and red plaid button up, and holds it up to my neck to see how it works with my jeans. "I know it seems like fitting in is the way to go." She hands me the shirt as confirmation that it works. "But being like everyone else robs the world of the real gem, and that's you, Percy."

The shirt works, and I'm thankful for her help because Lord knows how long it would've taken me to find the right combination on my own.

"This is the hardest part of being your—"

"Mom," I say.

She beams at this, so much that I wish we were behind on

the electric bill because that smile would light up the whole house.

"Okay...um, wow." I laugh at how flustered she is, especially for someone that's always so calm. "Alright, I can roll with that. Anyway, the hardest part is watching you learn about the world and not being able to protect you from what I know is coming."

"Like what?"

"It's hard to explain, but I'll try. Let's use girls as an example, since a girl is the reason you're going. Last week you went on your first date, and while I was at work, all I could do was pray that she saw how great of a person you are. As much as I wanted to be there and explain how wonderful you are, I have to accept that I can't protect you from heartbreak." She folds my collar down and undoes the top button. "And it sucks, because I can't stop it; I can only be there after it hits, and it makes me feel useless."

"Don't feel that way. I'd rather have you there after it all crumbles than not at all."

She wipes a single tear from her eye and takes a deep breath to compose herself.

"I guess what I'm trying to say is...the person standing in front of me right now, the one that laughs at fart jokes, and uses the washing machine as the snare when playing air drums. He's good enough to fit in anywhere while being himself, and if they can't see that, it's their loss."

She always knows the perfect words to say. "Thanks."

"One more thing." She picks up my phone and adds a number to the contact list. "I know you don't drink, but I was also a teenager once. Don't get into a car with anyone that's been drinking. Call the diner, it should be slow enough that I can pick you up. I'd rather be angry at a son that's alive than mourning a dead one."

* * *

THE PARTY IS at a house on the other side of Stratford, across the train tracks where the homes are more colonial in style. There aren't any streetlights, and if a serial killer jumped out of the bushes, I'd have to apologize for making myself such an easy target. I get more nervous as I approach the house, the sounds of the other students cutting loose making me rethink if I should even be here.

Christina texted me earlier to confirm our plans for tomorrow, and when I told her about the party, her response made me pause.

"*Be safe,*" she texted. Not 'have fun' or 'drink a beer for me.' She opted for the route of self defense, serving as a reminder that even if I was invited, I'm out of my element on this one. In a weird way, I want this night to get over with so we can hang out together tomorrow. I tell myself that if anything seems off, I can just head home. But the fear is balanced with the excitement of finally feeling like I have arrived. There are several cars parked in front of the house, fancy ones that look out of place compared to the types I saw while walking here. I recognize most of them from school, and I have the same feeling I had back home when suburban kids would visit my neighborhood for drugs. Would it kill them to have one night of hedonism in their own neighborhoods?

I knock on the door and wait five minutes, using the time to check my breath (passable) and body odor (good enough to slow dance). After realizing nobody is coming to the door I slowly open it, waiting an extra second in case someone objected. Nobody does and I'm greeted by the smell of weed and stale cigarette smoke. Drake is blasting through the speakers, and I wonder how anyone could function in an environment like this, let alone enjoy it. The crowd is dotted with familiar faces, mostly popular kids that eat lunch under the shaded parts while looking down on us like we aren't worth shit. I don't see Jade, so I smile and nod my way through the crowd in search of her.

The kitchen is interesting. There's a gate blocking the entrance, the kind you put to keep a toddler out of an area. Inside is an older couple, taking drink orders from frenzied high school students, while making drinks so fast you'd swear the world was coming to an end. I assume they're the owners of the house, and though I don't agree with their moral compass, I'm not gonna knock their hustle. The kids on the other side are rowdy, banging on the counters and making lewd jokes as they wait for their drinks. The focus the couple have is amazing, taking all orders by memory while filtering out the crude remarks from high schoolers that should be thankful that they're willing to break the law. I wait until the crowd disperses out of respect.

The woman sees me and saunters over. "What do you want?" she asks, clearly overwhelmed by our insatiable thirst for alcohol. I'm not sure if it's an invitation to order something or a challenge.

"Hi, how are you doing?" I reply. This disarms her, and I can see her shoulders slump in relaxation. I've always loved being the one kid that displayed manners and got adults to believe in the youth again.

"I'm doing all right. Thank you for asking; it's the first hint of manners I've gotten all night. What can I do for you?"

"Do you have club soda?" I ask, now sounding more out of place than I look and feel. She smiles at this request, grabs a red solo cup and fills it to the brim. "What do I owe you?"

"It's on the house sweetie, enjoy yourself. I'm Pearl."

Sweetie? Forty five seconds ago I thought she was gonna hit me with a right hook. "Percy. You guys seem to be raking it in." I point to the jar that once contained pickles, now filled to brim with illicit cash.

"We do pretty well with this," she says with a hint of sadness. "It's not my cup of tea, but Bob over there was forced to retire early after a back injury and the state wouldn't award him his full pension. You probably don't wanna hear my sob stories; go on with your friends." I watch Bob for a second, seeing him move gingerly to pick up the empty cups left on the counter.

"Well, you're in luck because I can relate to the state screwing people over, and I don't know anybody here. I'm starting to wonder why I'm here in the first place."

"I was gonna say, you don't seem like the party type we usually get from the high school."

"What gave it away? The club soda?"

She shakes her head and points to my headphones, draped around my neck like a dog collar. "In my year and a half of running this little speakeasy I've never seen a kid show up with headphones."

If only she could see my music collection. "Does this ever bother you?"

She takes a sip of water and ponders this. "If you're talking about serving alcohol, then yes. But they're gonna get it either way, and I tell myself that since it's a controlled environment, it's not as bad. But I tell myself that my social security starts in two years, and by that time my grandson will have graduated, so we can retire in relative peace."

"I'll toast to that," I say, raising my glass which she greets with a water bottle of her own. "Hopefully it all works for you guys, Pearl."

"I appreciate that." She looks around and beckons me in as if she's got a secret. "You said this isn't your thing, well, the football team lost and the players will be here soon. They're assholes and you're one of the good ones. I'd head out soon if I were you."

A part of me feels happy hearing they lost.

The other side of the kitchen starts to fill up with students, so I retreat to a corner and observe for a bit. Momma always told me to be nice to everyone because we only see what's on the surface. Pearl and Bob are the perfect example of that. They should be enjoying their retirement, maybe in an RV camping across the country, but instead they're putting their freedom on the line so that ungrateful students can have a good time. It's moments like this that I wonder how politicians manage to sleep at night knowing their decisions force good natured people to risk everything they worked for just to survive. It's jarring because I thought circumstances like that only existed in my neighborhood, but I'm learning that the fight for the bare minimum isn't confined to any particular zip code.

I finish my drink around the same time my patience runs out for the music. I'm not a snob or anything, but "I got your bitch in my Jeep" isn't exactly the most compelling narrative. Top 40 rap falls into a category I call direct deposit music. It sounds great when the direct deposit hits your bank account, serving as the proper soundtrack for spending new-found riches. But the week leading up to said deposit, when there isn't enough peanut butter to cover the whole bread slice, it's the last thing I wanna hear because I'm hungry and not interested in sharing with the stranger in my Jeep. But as I watch the party, maybe they enjoy the music because they can relate to the shallowness of it.

While there's laughter, nobody seems to be having fun. It feels like one big contest to see who can get the most drunk, while documenting it for social media. What's the point of going out and making memories if you get too blitzed to remember them? Then, in a corner tucked away near the back patio, I spot Jade, laughing with a group of kids I vaguely recognize. My heart skips as suddenly nothing, from the music to the fake smiles plastered on everyone, feels out of place. I approach cautiously and when she spots me I'm greeted with a look of alarm, making me confirm that it was indeed her that invited me here.

She puts her arm around me and diverts my path away from her friends, who notice that something far more interesting is taking place. "Hey," she says. "I'm so happy you made it." Her voice is slurred, and I know instantly she's made more than a few trips to Bob and Pearl's kitchen. She looks great in her school sweater, coupled with tight fitting jeans that send a tingle through my body that I'm sure isn't school spirit. "Would you like a drink?" She offers me her cup and I take a swig, because its' as close as I'll get to kissing her.

I'm not sure what it is, but it burns all the way down, like when you drink a soda too fast. At least the kids can't complain that Pearl is short changing them on their drinks.

"That's an interesting drink," I say, as my esophagus pulls the fire alarm to alert the rest of my body.

"Just a little vodka."

"A little?"

She smiles, and the burning turns to a warm sensation. "Okay, maybe more, but these are the best days of our lives, right?"

I'm holding a one on one conversation with my crush, I'd definitely agree with that statement. "So, are you gonna introduce me to your friends?"

She looks back at them, as do I, throwing a wave in there to let them know I come in peace. "Percy, I don't think that's a good idea."

"Why not? Is this about the first day of school? Because if

it is, they should know that I don't hold grudges. Even Dorothy and Blanche eventually became friends after their rocky start."

"Who?"

At this moment I decide to take advantage of our cable subscription, if only so I can update my pop culture references. If I told that joke to Pearl, it would've killed. "Never mind, why isn't it a good idea?"

"It just isn't."

"If you and I are friends, and they're your friends, it should be easy if you intro—"

"We're not the same, all right," she says. I'm thankful for the music being loud so that my humiliation can stay between us, just like our 'friendship.' Funny, I always dreamt up my humiliation to a better soundtrack. The way this conversation is going, it's looking like the rest of my night will be spent at home curating it. "Look, we're friends, just...away from here. You're cute and sweet and—"

"Not good enough. You can say it, I won't get mad." She's staring at me pitifully, and I search her face for any signs of the girl that has dominated my thoughts from the moment we met, but I don't see her, and I realize that maybe she never existed to begin with. On a positive note, my erection has decided that he's out, even if my heart is slow to follow, so it's not all bad. "If you don't wanna really be my friend, then why did you invite me here?"

"I wanted you to have some fun."

"You think my idea of fun on a Friday night is guest starring in this episode of the Neanderthal's of South Jersey?" I'm frustrated, because I'm usually right about people, but the one time I wanted more than anything to be right, I got it wrong. "I'll see myself out. Make sure you tip Pearl and Bob well; Lord knows they deserve it."

A hand claps me on the back firmly, like you'd greet a long lost buddy. "Don't go, you haven't met the gang yet," a voice says.

I turn and come eye to eye with our illustrious quarterback, fresh off a loss with his eye black still smeared around his eyes. I try to pull away, but his grip tightens.

"Let him go, babe," Jade says. "He was on his way out."

"No way, you kidding me." He looks me in the eye and smirks. "I think the party is just beginning. I won't hit him, I swear."

They lead me to the corner group that she was terrified of bringing me to meet. Its grown with the influx of football players, all presumably pissed off and itching to make someone else share in their failures. Except this time Eric isn't here to share the can of whoop ass with me, it's a table for one. The only available seat is in the corner, where all escape routes are blocked off, and I sit, nervously eyeing all of them, especially Jade.

"What are you drinking?" Casey asks.

"Club soda."

"Not a drinker, eh? James, get my man here another club soda," he says. James, who in my head was known as the guy that drilled Eric, heads off to the kitchen. "Relax, Percy, nobody is gonna hurt you."

Well, there's a load off my mind. I can deal with a little embarrassment, it builds character, at least I think that's what the fortune cookie said.

"Sorry about the first day of school, didn't mean to take it that far."

"We're good."

What the hell am I supposed to say? It's not like I'm in any position to disagree. James comes back with a fresh club soda, though I'm hesitant to drink it.

"Percy just moved here from Camden. Did I get that right, babe?"

Jade nods. It's obvious they've talked about me, and though I wish it were because she yelled my name out while they were having sex, it's clear he knows my story. I wonder if the ass kicking option is still on the table. "His mother is a heroin addict, so he's living in a foster home now."

I can take being mocked about my situation, hell, growing up poor that came with the territory. But it's another feeling hearing it from someone you care about, and up until ten minutes ago, that you felt cared about. She's laughing with the rest of them, just like she does in class, and now I find myself smiling along with them. Because I'm willing to bet they don't know that Jade has more in common with me than them, and though I'd love to see the look on Casey's face when he finds out about her past, I keep her secret to myself because she told me that in confidence. Being the bigger person sucks.

"Jade here was gonna send him home before I got here..." he lets it hang there for a second. "...but he doesn't have a home to go to."

They roar with laughter at the punchline, Jade included, and I sink lower in my seat, wishing I could disappear.

"...his own mother has to shoot dope to cope with having him around."

"...he's probably looking at things to steal for her next fix."

The jokes are coming with the swiftness of a tsunami, each barb cutting deeper than the last. My mind wanders to the old Dangerfield album I used to check out at the library. "*I get no respect*," he'd say. Now I am living it. A living, breathing example of life imitating art. To keep from crying, I stiffen my grip on the solo cup, and it shatters under the pressure, spilling my soda all over the floor. I'm not certain if the puddle on the floor is more club soda or tears.

"Maybe when your mom wakes up from nodding off she'll take a couple of dollars to come clean it," someone says.

I can't put a face to the person because the tears blur my vision. Wasn't Alex supposed to protect me from this? It's stupid to blame him when I'm the one at fault. I didn't hand Jade the gun, but did give her the bullets that they were taking turns pumping into my dignity.

"Percy, your Uber is outside," a voice says above the crowd.

I wipe my tears and see that it's Pearl, throwing me a life-line like the angel she is. Before they can stop me, I rush past the crowd, apologizing to her about the rug and thanking her for saving me before heading out.

Out of habit I run, unsure if I'm headed toward home, but sure that any path away from that house is the right one. I make it to the main road before I collapse on the wall of a dental office, letting out a wail that feels like a long time coming. I long for my old life, where I was comfortable biding my time in poverty and obscurity until college when I could strike out on my own. This foster care thing is a joke, a cruel one at that, where the good moments are illusions and the bad ones permanent. The worst part about this moment is I've gotten so used to being in a loving environ-ment with Grace that the loneliness hurts more than it did before.

I pick up my phone and dial Eric.

He picks up on the second ring. "My guy," he says. Clearly his date went well. "Let me call you when I get home."

"Why do you want to be friends with me? If it's to make yourself feel better just tell me now and I swear I'll never bother you again."

"What? Percy, what's going on?"

"I'm sorry, Eric, okay? I'm sorry I did this to you. I just

wanted to have friends, man, I didn't mean to ruin everything for you."

"You didn't...ruin anything. What happened at the party?"

Jade flashes in my head, the image of her laughing at my life playing on a loop like a scratched CD. "I just wanted to be like everyone else. Will you still be my friend?"

"Where are you?"

"I'm at the Wawa off Main Street."

I hear the acceleration of his Dad's Camry. "Don't leave, I'll be there in five minutes."

* * *

THE BACKYARD HAS an eerie silence to it tonight, almost like the crickets learned from their friends about my night and are giving me a moment of silence to pay their respects.

It's unusually warm for an autumn night, so we sit in silence on the patio furniture, occasionally taking sips of beer but otherwise passing for Buddhist monks. After Eric picked me up, we stopped at his house, parking on the street so he wouldn't wake his parents as he snuck in to grab some beer for us. We headed back to my house, where we drink in silence and wonder who's gonna speak first.

I count no less than ten text messages from Maria since we've been here, but he's empathetic enough to my plight that he hasn't responded yet. He seems as content with the silence as I am, but it is getting late.

"You didn't have to stay," I say.

He frowns at me and takes a drink. "I know, but it felt like you could use someone right now." He waits for me to crack mine open and we toast. "So, when are we going to talk about the party?"

It's a sore subject, and in a perfect world I'd never speak on it again, but he literally dropped everything to make sure I was all right. "It was humiliating."

"I got that part, genius. But there's a difference between being humiliated and the person that called me on the phone."

He's got a point. "Long story short, I told Jade some things about me, things that I haven't told anyone, and she told her boyfriend, who then used it to make fun of me."

"What a bitch."

I look over at him.

"What? She's not my crush, and you're being awfully protective of someone that betrayed you like that. You don't have to tell me what the big secret is..."

"I'm a foster kid."

I'm not sure if everyone at the party learning this is a factor, but for the first time I feel at ease with saying it. Hearing it out of my own mouth makes it easier to come to grips with than thinking about it all the time.

"That's your big secret? Well, if it makes you feel any better you didn't do a great job of hiding it."

This is news to me as I think about all the time we'd spent together, trying to find a point where I slipped up. "How'd you know?"

He finishes his beer and lets out a loud belch. "I didn't know what it was exactly, but I could tell while having dinner with my parents that something was off. You almost shit your pants when my Dad asked about your past." We both laugh at this as he cracks his second beer. "So like I said, it was obvious something was off."

"You want the whole story?"

There's a long silence, with both of us thinking about the consequences. It's the most pivotal moment of our friendship yet, where we'll both know if the other is all-in. Two swigs of beer later, Eric decides he wants the full story.

I start with Momma's overdose, a memory that gets more replays than the movie Elf in December. His posture is firm as I give him all the details, even though it's obvious how uncomfortable it makes him. I talk about meeting Jade in the record store, leaving out our encounter at court, before bringing him up to speed on where my case stands at the moment. It feels surreal to be this open about my life, but it's also freeing, because I've filled in the blanks for the one person that's been solid with me since the day we met.

"I have a question," he says. "Why were you scared to tell me this? I get that your situation is...well, I'm not sure what word to use there, but if we're friends, why wouldn't you tell me?"

There isn't an answer I can give him that could justify it, but I'm reminded of the talk that Grace and I had at the taxi stand in New York, and how I laid bare my feelings about living with her. This feels eerily similar, so I go for broke again."I didn't think you'd wanna be friends with someone that might disappear one day."

He laughs at this. "Are you kidding? My dad is already asking when you're gonna come over again."

"And your mom?"

"She's ex..." He sees me preparing to call bullshit and stops. "...well she'll come around eventually, but don't feel bad, she doesn't really like me either."

Hearing about his parents reminds me of how late it is. It's almost two in the morning. "You should probably get home before your parents start worrying about you."

He blows raspberries out of his lips from the suggestion. "Yeah, maybe if I had skate practice in the morning they'd care."

My suspicions from dinner at his house is correct, and it makes me wonder if that's why we got along so well. He understands what it feels like to be an outsider as much as I do, even if he has two parents. That's what's funny about having a screwed up home life, the circumstances don't have to match up perfectly for someone else to understand them.

"Your parents love you, Eric."

"My dad does, sure." He finishes his beer. "But it feels like my mom doesn't even know I'm there, and if she does, then she doesn't care."

"Look, I'm not gonna pretend that I know what it feels like to walk in your shoes, just like you don't know how to walk in mine. But you have no idea what I would give to wake up in a world where my mom isn't strung out on dope. You can get up tomorrow and hug your mother, even if she doesn't want you to. I gotta go through a social worker and get clearance to hug mine, and even then I have to hope she's coherent enough to remember it."

I can tell my point hits the mark because he just stares ahead for a second, acknowledging it with a shrug that says, 'I understand, but I'm not trying to hear that shit right now.' "Do you ever get angry about your life and wish for a new one?"

I've never been asked that before, and come to think of it, I'm not sure anger has ever crossed my mind. My focus has always been on survival, and anger isn't something I can eat or use to keep warm, so yelling at the clouds seemed useless. Plus, knowing my luck, they'd talk back by snowing on a day I didn't have a coat on. Even on the rare occasions that I'd pray, I never wished for a different mother—I love the one I have, warts and all— I just wished that she'd get better.

"No, because I believe everything has a purpose. I ended

up with two mothers that love me. Even the most cynical person would find that hard to frown at."

"Two mothers and a brother."

"Brother, what brother?"

"You got me, you idiot."

We bump fists and I down the rest of my beer. "Thanks for coming to get me, I was in a really bad place."

"That's what family is for, and I kinda owed you one after the Halloween fiasco."

"Oh shit," I say, remembering my plans with Christina. "I gotta get to bed. I'm hanging out with Christina tomorrow, well, today."

"Are you serious? You don't have to play along anymore. Maria and I are a couple now."

I'm partially offended at the suggestion, but I can't be mad because he wasn't privy to how deep our conversation had gotten. The same rules I applied to Jade go for Christina, her secrets are safe with me. "I'm actually excited; we're gonna check out a bookstore together."

"There you go, don't let heartbreak hold you down."

"It's not like...that. We're just friends."

"That's how it starts, then before you know it, you're playing tonsil hockey behind the Rite Aid."

I really could've gone my whole life without that visual. He collects the beer cans and I walk him to the car. He pulls something out of the glove box. It's wrapped in newspaper, but from the shape I can tell it's a disc. "Remember that conversation we had by the linen closet at my house last week?"

I glance at the paper and back at him, realizing what I'm holding. "You gotta be shitting me."

"Afraid not. Enjoy yourself, and thank me later. I need you to have a clear mind when we plan the get back."

"Get back?"

"Those pumpkin spice sipping assholes will regret the day they fucked with my brother." He pulls off and rounds the corner, leaving me with a porno movie and a bittersweet night that he helped salvage.

EIGHTEEN

THROUGH THE STACKS

If the residents of Cherry Hill thought they were rich because they lived next to Camden, then the residents of Haddonfield *knew* they were rich by living next to Cherry Hill. The houses are astounding, each one bigger than the next, like the men were constantly competing to see who could be more extravagant. They probably meet at their mailboxes every morning and have a dick measuring contest while picking up the morning paper. People with money are weird like that.

Walking through neighborhoods like this is an out of body experience. I feel like every step is being monitored, even when I don't see anyone. When people pass by I don't know if I should nod at them, putting them on alert that there's an imposter in their midst, or ignore them, putting them on alert that a suspicious character is roaming their neighborhood. Either way, I'm scared of making the wrong move because the residents will view me the same. What has always fascinated me about neighborhoods like this isn't the amenities of the homes, though there are plenty, for example, I didn't know bushes could be trimmed to the shape of an animal. Now, as I look around, I always wonder the same thing.

What kind of problems do these families deal with?

They seem to have everything, more rooms than they can fill, multiple patios and decks to separate oneself from everyone else, one house even had a full street hockey set in the driveway alone. I wonder what their worries are, what keeps them up in the middle of the night, because to me they seem to have everything. I know their life isn't perfect, given that I've seen enough of their kids drive exotic cars into Camden for the best heroin. But they're afforded the opportunity to deal with the fallout privately, while our struggle plays out on the evening news. Sometimes I wonder if I would want to live in a place like Haddonfield if I could. There's no simple answer, but I think I'm more of a middle class type of guy. I couldn't imagine living here and having it all taken away from me, because a fall from the middle of the ladder hurts less than a fall from the top.

The Main Street in Haddonfield has a calm to it that reminds me of Costco. People move at a slower pace, taking extra time to admire merchandise in the storefront windows. I can see the sign for Cliff's books from a block away, and as I get closer I recognize Christina standing out front. The failure from last night gives way to nervous excitement the moment she looks up and greets me. She looks amazing in a real outfit, her jeans fitting perfectly and complimenting her blouse well. It's also the first social event that I'm not overdressed for, so that's a good thing.

"I was beginning to think you were gonna stand me up," she says, even giving me a hug for good measure. The cocoa butter in her lotion smells great, lingering in my nostrils long after I let go.

"You're kidding, right? I couldn't turn down the chance to actually meet up without having to be a chaperone." She smiles again and I wanna punch Ashton in the face for treating her like shit. I know she likes someone else, and I'm struggling to tell her how pretty she looks while respecting her feelings for him. "You look great." Not the most original line, but she doesn't protest, so I guess we're alright.

I can tell she's passionate about books, seeing as she practically pulls me into the shop and wastes no time bringing me up to speed on its history.

She explains that Cliff's has been around since the 80's, and in her opinion, arguably the best bookstore in the city. If you didn't know that Cliff's had been there for almost thirty years you're quickly reminded by the decor of the place. The shelves are made of wood that I assume at one point matched the color of the floors. Every section is organized by genre, but there isn't any sort of order like you would see at one of the larger chain bookstores. In some sections books are stacked on the floor, a real life example of the supply and demand curve we learn about at school. The lights hang from a string on the ceiling, which make browsing certain sections a challenge because not all of the lights worked. The stacks are close to one another, giving the place an intimate feel. Friendships have been forged in these stacks, and I can almost hear the banter of strangers discussing literary merits with each other as they navigate the cramped space.

After last night, it's refreshing to meet someone that has a passion for something that doesn't involve alcohol or sex. Her feelings for this place mirror mine for Randy's shop, with each of us discovering places where our social standing doesn't matter.

She explains that Cliff himself is working the register.

He's a heavyset guy, with his white hair and beard making him pass for an out of work Santa biding his time until the holidays roll around. He has a warm presence about him, stopping his own reading to greet Christina and I.

"I was just remarking to my wife last night about how you haven't been by in awhile," he says to Christina. They share a hug, and it's obvious that she's spent a decent amount of time here.

She pulls three books from her messenger bag and slides them across the counter. "Been super busy with school, but I finished these classics up."

He inspects each one before putting them under the counter. "What did you think of Raymond Chandler?"

"Not really my cup of tea, but I can see why he's popular." She smiles at me, conveying that she hated the book but didn't want to offend him. I felt the same way when Randy introduced me to Frank Zappa. "Cliff, this is my friend Percy."

I shake his hand enthusiastically, ecstatic that I've officially graduated from an awkward blind date to friend. "Do you have any music biographies?" I ask.

"Got a whole section," he says. "Anybody you looking for in particular?"

"Prince would be my top choice, but beggars can't be choosers either."

This makes him laugh. "I wish more customers had that attitude." He rolls over to his computer and starts typing furiously. "I don't think Prince ever had an official biography." He types a few more words and waits for the screen to load. "Yeah, I didn't think so. I do have a copy of the autobiography of Questlove; he's the drummer for Jimmy Fallon's house band, The Roots. I know it's not exactly what you were looking for, but he was inspired by Prince, and he leaves a playlist at the end of every chapter to let folks in on what he was listening to."

Did he just say the book had playlists? I can excuse his verbiage on the strength of us never having met before. I feel bad about visiting a cool place like this without buying anything, so I tell him that I'll purchase it. Christina excuses herself to go to the bathroom, leaving Cliff and I at the front of the store.

"Hey, Cliff," I start. "Forgive me if I'm prying, but how do you go from loving books to opening a shop?" It's unfathomable to me, at least the logistics of finding a million books.

"In all my years of running this place, I've never been asked that. Been asked the who, what, and why, but never the how." He looks around the store smiling, almost like he can't believe it himself. "This started as a way of getting out of the house after I retired. I was a probation officer, and my wife was convinced I'd be dead in five years if I didn't find something to do. I had just under four hundred books in my garage, and that became my first inventory."

I love businesses that have real stories behind them, like it was divine intervention that made them come to fruition. It's sad because he's gonna run into the same issues that Randy is fighting right now, which is the digital world being more convenient than the physical.

Christina returns from the back with three more books, just as I'm paying for mine. I notice that Cliff doesn't ring hers out, and thanks her for taking part in his lending program. My stomach growls and I ask Christina if she's hungry. The question makes her nervous, and she dances around it before saying no. Cliff recommends the pizzeria next door, so we grab our bags and tell Cliff that we'll be back.

* * *

THERE AREN'T many customers in the pizzeria when we walk in, so we have our choice of tables. Christina chooses one in the back, away from the windows at the front, with enough privacy so that our conversation will be out of ear shot. Before she goes to set our things down, I ask again if she's hungry, and again it seems to throw her off, this time with a stutter before she says that she isn't. I don't believe her, and after she leaves I order an extra large cheese pizza and figure that I'll deal with her protesting it later.

Once I'm back at the table, her smile returns to normal, which gives me butterflies. There's something about her that I click with, I'm just not sure what it is. Maybe it's that we're both outcasts, which in a town like Haddonfield is the difference between feeling alone and feeling comfortable.

"So, what did you think of Cliff's?" she asks. Christina has an innocence about her that keeps me on edge, wanting to protect her in any way that I can. She'd taken the time to show me one of the places that's dear to her, and I don't take her willingness to open up for granted.

"It was awesome," I say. "I can see why you dig it so much, and Cliff seems like a good guy."

"He's the best." Our pizza arrives and suddenly she's nervous again. "You really gonna eat all that?"

I take a paper plate for myself and slide one across to her. "No, *we're* gonna eat all of it." She thinks on it for a second before relenting and grabbing a slice.

The pizza itself is cooked perfectly, with just the right amount of flop, and a commendable crust to sauce ratio. Speaking of the sauce, that's always been the make or break moment for me. Some people prefer the sauce to have a little tang to it, while others prefer sweet. I like a healthy mixture of both, the kind that fights for the affection of my senses while I'm chewing it. The sauce here is perfect, like the chef read my mind when we walked in.

An unfamiliar band is playing on the speakers, electronic by the sounds of the synth, but the singer is nailing an impressive falsetto. I notice that Christina is vibing to it, nodding along as she munches on her slice. "You know this band?" I ask.

"Mm-Hmm," she manages before wiping her mouth and finishing her bite. "They're called Passion Pit, one of my current favorites." She watches me take a note down about them. "I noticed your CD player, you a big music guy?"

I don't wanna bore her by taking her down a rabbit hole of what music I prefer and why, so I pull out my CD wallet and slide it over to her. She's hesitant to look through it, so I prod her along. "You showed me something you were passionate about, now it's my turn."

I'm always fascinated by watching people go through my music collection, and this time is no different. She loves Muse like I do, given that she tactically squealed when she saw the Absolution album. But even when she finds something she isn't familiar with, she never frowns or makes a sly remark, instead showing genuine interest, and if I were a gambler, I'd bet that comes from letting people see her book collection.

"Have you ever been to a concert?" she asks. Now it's my turn to be nervous, because it's the first question that starts the dive into my sorry excuse of a past.

"I haven't, but now that I have a job, I'm hoping to save up enough money to afford to do it the right way."

She smirks at this. "Okay, give me the band you'd wanna see and why."

"We don't have enough time for me to describe that."

She checks her watch. "You have somewhere to be?"

I shake my head.

"Well then, since you're free and we've only eaten two of the twelve slices on this pizza, I'd say we've got ample time."

For the millionth time I wonder why Ashton is so blind to how cool this girl is. "Fine, but you asked for it."

"Yeah, yeah, now spill it. I'm all ears."

"All right, gun to my head right now, I'd pick Muse. I heard them for the first time a couple of months ago and they've been heavy in my rotation every day since. This might sound like a stupid question, but have you heard the song Starlight?"

"Oh my gosh, yes." Her enthusiasm makes me happy. I let Eric talk me into that double date. To think that I would've missed out on getting to know someone like her is depressing.

"See, that was my exact reaction, well, it was lighter on the teeny bopper verbiage, but the emotion was still the same. Anyway, I checked out one of their lives albums while I was working at Backside and I heard a part where they let the crowd sing the chorus. I wanna be a part of that one day, with floor seats in a sea of people so I can lose myself in the moment. Now that's already perfect, but imagine that happening at Madison Square Garden."

She's no longer eating, and we're gazing into each other's eyes for what feels like an eternity. I realize I never looked her in the eyes the first time we met, and I'm happy I didn't, because I would've melted quicker than a Snickers bar left on the passenger seat in the middle of July. Now I'm conflicted, because she's making me forget about Jade, but she also has feelings for someone else. They say life is cruel, but I think I could make a compelling argument that its timing is much crueler. She blinks first, suddenly finding the menu on the table to be interesting, and I know she felt it, too.

"I'd love to be there for it," she says, still not looking up from the menu. "To see you living your dream like that. And for the record, I've never been to a concert and they would be my first choice as well."

I'm not letting her off the hook that easy. "Okay then. You describe your ideal concert to me." She's ready to shake her head before I remind her that there are still ten slices left on the tray.

She lets out a sigh. "Fine." She takes a sip of her water. "So you summed a lot of it up, but you made it about one particular moment. To me, something like that is an experience, with the whole day planned out. Since we're talking dreams, I envision it starting from the moment I wake up, researching the set list and making a playlist of it to listen to on the way there."

I see my work of changing the vernacular of the playlist is gonna take some time, but I like where she's going with it, and she's beautiful, so I'm not docking any points from her.

"I'd want to eat at a nice restaurant, the kind that's out of my budget. I figure if it's just one night I can allow myself to live beyond my means for a bit. I'll copy and paste your feelings about the floor seats, but I would wanna go to a merchandise booth and get a shirt. Eventually the night will end, but I'd love to have something to remember the night my dream came true."

With one more smile she snaps back into the real world, pulling another slice off the tray and munching on it while we both compare our respective fantasies.

"Is that why you invited me here so early?"

My question stops her mid bite, and I wonder if I've either said something wrong or misinterpreted the story she told. But instead of answering she just looks me in the eye, smiles, and gives me a shrug of the shoulders.

My mind goes blank, and if you asked me my name I'd only be able to babble incoherently. Two words float out of my soul and hang in my mind like a leaf in the wind before landing softly on my heart.

Jade who?

* * *

IT'S funny how coming back to your neighborhood has a way of reminding you that you're back to reality. It might be seeing familiar stores, or in my case, seeing my friend become a nervous shell of the person I spent the day with.

It's dark when we get back, and we hit a stalemate at the train station because Christina was insistent on walking home alone. Something about it felt off, though, like when she said she wasn't hungry but lightened up and eventually helped me finish that pie. The signs were there already from the first time we met and the jacket snafu, but I chalked it up to her detesting my existence. After stating firmly that I wasn't gonna let her walk home alone in the dark she relented, but became suspiciously quiet as we walked through our neighborhood in silence. Her head is down, and I wonder if we jumped in a time machine back to the night we met.

I use the silence of our walk to mine over every moment of our time spent together in search of answers. It's frustrating as it is fruitless until, without a word, she turns up the steps of a rundown house.

"Christina," I say. She stops and turns around, tears falling down her face as I realize it's her house, she's just embarrassed by the state of it. The lawn hasn't been mowed and there's trash strewn throughout the yard. The house was once a nice shade of red, but the weather and lack of upkeep has left it with patches of its former glory. It doesn't look like a house that would belong in Stratford, it actually looks like something you'd see in my neighborhood. But everything makes sense now.

She still isn't saying anything, and the silence makes my chest hurt because I understand exactly how she's feeling. But

I also know not to push these things, so I tell her goodbye and start to leave.

"Percy," she calls out. I turn around as she approaches me, stopping within inches of me. "Could you keep this..." she waves at her house, "between us, please?"

I promise her that her secret is safe with me and we share a long embrace, not nearly long enough for me, and then she starts to head in. Something hits me as I watch her walk away, and before I can talk myself out of it I go for it. "I'm living in a foster home," I say.

She stops when she hears this, turning slowly to hear me out.

"My mom is addicted to heroin and I got taken away from her."

"Why are you telling me this?"

While it might sound like a harsh question, I read it differently. Her tone isn't one of annoyance, but more of why would I volunteer such information. It's a fair question, and one that should've come from within instead of from her. But if I learned anything from hanging with Eric last night, it's that I shouldn't be scared to share my real life with my real friends.

"You just showed me your darkest secret and I want you to know that you aren't alone. Well, that and most of the popular kids took turns mocking me about it last night, and I'll be damned if they know it but my real friends don't."

She walks up and gives me one more hug, whispering that she'll never tell a soul, and crazy as it sounds, I actually believe her.

NINETEEN

THE EMPRESS HAS NO CLOTHES

I'm unloading boxes in the back when I hear the door open in the front of the store. Since Randy is at the front of the store, I think nothing of it. After some muffled conversation, he comes to the back saying someone has requested my presence.

"Who is it?" I ask. There's only one name I want to hear these days, like finding a new favorite song and leaving it on repeat.

"The girl that you like."

"Christina?"

"No, the one you met the first day you came in here. Jesus, kid, how many are there?"

I hadn't talked to Randy about the party, so I forgive him for being ignorant of the shortcomings in my social life. My first instinct is to have Randy send her off by claiming I'm busy with work, but I'm also intrigued to see how she plays this. I look down at the box cutter in my hand and briefly consider slicing my wrist and bleeding out knowing she has remorse for what she did.

Randy looks on, confused at why I'm so indecisive about talking to a beautiful girl.

With a long sigh, I head out to face her, with Randy patting me on the back for good luck while muttering something about not understanding teenage boys these days.

She sees me coming and gives her saddest smile, doing that thing pretty girls do that makes you wonder if it's your fault in the first place. But I also think of her face at the party, how she laughed even though she knew how terrible it was, and it gives me the resolve to be somewhat cold to her.

"Hey," she says. "Do you have a minute to talk?"

"I'm kinda busy at the moment. Besides, I think you've made it quite clear how you felt the other night."

She looks down at her toes, shuffling back and forth nervously. "I tried to tell you to leave, I didn't mean for..." she trails off.

"You were one of the people that made me comfortable with the idea of being in foster care. When you gave me your phone number, it felt like I'd won the lottery; that's how much I cared about you."

"I still care about you." Our eyes meet and she sees I'm not convinced. "I really do."

"You can't honestly expect me to believe that."

But here's the thing, I do believe it. She wouldn't have showed up here, when she knows her boyfriend is at practice, and her friends are somewhere else sucking the life out of hard working people. In all honesty I don't hate her; we're just two people that dealt with shitty circumstances in different ways. But not hating someone and wanting them in your life is another conversation, one that I'm not in the mood to have.

"I saw you've been spending time with Christina, is something there?"

The question throws me off my game, and I don't know if I should be ecstatic that people notice us together or appalled that she had the guts to ask. Part of me wants to tell her that we're dating just to see her reaction, but the thought of having Christina play a part in whatever game we're playing doesn't sit right with me.

"What does it matter to you?"

"Believe it or not, I care about your happiness, Percy."

You've got quite a way of showing it. "Not that it's any of your business, but she's just my...friend." Her eyebrows raise with the way I emphasized 'friend,' cutting her deep. "She's in love with someone else anyway. Seems to be my luck these days, right?"

She nods at this, making me sad because I'll always believe we could've been amazing together. "Are you going to homecoming?"

"You're asking a lot of questions for someone that has a boyfriend."

"I'm not asking you to go."

"Look, we can stand here and do this all day, so let me save us both some time. I don't hate you for what you did, but I don't love you anymore either. If that hurts your feelings, I can assure you that it comes nowhere close to how I felt the other night, and as a bonus, your feelings can play out privately in your head."

"Percy, I'd like us to be friends,"

"There is no friends," I say, more fierce than I mean to be. "We tried that, and I ended up having one of the worst nights of my life at the hands of someone I cared about. I mean, at least my mother has a heroin habit to fall back on as an excuse. What's yours?"

She doesn't say anything, instead she just looks around the store, probably hoping a car would crash through the front so she can get the hell out of Dodge. "They're all I have, Percy. Without them I just have my mom, and you under-stand more than most how delicate that is. My best hope is to get a scholarship to whatever school Casey goes to and hold on long enough so that he'll stay with me."

I always thought watching my mother struggle with a habit she couldn't kick would be the epitome of hurt for me, but this moment is definitely on the list. She's not dating him because she loves him, she's just looking for a way out, and I get it. "Did you come here because you're sorry, or are you trying to gauge if I'm gonna spill the beans on your secret?"

She seems hurt by the question. "I really do care about you; I can't leave here until I'm sure you know that."

I shrug my shoulders at this. "Your secret is safe with me. Outside of that, I think it's best if we pretend like we don't know each other. You seem more comfortable in that role anyway."

Randy comes out of the back with impeccable timing.

"Is there anything else I can do for you, ma'am?"

"No, I didn't find what I was looking for. Maybe next time."

She leaves quietly, stopping at the door to look back one more time, giving me a sad smile that'll always be beautiful to me, then heads out into a life that doesn't include me in it. It's a confusing moment, because I thought I'd relish cutting her out of my life. But, on the flip side, it doesn't hurt like I thought it would either. See, that's the thing about closure, it's not about giving way to any certain emotion, it's about soothing the mind and soul, clearing a path to a better place.

I can only hope that path is to Christina's heart.

TWENTY

BATTLE OF THE BULGE

For two weeks, the "movie" sat hidden, placed inside the CD booklet of Morrissey's Bona Drag album, which was stashed inside an issue of Rolling Stone. I was confident in my smuggling tactics, knowing that if Grace found them I could have a plausible argument that a customer had traded the CD in with a little extra. My hormones were raging, and I knew that if I didn't do something about it soon, I'd go off like a firecracker, so I made a plan for Saturday night.

Since Grace's room was the only room with a television and DVD player, I had to ensure that my time would be uninterrupted. She worked the overnight shift on Saturdays, so I had free rein once she headed to work. I used Google on Eric's phone to get an idea of what I was in for. Eric found this hilarious to no end.

"Trust me, dude," he said. "When it's time, you'll know exactly what needs to be done. You're making it out to be way harder than it really is, no pun intended."

"Do you think I need a playlist?"

"You and your damn playlists. No, you don't need a

playlist. In fact, given your history, I doubt you'll make it through a song."

I decided that while it didn't require one of my renowned mixtapes, it wouldn't feel right without music. Randy noticed that I was paying extra attention to the R&B section that week. I asked him what he'd recommend for a romantic evening. He lit up like I told him MP3's were a thing of the past.

"My little guy is growing up." He slapped me on the back. "It's Christina, isn't it? I knew you two had a thing going on—"

"Stop right there. No, it's not Christina," I stammer. He's the second adult figure in my life convinced that Christina and I were destined to date, and though she was pretty, out of respect for her feelings I owe it to her to let the Ashton situation play out, even at the expense of my own feelings. "Look, I just need something to set the mood."

"For a date?"

I thought about the movie stashed in my sock drawer. "Something like that."

He headed to the soul section of the store and dug around for a few seconds. "This," he exclaimed, "is exactly what you need to get the job done." A man with a receding hairline graced the cover, hand on his head in a way that reminded me of the Willy Wonka meme, the backdrop of the big city behind him. The title proclaimed it to be *Midnight Love* by Marvin Gaye. I was familiar with the name, even tried to check out one of his albums but there was always a waiting list at the library. "The album you're looking for is right here...trust me, women go crazy for this album."

"Aren't you getting divorced?"

"You asked for an album to get a girl, not keep one."

"Point taken."

He sauntered over to the big stereo, delicately placing the

disc in the tray and skipping to track two, holding the button pause button for dramatic effect. "Percy," he shouted, like he did whenever he got overly excited about something. "Are you ready?"

I gave a shrug of indifference and he muttered something about millennials and pressed play. My indifference held firm through the person whispering 'wake up,' but the bass line dropped and it made all the hair on my body stand up.

There are times when pieces of music defy the label of a particular genre, when the music is so perfect it almost feels like you're underselling its greatness by putting a label on it. This song, and I suspect the album as well, is one of those times. His voice floated above the instrumentation like an angel, and when I closed my eyes, it felt like I was in the studio with him, damn near playing the bass alongside the band. Other than watching Randy sway, no doubt reliving a time when he didn't have to pay attention to Viagra commercials, it was a great day, and I couldn't help but notice that they were coming more frequently.

But underneath it all, there was a sense of sadness that kept me up at night. Sadness because Thanksgiving break was around the corner, which meant I had seven or so months left in foster care. It hung above my head like a dark cloud, knowing that soon these people I had let in my life would fade away, little by little, almost like I had lived in a dream, and that the walls I had built for myself and became comfortable in would rise again. Only now I knew what lay outside of them, and I would become one of the winos I'd see outside the liquor store telling stories about a better time. But I couldn't turn back now, after all Momma and I had been through, there's no way I could let her live alone like that, I owed her that much.

Randy noticed that I wasn't in the dancing spirit anymore. "You all right, Percy?"

"Yeah...I'm good." My work had been completed for the day, and if I was gonna be in a funk, I preferred to be alone. "I unloaded the pallet, can I borrow that cd and head out?"

"Sure thing." He removed it from the stereo and handed it to me with a knowing smile. "Knock yourself out, kid."

* * *

IT WAS FINALLY time to strike.

Two weeks of meticulous planning was on the verge of coming to fruition and I was nervous as hell. You'd have thought I was planning on robbing a bank with how precise I was in every detail. The magazine holding the movie had graduated from my sock drawer to the prime position under my pillow, right next to the sheet I would cover the bed with to catch any spills. On my dresser sat a box of Kleenex, infused with Aloe Vera for maximum softness according to the box, with a bottle of vanilla bean lubricating lotion from Bed Bath and Beyond as its companion.

At 8:45 I bound down the stairs to kiss Grace goodbye and make sure she was actually gone.

It's go time.

I bound back upstairs and gathered my things, nervous excitement rushing through my veins. After laying the sheet down I dimmed the lights and started the album, begrudgingly admitting that Randy was right about how great the album was for the mood. I loaded the movie into the DVD player and took my position on the bed, unsure of what to do next but excited to find out. The menu music for the movie was awful, a clumsy mess of guitar riffs with no semblance of cohesion with the drums, like the director gave two monkeys instruments and just hit record in the studio. A blonde girl stared at me through the screen, sitting on a couch between two guys, both of them clearly at ease with the situation.

'Meat my Girlfriend: Because the best friends are the ones you can share everything with' was the tagline, and it made me laugh because I couldn't picture Eric and I sharing anything more than a meal with Maria, let alone anything else. There was also an advertisement for a bonus scene, and I'm wondering if I carved out enough time.

I press play and pull my shorts down to my ankles, sitting Indian style with enough lubricant on my hand to run the Indianapolis 500. The opening is innocent enough, with the couple meeting at a house with his friend. I could tell the actress was a lot older than she was portrayed to be, which ruined the authenticity for me.

"He's just having problems satisfying me, and we wanna try something different," the girl said.

They hadn't started having sex and I was over it. The entire premise made no sense, and it was funny even thinking people got aroused watching something like that. With my free hand, I ejected the disc and put it back in the case. I flushed the glob of lube down the toilet and stared at myself in the mirror, pitying the sad sack of shit I saw staring back. After throwing the sheet in the laundry hamper I called Eric. He picks up quickly, sounding agitated by the interruption.

"Man, you must've beat the skin off that thing, your voice even sounds deeper."

"First off, go to hell. And secondly, I didn't go through with it. The dialogue was choppy and the narrative made no sense."

"Dude, it's a porno. The dialogue shouldn't matter. It's about getting your rocks off, and you're acting like you're voting for Best Picture at the Oscars."

"Whatever man, you free to hang out?"

"Um...now isn't the best time."

I sucked my teeth in frustration. "Again? We haven't really hung out since you and Yoko Ono got together."

"It's a two way street, Percy."

"What do you mean?"

"You have your little girlfriend, Christina," he sneered. "Say what you want about me, but I'm calling my situation what it is. You two are sneaking off to bookstores, doing things couples do, and masking it as a platonic friendship."

There's a long silence on both ends of the phone before I hear Maria start complaining. "Look, my dad wants to know if you're coming over for the bird's game tomorrow night."

Awkward as it might be between us, I still loved hanging out with his dad. "Yeah, I'll be over after I leave the shop."

"Cool, see you then." He hung up and I stared at my phone for awhile, wondering if our friendship was disintegrating, or if we'd just hit a rough patch like high school friendships do. He was my first real friend, so I didn't have a history to pull from. Was he really that angry about me not wanting to go to homecoming? Hell, we'd laughed together about how lame the idea of high school dances were. If I knew it meant so much I would've gone.

But even I knew things were changing. Our conversations were stilted, with the laughs that once flowed freely from the belly now being forced from the chest. Maybe he finally understood my situation and figured I was leaving at the end of the year anyway, so there was no point in continuing with our brotherhood, and I couldn't blame him.

It wasn't him that had a list of New York City shelters committed to memory, or a growing stash of runaway money in case his mother couldn't regain custody of him. What I envied most about him wasn't his family life; it was that he was free to cultivate relationships without looking over his shoulder. He could screw his whole life up tomorrow and still have a place to call home. Maria could break his heart and he could afford to take that loss because he had relatives ready to replace whatever love was lost.

But he was the closest thing I'd ever known to having a brother, and if this was it, I'd stay until the end.

* * *

IT'S funny how the smell of breakfast cooking can make you forget the failures of yesterday, if only for a moment. I wake up with the emotional hangover from the pity party the night before to the smell of maple sausage, the aroma wafting up to my room and teasing my senses. I dress slowly and head to the kitchen, where I find Grace dancing to her salsa music. She yells my name when she sees me, pulling me into a dance in which I lack both the coordination, and the motivation. Sensing an unwilling dance partner, she spins me toward the table and begins plating the food.

She makes her plate and lowers the music before joining me and leading us in grace. "Why are you looking so down, Percy?" she asks.

Much to my chagrin, I was realizing that letting all these people into my life was robbing me of the ability to hide my emotions. It was the one defense mechanism I could always count on, and while I seemed to be growing as a person, I felt like I was losing part of myself in the process. Summer couldn't come soon enough.

"I'm all right, just a little tired."

She could barely contain her smile. "I bet you are, with your exploits in late night cinema."

And just like that, breakfast isn't appealing anymore. I

thought my plan was fool proof, but I'd let my penis down, I'd let Marvin Gaye down, and apparently I unknowingly netted a hat trick by letting Grace down.

"Yes...but it's not how you thin—how did you know?"

"Well, you always seem to forget that I was a teenager at one point. But just sticking to you, no pun intended, the balled up sheet in the laundry basket was a dead giveaway, and that's without even mentioning the glob of what I judged as vanilla lotion caked at the bottom of the toilet, or the fact that I came home to Sexual Healing playing on a loop." She laughs and takes a bite of her food. "Would you like to talk about it?"

No, I wouldn't. In fact, I'd like to crawl into a cave and be adopted by a pack of wolves as one of their own. "Not really, but I...uh...I found out that it's really not my thing."

"The movie or playing with yourself?"

It feels like we we're playing poker but gambling with awkwardness instead of money. And she's holding a hell of a hand, one she's content with pushing everything all into the middle of the table. I decide to fold."Both," I said. "But I was so turned off by the former that the jury is still out on the latter."

"What you're going through is normal; you have nothing to be ashamed about. Well, maybe the ambiance was a bit much..."

"Please stop," I said, vowing to myself that the next time I masturbated it would be into a dirt hole deep in the woods.

"All right, all right. In the future, at least leave me the option of plausible deniability."

"Done. And can we maybe not tell Alex about this?"

She turns serious. "Funny as that would be, I believe some things are best kept in house."

"Thanks."

"On that same note, I was thinking. Would you like to take your mother out for Christmas dinner? My treat."

I could think of a million reasons why that was a bad idea, chief among them being I didn't know what version of my mother would show up, and I'd seen her strung out for so long it was still eerie seeing her clean. On top of that, I'd come to care about Grace, and it felt like giving love to her was taking it away from my mother, and I've never been good at juggling. She seemed to sense I wasn't too keen on the idea.

"I don't really know her, but I care about you so much, Percy. So by extension I care about anything that I know makes you happy."

I've always heard there's a difference between telling someone you care about them and actually showing it. I'd always been content with the former, and for most of my life that has sustained me. But Grace was about both, from making sure I was comfortable with how she introduced me, to something as simple as making sure I could have a holiday meal with the person I cared about the most. Like Eric, Randy, and even Christina, I was finding it harder to disconnect myself from them emotionally. Which I know is a recipe for disaster.

"All right, I'm in."

There's a knock at the door, and Grace practically skips to answer it.

"Percy, you have a guest," she says from the other room. She enters the kitchen followed closely by Christina.

I jump from my seat like a cadet whose drill instructor just walked in.

"So, this is the girl that has you staying up late on the phone." She's enjoying seeing me blush, and while I can't confirm it, it feels like she got in the foster care business for moments like this. "He told me you were beautiful, but he talks about you so much I was starting to believe you weren't real."

"Thanks, Mom." Christina is trying her hardest to suppress a smile, while I'm wondering if diving headfirst through the sliding glass door will be a quick enough death to spare me any further embarrassment.

"Well, he's the perfect gentleman," Christina says. "Clearly it's a product of a loving home."

This makes Grace smile and she exits the kitchen to give us some privacy. "Help yourself to some breakfast, there's plenty," she says on the way out.

She obliges, and I pull a chair out for her, getting a whiff of her hair so strong Joe Biden would donate to my GoFundMe.

"Sorry to barge in unannounced, but I needed to talk to you in person."

You can show up anywhere and I'd only be mad you didn't get there sooner. "It's really no problem at all, I enjoy hanging out with you. What's up?"

"All right so something crazy happened last night...I'm sorry, how rude of me. How was your Saturday night?"

"Oh you know, nothing crazy, just let it hang out...not my penis or anything." I fumble my fork onto my plate. "I didn't mean anything by...because my pants were definitely on. I...um...what did you want to talk about?"

A laugh comes from Grace in the living room before I can explain myself.

Christina just smiles at the awkwardness while I'm trying to understand how last night's embarrassment carried over into today. "I wanted to talk to you because Ashton asked me to homecoming."

In an attempt to not look distraught at this, I stuff my mouth with oatmeal, giving her two thumbs up in support.

But inside, there's a deep sadness that the train is about to leave the station. Ashton has finally smartened up, so it's only a matter of time before they're a couple. Eric and Maria are one convenience store run away from consummating their relationship, and Jade, well, she's off planning her happily ever after. That leaves me, alone with nobody except Grace, which isn't a bad consolation prize, but my social life shouldn't revolve around dance parties with her.

"That's great," I say, dribbling Quaker Oats down my shirt.

It's not great. In fact, it's so far the opposite that if you dropped an anvil of great on a see-saw, the 'not great' couldn't go high enough to represent how devastating this is.

"Really, you think so?" She doesn't sound sure of herself, which casts me back into my double agent role of genuine friend, versus friend that really likes her.

"Yeah, it's what you've been wanting, so I'm happy for you." *There you go, buddy, let her be taken off the market so you have one less thing to worry about.*

"You don't sound so sure?"

You just couldn't help yourself, you idiot.

"I mean, it's great...I just thought that maybe y—" She eats a spoonful of her oatmeal. "That's good stuff. You're right, maybe I'm just overthinking it."

Don't get me wrong, Grace makes great oatmeal, but I feel like she was trying to say something else, something more pleasing to my ears. Our mutual longing for specific people is what helped us become friends in the first place, and I'd be doing her a disservice as a friend by showing displeasure in her moment of triumph. I change the topic to talk about what she might wear, hoping to make myself excited for her as a way of masking the budding sadness in my heart. As she describes her dark red dress, my mind drifts into a daydream about her taking me to the mall to find a shirt to match. I imagine trying on different shirts and ties, with each walk from the fitting room being greeted with a shake of her head, until I find the one that makes her smile.

"So what are you gonna wear?" she asks. This removes me from my daydream where she's my date and into the real world, where I'll buy a couple of pints of Ben and Jerry's and watch "Meat My Girlfriend" on a loop.

"I'm actually gonna sit this one out."

She throws up a hand and frowns, the universal sign for 'what the hell?' "You're not going?"

"Christina, you need a date for these things."

"I'll be your date then," she says, pretty quickly.

"You have a date already, and besides, all you've talked about is your chance to see if there's something there with Ashton."

"Eric and Maria are going together, I can't stand the thought of you being home alone."

"So, you'd rather me walk around the gymnasium by myself?" It came out before I could stop myself, and now I feel like an asshole. "I'm not really the best dancer anyway."

She seems disappointed in my response, making me wonder if I missed some pertinent detail while I was daydreaming. As much as I appreciate the thought, in a nutshell my night at homecoming will result in me sulking over her while listening to a god-awful playlist curated by a DJ that couldn't put together a mix if Quincy Jones was guiding him.

She finishes her plate, and to my dismay she has to run.

"You're leaving already?"

"Yeah, if I'm gonna go to homecoming I gotta make sure I can afford to get in. I'm helping my Mom on her Amazon route and she'll give me the money to go."

She's leaving when a thought crosses my mind. "I'll buy your ticket," I say, wondering why I feel the need to torture myself. "Think of it as my way of celebrating with you."

"You don't have to do that."

"I know I don't, but I want to, and it'll be awesome knowing that you're finally happy. Go get 'em, champ."

She bites her lips and stares at me for awhile, making my blood pressure rise as I picture her staring at me under different, more erotic circumstances. It's funny that since I'm in a position to afford being a real teenager, my hormones are determined to make up for lost time.

"All right, I accept...but on two conditions." She walks slowly toward the table.

Down, boy.

"First, you agree to go to homecoming. I don't wanna hear about you not having a date. Second, and most importantly, you promise me one dance." She reaches her hand out. "If you don't accept, then I won't go to homecoming and we'll be miserable together."

My first instinct is to ask her what movie she wants to watch, and if she prefers movie butter or kettle corn. But it isn't fair to hold her happiness hostage because my crush turned out to be awful. If the tables were turned, I know she'd jump at the chance to make sure I had the best chance of being successful with Jade. I shake her hand in return. "Deal."

She smiles, showing no signs of letting go, or breaking eye contact for that matter, so I break first, because any longer and I would've melted into a puddle and Grace forgot to get more pads for the Swiffer mop.

After she leaves I sit at the table in a trance, wondering what the hell I agreed to, and more importantly, if I'm even prepared for whatever it'll entail.

"Now I'm not up to date with the current dating trends,"

Grace says suddenly. "But it sounded to me like she came over hoping you'd ask her to homecoming instead of him."

"You were listening the whole time?"

She puts her hands on her chest, feigning ignorance. "Who, me?"

"Yeah."

"You just had your first girl come over. Did you really think I was gonna give you privacy and wait for your shoddy play by play afterwards?"

"No, not really." I can tell this mother and son dynamic is real because any mention of the opposite sex makes me cringe. "Christina likes someone else anyway, I'm just trying to be a good friend."

"She likes you as well, and I'm willing to bet she's just struggling with how to say it." We start clearing the table together. "Now this is my first mother rodeo, so forgive me if this comes out wrong. But it's ok to be selfish about your feelings, Percy. If you have feelings for her, then watching her parade around is only gonna leave you miserable and wondering what if."

"Maybe one day I'll take you up on that advice."

"Well, on a selfish note, make it soon, because you guys are so cute together."

TWENTY-ONE

IT'S HARD TO RIDE THESE EMOTIONS WITH TWO LEFT FEET

"How the hell are you so nervous and you don't even have a date?" Grace asks. She's adjusting my tie, dark red in color to match Christina's dress, and from her silence mixed with constant eye contact I get that this isn't a rhetorical question.

"If I knew the answer to that you could retire tomorrow and we'd be flying around the world going to concerts by next week."

"I'm being serious, Perseverance." Grace has never called me that before, and now that I think about it, my own mother only calls me that when I screw up. "You're moping like you got your heart broken and you haven't left the house yet. Talk to me."

Eric will be here in about fifteen minutes, so I decide to handle the big issue now and have a self therapy session while I'm at the dance to deal with the rest. "It's my first high school dance and I wish my mom was here to see how well I'm doing."

Talking about Momma with her always feels weird to me, and the thought of our upcoming dinner weighs on my mind. Sometimes I wonder if these milestones even count if she's not here. But at the same time I'm happy she's not here, because my presence only serves as a reminder of our past, and though she's passed every mandated drug test, I'm not sure she's actually clean. Even our court mandated visits, closely monitored by Alex, have done little to ease my fears that her sobriety is an illusion. Her addiction has had more false starts than a track meet, each relapse making the next brief moment of sobriety harder to trust. Grace does her best in the awkward position I've put her in, forced to be a mother while consoling me about my real mother. Some days I wish I'd never ended up in her home, because every moment spent with her, for every forehead kiss and impromptu jam session, comes a moment of resentment for Momma because she's never shown me a love like that. She's gone from a creator of my life to a spectator in it. Lately she's taken to calling my phone late at night, always from a blocked number, but never saying anything. She just listens to me talk about my day, and by the end of the call I can hear her sobbing, knowing I was trying to figure stuff out without her.

"You know she would be here if she could, Percy. But letting this whole situation get you down isn't gonna help her get clean any faster."

"I know it won't, but I still think about it."

"Well don't think about it then."

"It's not that easy."

"Yes, it is." Her adjustments on my tie are getting rougher. "Every moment you spend thinking about something that may or may not happen only enables her. When you enter some-one's life and allow someone to enter yours, there's a responsi-bility we have to do our part. My responsibility to you is to make sure you have no excuse to fail, and when you do fail it's my responsibility to hold you accountable. That's what I accepted the moment you stepped foot in this house. Do you know what your responsibility to her is?"

I shrug my shoulders halfheartedly.

"Your responsibility is to succeed so that she knows that everything she's going through is worth it at the end. You have to be her light at the end of the tunnel." She finishes tying the tie and steps back, giving me the up and down once more, her smile confirming that I'm dance ready. "This night isn't about court or going back home. We can deal with that in the morning. This night is about you and your girl."

"What girl?"

She looks at me like I'm crazy. "Men's Warehouse had more tie colors than the Crayola factory. You expect me to believe you landed on that color by accident?"

I give myself away with a smile. "It's a great color."

"It's *her* color." She goes over me with a lint roller, and I can tell she's soaking this moment up. "Now, is there anything else on your mind? I figure you're gonna be in your own head at the dance, so the least I can do is make sure you get there with a clear mind."

I think real hard about this, embarrassed that I even have to ask. "I don't really know how to dance."

Saying she doesn't respond would be lying, because she definitely had a response, just in the form of a laugh. Instead of smoothing over my fears she pulls me close. "Alexa, play Kiss From A Rose by Seal." I'm expecting Alexa to say that I'm a lost cause, but she does her job and plays the song. As the melody fades in she places my hands around her hips, and places hers around my shoulders. "Okay, so the first thing you need to do is sway with the beat."

I can only do what I think she means, and I feel like I'm doing it well.

"You dance like you're having a stroke," she deadpans.

Okay, so maybe I'm not doing as well as I thought.

"Stop moving your feet," she says. "Think of it as rocking back and forth...and stop looking at your feet." She moves my head up and now we're face to face. By the time the chorus is over, I think I've got the hang of it. Apparently I'm doing too well, so Grace takes it up a couple of notches. "Oh, Percy, I've never met anyone like you before," she says, batting her eyelashes.

"What are you doing?"

"You owe her a dance, and I'll be damned if you stutter through it like you did when she came over last week. Focus."

"Mom, this is awkward."

"No, awkward is when she says that to you and there's no oatmeal to stuff in your mouth on the dance floor. Now, I've never met anyone like you before," she says again, sounding less like Christina and more like Pearl the first time I ordered a drink.

"Um...I've never met anyone like you either. In fact I—"

"You're talking too much. Speak from the heart, you paid twenty dollars for that ticket."

"Right. Um...well, I feel like you just get me, and when we hang out, my life just makes sense."

Grace smiles at this. "That's what I'm talking about. You say that and that imbecile she's going to the dance with doesn't stand a chance."

I say that and I'll faint from anxiety before she even responds. We mercifully separate and I start to gather my things so I can leave.

"Where are you going? There's three parts to dancing with girls."

"There are?"

"And we've only covered the first."

"We have?"

"Alexa, play Got to Give It Up by Marvin Gaye."

The song starts playing, and immediately it puts me in a groovy mood. The bass line is perfect, with the sound of what I think is two bottles clapping together to create magic. Grace is grooving along, making me forget about the dance and taking me to our Sunday mornings cleaning together.

"All right, Percy, now everything can't be a slow dance, so you gotta show your moves all night so that when it's time to close the night out, she's looking for you. This is called the two step, it's easy and doesn't require much thinking, but it does require you to catch the beat. Now, follow me." She's moving side to side, and apparently I'm supposed to move my feet this time. I try matching her, but miss the beat in the process. "You're dancing like a robot that was dunked in water. Loosen up and stop thinking so much. Would it help if you imagined I was Christina again?"

"Please don't."

"Well then, focus."

So I do, and sure enough I start to get into it, moving so well with the beat you'd think I was in the studio when they made it. Grace cheers me on, teaching me how to incorporate snapping my fingers, all while staying on beat. However, I forgot about one thing.

"Do you have to take a shit?"

I shake my head.

"Well fix your face then." Apparently my 'concentrate while dancing face' is interchangeable with the one I'd make an hour after downing a bottle of prune juice. After she's sufficiently happy with my progress, she tells Alexa to stop playing.

"Okay, now we've got two types of dancing out of the way. So this next question is the most important one of all." She pauses for dramatic effect, leaving me to wonder what could possibly be more important. "What are you gonna do if she starts popping it?"

"Popping what? Like...a hamstring? Because they have nurses there I bel—"

"Alexa..." she says, grinning from ear to ear. "...play Get Low by Lil Jon and the Eastside Boyz."

There's a game at every county fair, the one where you hit a target with a mallet as hard as you can to make the puck go as high as you can. Right after the song starts playing is that game, except instead of a puck shooting up its my anxiety and awkwardness, and the person holding the mallet might as well be Hercules because it's shot up way past the top. Grace finds her groove again, and I learn quickly that the popping she was referring to isn't a hamstring. She starts backing up into me, meanwhile I'm wondering who is this woman and what has she done with my mother?

"You have to be in tune with her," she says. "If she's throwing it back, you have to catch it. You're dancing like you're scooting your chair up to the table. This is the ass of the girl you're crushing on."

Or the ass of my surrogate mother.

The music fades out, and Alexa informs us that someone is at the door; I believe they call that a mercy killing. Thankfully this concludes our little dance class. I grab my keys and phone, confident that the last twenty minutes have prepared me for anything that might happen tonight. In the living room, I kiss Grace on the forehead and open the door expecting to find Eric, but to my surprise and bewilderment it's Randy. His face is as surprised as mine as he stands there with a bouquet of roses.

"What's up, Randy?"

"Hey, Percy. I uh...just came to see you off for your first dance."

"With roses?"

He looks down at them, then back at me. "Yeah, figure you could give them to your date."

"I told you she was going with the other guy, remember?"

He smacks his hand against his head. "Oh my goodness, you did tell me that. Well, give them to her anyway, so you're always at the front of her mind. You can't take any chances with a girl like that." He hands me the roses, but it's in a weird way, like he doesn't want to. Maybe he's just embarrassed, but I have to pry them from his hands.

"Randy?" Grace asks from behind. "What a wonderful surprise." She looks at the roses and smiles, making me feel bad for being angry with him when he was just trying to help me.

Eric pulls into the driveway, Maria in the front seat, and to my surprise, Christina is in the back. She steps out of the car and if someone handed me a dictionary I wouldn't be able to describe how beautiful she looks. Her dress—which matches my tie perfectly—fits perfectly down to her knees, with her now straightened hair flowing freely down her back. It's kinda fitting that the one piece I have that matches hers is closest to my heart, because that's as close as I'll get tonight. As she strides toward me, her smile more beautiful than the last time I saw it, I wonder if Grace was right and I made a colossal mistake by not asking her. But in the spirit of friendship I'll bury that deep in my subconscious for the evening.

"Are those for me?" she asks. I nod and she's genuinely moved, giving me a hug and frustrating me because her scent is gonna be the only part of her that keeps me company tonight.

"You're not riding with Ashton?" I ask, hoping that he got food poisoning and wouldn't make it.

"He's meeting me there."

"Awesome." Not awesome.

Eric and Maria get out so Grace can take pictures, first as a group, then of the actual couple. When it's my turn I take a pose by myself, but to my surprise Christina jumps in. "We're matching, so that makes you my date for the moment," she says. Grace snaps the picture, winking at me afterward, and full disclosure, I'm grinning like an idiot, too.

Since Randy can't leave because Eric's car is blocking him, we head out, the last thing I see is them waving us off from the porch. Christina holds my hand on the car ride to the school, both of us looking over at the other every few seconds, always checking if the other is there, and I'm at peace with the night.

Because I know that moment in my front yard will be with her the rest of the night.

TWENTY-TWO

HEY MR. DJ

It's a good thing we had that moment back at my house, because now I'm lonelier than a prisoner in solitary confinement at Alcatraz. Ashton was waiting just inside the door when we arrived, wasting no time sweeping her away. He didn't even bother to match with her, leaving me seething with anger while she followed him around with his band of sycophants.

"I should whip your ass for letting her go with that idiot," Eric says. "But I have a feeling you're doing a pretty good job of that on your own."

Truer words have never been spoken. He's asked me at least ten times if I need him to stay with me, like I need a chaperone, but I can't be too mad at him. Last time I was on my own around most of these people, I called him crying at the end of the night. I assure him I'm fine and Maria hands me their coats to check in and takes him straight to the dance floor. After watching him dance for two songs, I'm convinced that he needed Grace's dance lessons more than I did. He's a step behind the beat, like one of those Kung Fu movies that was made overseas and they overdub the vocals. His mind is thinking one thing and his body is doing another. He doesn't need a dance lesson, he needs a goddamn exorcist.

Since the dance is in a school gym, there's not a lot of room to maneuver, so I'm limited to the outskirts near the restrooms. It feels like a PG version of the party I went to a month ago. Knowing most of these kids they've probably managed to sneak in alcohol, taking sips between songs while others keep lookout. At the punch table, I find Mr. Jones serving drinks and dressed better than everyone in the place. He greets me with a fist bump, and I can only hope some of his cool rubs off on me.

"My man, Percy," he says. "Big man on campus at the dance. Where's your date?"

Why does everyone have a fascination with me bringing a date? People don't come to these events on their own? Am I forever doomed to being a party of one? My situation with girls is too complicated to explain, so I just tell him I couldn't find one.

"Don't feel bad, kid, your mind is too great to be confined in something as shallow as this." He gestures to the dance floor. I'm puzzled by the remark, and he picks up on this. "I'm not saying you're incapable of finding a date. But I've been reading your papers...and you see the world in a way that most of these cats in here can't."

"You actually read them?"

"Yeah," he replies, his Brooklyn accent coming through heavy. "I can tell by the way you articulate your thoughts that you've probably seen some heavy things growing up. That and I've noticed kids mocking you by tapping their arms when you walk by."

Ah yes, the residual effects of the party from hell. "I've never thought of life as being heavy, I just deal with it and find my happiness in the simple things."

"That's what I'm talking about. You're operating on a different frequency, one that's years ahead of everyone else. Trust me, when college comes, that'll be your time to shine."

He hands me a cup of soda, and I sip for a while, begrudgingly admitting to myself that the DJ is killing it. His mixes are perfect, playing just enough of a song before fading the next one in. Another understated part of his set is he's conservative with his scratches, letting the song be the star of the show instead of making it about himself like the radio DJ's. He really gets into it by playing a current song, then fading in the original song it was sampled from, with the students on the dance floor none the wiser, thinking he came upon an unreleased remix.

"This DJ is killing it," I say, excited to hear the sounds of Charlie Wilson and the Gap Band coming through on his mix.

"You like that?"

"I'm a big music guy, it's kinda my thing."

"Man, you're an old soul to know about this music here. This is my generation right here, youngster. The DJ is my man from Brooklyn. He comes down for the dances to make a couple bucks. If you get bored, go tell him Desmond sent you; he's good people."

This trip to the booth is the most exciting prospect I have this evening. "I'm definitely gonna do that. My customers at Backside come in and request stuff like this all the time. It's hard not to be curious about it."

"You work over there? I might have to stop in and see you one of these days. My old lady loves vinyl, and y'all are the only place in the area that has a nice selection without having to go into Philly."

"Please do, even if it's just to chat."

A large group of students come over for drinks, so I step to the side and let him do his thing, searching for Christina in the crowd. As one group is leaving the dance floor, I spot her on the other side. She looks out of sorts, probably how I did the night at the party. Now that I've been in that circle I find it hard to believe that they were who I aspired to be friends with. For a lot of them, these four years are going to be the highlight of their lives, the peak of the roller coaster, and it's funny to think of them having to navigate a world where their letterman jackets don't mean shit. Understanding this makes all the jokes worth it, because this is their endgame, and mine is just beginning. Hopefully Christina is able to figure this out without going through what I did. But if she does, I'll be there to wipe her tears away.

It's one thing to know the girl you like is with someone else, but having to watch her with him is a cruel exercise I wouldn't wish on anybody. To watch someone so amazing get dressed up for a guy that couldn't be bothered to match colors and make her feel special infuriates me. Ashton is barely showing her any attention or affection, as if she should be thankful that he asked her.

"He only asked her to the dance because his friends said he couldn't sleep with her," a familiar voice says. I turn to see Jade, in a dark green dress that matches her name, staring at the same events as me. Before I can tell her how great she looks, a switch flips in my brain, reminding me that we're not supposed to care about her anymore.

"That sounds like the kinda game you would play," I reply, coldly. "In a way I should be thanking you for doing it at a house party instead of at the school dance."

"All right, I deserve that." She stares into her drink. "Will there ever be a day when you forgive me for that?"

"Yeah, it'll be the night your boyfriend actually wins a football game."

To my surprise she smiles at this, given that we're o-6 as a school and word is we got our ass kicked last night. I'm shocked the players even showed up here tonight. But with all my quips, it says something that she's still trying to make things right with me.

"How's your mother?" I ask.

"She's doing well...still clean, and it's looking like this time I'll stick around." She looks defeated when she says this, like she doesn't really believe it'll last. As the child of an addict I know that face. "What about you? They sending you back home or what?"

"I wish I had an idea, it would help me navigate my friendships."

"You'll probably go back. My social worker told me that the department seeks to have an eighty-twenty ratio on kids. Eighty percent of them should be returned to their families, with the other twenty percent being adopted. At your age, they'll probably push for the former, which you should hope for anyway because adoption terminates your birth mother's rights. Just something you should think about."

"Thank you for that, and for telling me about Christina; it means a lot."

I see Casey coming out of the bathroom and decide to make myself scarce.

"Are we good?" she asks as I look for an exit.

Momma always told me that sometimes good people make mistakes, and that you can tell if they were really contrite with how they tried to rectify them. Jade could've left our conversation in the record store and acted like I didn't exist anymore. But here she was, still trying to make it right in the midst of the chaos.

"Yeah, we're good." She gives me a hug, and I swear I can feel the tension she's been carrying evaporate. She will never be my girlfriend, but I committed to being a friend early on, and this just feels better.

"Go get your girl," she whispers. "You guys look really good together."

I let her go and fade into the dance floor just as Casey is getting to her. With nowhere to go and nobody to talk to, I make my way to the DJ booth, which is situated at the far end of the court at the bottom of the bleachers. He looks annoyed by my presence, until I tell him that Desmond sent me, then he invites me up.

"Sorry about the mean mug, but some of your classmates are little shitbirds, asking for any song they think will lead to a handjob. I'm Marlon."

"Percy." We pound fists and he shows me his setup. There's two turntables for mixing, with a monitor on each side showing his large and pretty impressive library of songs. It spans decades, and at the proper event he could spin a party that would make people of all ages happy. He walks me through his setup, impressed by my knowledge of music, and sighs when I ask him why he leaves so many good songs unplayed.

"These kids wouldn't know who Rick James is if he walked up and stole they girl right in front of them."

"I'm sensing a theme amongst you adults."

"It's true. For every kid like you, there's another twenty that swears Justin Timberlake invented R&B. Kids like you must be protected at all costs."

He would've really come in handy at that house party.

"So, where's your date?" He looks around, with my silence letting him know there wasn't one. "Damn, Percy. Didn't mean to hit a sore spot for you."

"You're good. There is someone, but she likes someone else, and instead of asking her, I encouraged her to go with him. So, now I have a front row seat with you to watch him treat her like shit all night. But she did make me promise her a dance, so I just gotta wait for the right song."

"You got one in mind?"

"I thought you were annoyed by students asking for songs."

"Man, you're different, and you funny as hell. What you got?"

This is a tough question. Since I never got the hang of 'catching it' Lil Jon is out of the question. Anything that requires the two steps is too basic to waste on my one moment with her. There's gotta be a song that can bring us close together for an uninterrupted period. I laugh, because it's almost too funny. "You got Seal, Kiss from a Rose?"

He says nothing, instead logging into his computer and pointing to the track inside one of his files, before dragging it down the playlist to the last song. "Last song is at eleven-forty-five it's all up to you now, kid."

This being nice to people may not be paying off with the girls I like, but with everybody else I'm striking gold.

I thank him and set off in search of Christina, knowing I got about thirty minutes to make it happen. She isn't on the dance floor, or in the section with the refreshments, and in a desperate bid I walk through the popular kids section, dealing with their usual jokes about my mom while I look around frantically to find her. But she isn't there, and I realize that I waited too long too long to make a move. That's pretty much been the story of my life. I walk out into the hallway, hoping to find Eric and tell him I'll walk home and I find her. She's standing alone near the section where the pictures are being taken. She's got tears in her eyes, and a quick scan of the scene lets me know why.

In front of the camera is Ashton, cheesing with that same

shit eating grin all the popular kids seem to have, except the girl on his arm isn't Christina. It's another vaguely familiar girl from the section of the school that I stay away from, but the colors of her dress match his suit. I feel a deep sense of regret for not seeking her out the minute Jade told me what his plans were. Even though I wish I could've been her date, seeing her go through this brings me no joy. I saunter up next to her, and her head finds my shoulder because we both have nothing to say. Just two friends learning about love and the heartache that often accompanies it. But somewhere between her tears streaking down my jacket and the flash of the camera, an idea strikes.

"I may not be your date," I say, "but we just so happen to be matching, so I think I'm good for a flick and the dance I promised you."

I know, I can't believe I manage to say those words either, but my rapid heartbeat and her lifting her head confirm that I really said it. She smiles at me, so I take the handkerchief from my pocket and wipe her tears away, and she checks her makeup while we wait our turn in line for pictures. She still hasn't said a word, but in this case her actions are doing all the talking. When it's our turn, we take our places in front of the backdrop like the photographer tells us, and smile on his count. In this case a picture really is worth a thousand words, because once it's developed, it'll tell the story of two friends that found a way to be there for each other when it mattered.

"Thank you," she says as we're walking back to the gymnasium. "I really needed that."

Right on schedule, like Cupid himself was working the turntable, the song starts playing and I lead her to the dance floor. My hands find her hips while her arms find my shoulders. The dance floor has cleared, not because it's a Hollywood moment, but because none of the kids know this song, or the DJ for that matter. I can feel the stares of the popular kids, but my eyes stay on Christina, where they always should have been.

"Why do you let them treat you that way?" she asks. No need to ask who she's speaking of.

"Trust me, I want nothing more than to dish it back. But I was taught to be the bigger person, and sometimes that means the things that I want go unfulfilled."

She looks up at me, and if it wasn't for Grace's lesson of not moving my feet during a slow dance my knees would buckle. God bless that woman. "Well, what do you want? Because sometimes you have to reach out and grab it, even if it scares you."

The moment feels infinite, even though the hook of the song lets me know it hasn't been that long. I really want to kiss her, but she's dealt with enough for one evening. The moment passes and she rests her head on my chest.

"I know you could never see me as being more than a friend," she says. "But I'm happy you pretended to be for a little while."

I want to tell her how I feel about her, about the moments when she runs through my mind like a Kenyan in the New York City marathon, but I can only think about the 80%, and it's not fair to lead her on knowing I'll be leaving one day. So I stay silent. It hurts like nothing I've ever experienced, and I pull her closer, wishing that I would've chosen a live version of Led Zeppelins's Stairway to Heaven so the moment could last longer. But we hold each other, long after the song ends and the lights come on.

It was as close to forever as I've ever known.

TWENTY-THREE

SAD BOY HOURS

The middle of the night is usually my favorite part of the day, a time when I can dump all of my emotions out and sift through them one by one, pairing them with a song that fits the mood. But tonight, hours after my first school dance, my mood is bittersweet as I replay the night over and over in my head. I feel like the basketball team that loses on a last second shot. Sure, I played a good game, but the little mistakes led to a breakdown and ultimately, a loss.

But is it really a loss?

Christina left with us, falling asleep on my shoulder on the drive home while I held her hand, wishing Eric would jump on the highway and just drive, but he and Maria had plans of their own. So my hesitation on the dance floor dissolved into a hurried goodbye on her doorstep, followed by a brooding ride to my own house, culminating in me laying in a mess of CDs. Normally I prefer whole albums, but right now my emotions are all over the place, so I'm changing discs after every song, frantically searching for specific tracks to match each emotion.

Right now, Wonderwall by Oasis is the flavor of the moment.

The lyrics play over and over in my head, hitting even harder when I close my eyes to match them with specific moments from the dance. My heart races as I replay our moment on the dance floor, the softness of her wrists as they clutched my shoulders, or how she averted eye contact when she assumed that I couldn't see her as anything more than my friend. She was so firm in her beliefs about my feelings toward her that she couldn't stand to look me in the eye, preserving the moment for both of us and leaving a sliver of hope for a miracle. She's right about my feelings, but for the wrong reasons. Like putting together a puzzle without the box, she has an idea of what my feelings are as a whole, but without the details it's never complete, so there's no way for her to understand that I'm doing this to roteher in the long run.

From the moment I became a foster kid, I thought the worst part of it would be living with a stranger while worrying about my mother. Thanks to Grace that's been the easy part. The worst part is being forced to love all of these new people half-heartedly, entering every relationship with one foot out the door already, leaving each of them to ask 'why not' while leaving me wondering 'what if.'

A light flashes against my eyelids, and I open them to an incoming call from an unknown number. Momma always has a sixth sense of when I need to vent, and I know she's wondering how my first school dance went.

"Hey, Mom," I say.

She greets me with a sniffle, my cue that she's listening.

"So, the dance was great, well, as great as it could be for a guy without a date. But the DJ was amazing and I finally forgave Jade, just like you said I should."

More silence on her end, except for a TV running in the background.

"But I'm in limbo because..." I trail off. "...because there's someone else. She was supposed to be this blind date I went on to help Eric out. I even thought she hated me, and the feeling was mutual, believe me. But somewhere along the way I've found it hard to think about my life without her in it, and it hurts because I know you're working super hard to get me back."

My music was up so loud I could hear Coldplay playing clearly through my headphones on the floor next to me. She hasn't hung up yet thankfully, because I enjoy being able to spill my feelings out to someone without having to listen to advice. Don't get me wrong, consulting with the people in your life is perfectly fine, but only for certain topics. Talking about girls isn't one of them, mostly because the advice you get is one size fits all type of advice, like when you call Comcast and tell them your internet isn't working and they tell you to unplug your router. With people there's a human element to account for because people react differently.

"I'm still committed to coming back home, but it can't be like last time, Mom. If I'm gonna leave her, I need to know that you're as committed to staying clean as I am to staying with you. All I want is for my love to be enough for you." My eyelids are starting to get heavy, with Chris Martin's voice fading in and out like a bad radio signal. "I'm fading fast, but I'll see you in two weeks for dinner with Grace. I love you, Mom." There's a faint beep letting me know the phone call has ended, and I drift slowly into my dreams, at peace that my decision is for the right reasons.

TWENTY-FOUR

LET'S GET READY TO RUMBLE

My anxiety is running at an all-time high for tonight's dinner. In two days I'll meet with Alex to figure out the next steps, so it feels like everything is on the line tonight. This has turned what should be a simple dinner into what feels like a titanic clash of circumstances. In light of that, I'll let Michael Buffer handle the intro.

Ding Ding Ding

Ladies and Gentleman, we have arrived at our main event of the evening. Brought to you by Olive Garden, where you can get all you can eat pasta with unlimited salad and breadsticks for 9.99, with curbside service so you never have to leave your car to get a taste of Italy.

Tonight, we are going to witness...the most anticipated match in the history of Percy's life, a titanic clash of two juggernauts, each one qualified to be here this evening. Are you ready?

Imaginary crowd roars

I said, are you ready?

Imaginary crowd roars even louder

This bout will be contested at one meal, and it's for the

undisputed loyalty and eventual custody of Perseverance Martin.

Introducing first, the challenger. From upstate New York, she comes in with a record of one foster child, no biological children, and an undying love for the child who's growing up way too fast for her. Grace "We got food at home" Wilson.

And her opponent. From Camden, New Jersey, entering the ring with a record of one biological child, no foster children, and a complicated relationship with the one she's got. She is the reigning, defending, champion of Percy's heart, Wanda "Maybe tomorrow will be better" Martin.

LET'S GET READY TO RUMBLE!!!!!!!!!!!!

* * *

I SPOT Momma sitting in front of the Olive Garden as we pull into the parking lot. Grace lets me out to greet her while she parks the car, and I decide to use these precious moments to lay a foundation for a pleasant evening. Admittedly, it's a weird arrangement, the fact that I get to have dinner with my mother, accompanied by my other mother, and I'm in the awkward position of making them both feel like they're getting an equal share of my love.

She's excited to see me, gripping me in her embrace before I make it to the curb, and I can admit that I've never seen her so happy. Her hair is picked out into a mini Afro, with a tight fitting sweater that tells me she's gaining weight, a telltale sign that she's healthier than she's been in awhile.

"I'm so happy to see you," she says, releasing me from her grip and getting a good look at me.

"Me, too, Mom." I reply, and I mean it. I pull her Christmas gift from my pocket. It's one of those Visa gift cards, since I don't know where she's staying or the places she frequents. She's overjoyed by this, promising to give me my gift at the end of the night.

"I promise this won't be like the last time we went out to eat," she says. This makes me shudder, because I've tried to act like that night never happened.

The last time we went out to eat was my tenth birthday. By this time I no longer referred to her heroin habit as medication; it was a disease that was ruining both of us, and I went to extreme measures during this time to shield her from anyone that could report us to social services. But when my birthday came around she always tried to make it special, using it as a day when she swore that she would get clean.

She took me to a run of the mill diner, nothing extravagant for obvious reasons, but it wasn't the shelter or anything that had to be cooked in the microwave, so I was all in. Unfortunately she was going through withdrawals, and though she tried to make it through the meal, she ended up throwing up everywhere as the waitress sang happy birthday to me, her vomit blowing out the candle in a cruel representation of how her addiction would always dim any light that shined in our lives. The waitress was horrified, and I'm not sure she bought my story of Momma having food poisoning, but she let us leave without paying. Momma ended up leaning on my shoulder as I guided us home, and after I laid her on her stomach, I vowed to never go through that kind of embarrassment again.

Grace makes her way to us and Momma eyes her suspiciously, giving a fake smile as they shake hands and walk into the restaurant.

The hostess greets us with a smile, and I wonder if we look like any other family coming in to share a meal together. Since it's their busy night we end up with a table instead of a booth, and I take a seat at the head of it, in the middle of both so neither of them can feel like I'm playing favorites. The hostess says our waitress will be with us shortly and leaves us to study the menu.

"You guys get whatever you want," Grace says.

"I can pay for my own meal," Momma shoots back. *Just gonna dive into the bullshit I see.*

Grace pretends to not hear the remark, nodding and studying the dinner combinations, living up to her name by the second.

Our waitress arrives before any potential bloodshed can occur, taking our drink orders and promising to return with breadsticks. I'm tempted to ask her to hold the butter, seeing as the tension was thick enough to slice and spread around. Grace tells me what to order and excuses herself to go to the ladies room.

"Mom, what gives?" I ask. "Why are you treating her like that?"

For a second I can see she's going to defend her behavior, but once our eyes meet she drops the facade. "I'm sorry, this is just weird for me because I'm not used to sharing motherly duties with someone else."

Well, if you had done what you were supposed to do in the first place, we wouldn't be sitting here. "I get that, Mom, but Grace is awesome and she's trying really hard to make this special for me. She's bent over backwards for me, and what you're doing isn't fair to her or me."

"I'm still your mother, Percy. Until the Lord calls me home, I'll always have that title."

"And she's not trying to take that from you."

She looks away, tapping her spoon on the table like a child being scolded.

"Look, if you can't appreciate what she's trying to do for

me, at least play nice because it would mean something to me."

I can tell this hits home. When you live with someone for years you learn what buttons to press and when to press them. It feels like my love is being auctioned off to the highest bidder, and I feel bad knowing that she's watching someone else doing things for me that she should be doing. But I do a good enough job comparing them to each other on my own, and knowing that they don't hate each other would go a long way with me since Grace made it clear that she'd be in my life for as long as I wanted.

"Loving her doesn't mean I love you any less." I grab her hand. "I need you to know that."

She starts to say something, but Grace returns to the table commenting on how the bathroom wasn't stocked with toilet paper, a symptom of being a waitress. "Grace," Momma says. "I want to apologize for my remark. This is hard for me, but I appreciate you taking the time to do this." She looks at me as if to ask, "Was that enough?"

"I totally get that this isn't everyone's cup of tea, but I love Percy and naturally that means I love you, too, so it's water under the bridge." With that, we're back at square one. "Now that we got that out the way, who wants to split a sampler platter with me?"

Miraculously, the sampler platter has something we all like, and after our orders are taken, they get to know each other better.

"Percy tells me you're a waitress," Momma says. It's her first remark delivered without a hint of bitterness. "I used to waitress before he was born. It was an interesting gig."

I never knew Momma to have any job outside the unspeakable ones, so this is quite informative.

"What shift did you work?" Grace asks.

"Usually dinner rush, that's when you got the best tips."

"Amen to that." They clink glasses to their shared occupation before turning the conversation towards me.

"How was homecoming, Percy?"

The question stops me just as I bite into a piping hot mozzarella stick, shooting scorching cheese into the roof of my mouth and causing me to choke. After regaining my composure, I don't know how to answer the question. I literally laid on the floor in my suit and told her everything right after Eric dropped me off. I know I told her to play nice, but this was pushing it.

"Don't you remember I told you..."

She looks genuinely puzzled by this, and her confusion scares me because her lack of recollection has always been a sign that she was using again. I've suddenly lost my appetite, and judging by their looks, I've also lost the ability to form coherent sentences. To save face I excuse myself and rush to the restroom.

I splash cold water on my face, as if it would give me a do-over on the evening. She couldn't be using again, could she? No way, I mean, she looks healthy and full of life. From what I know, she's passed every random drug test she's submitted. But even I know how easy it is to beat that, hell, in the past she's used my urine to do it.

The worst part of knowing an addict is trying to discern the real from the fake. Nobody likes to be known as a substance abuser, so they become adept at hiding it any way they can. For Momma, it's always been long sleeve sweaters to cover up the tracks in her arms. But she took her coat off at the table and seems to be going the extra mile to prove to me that she's clean. It's all too confusing to mull over in the bathroom of an Olive Garden, and I return to the table with the same confusion I left with. I'm watching her every move, every tick of the face and sip of a drink, looking for anything that will confirm my suspicions, but I see none.

Our food comes and I barely touch it, faking that the mozzarella stick scalded the roof of my mouth, making every bite painful. Neither of them seem to believe this, but they leave me be. As Grace talks about my accomplishments in school, I notice a change in Momma. She's saying all the right things, like how she's proud of me and that she expects nothing less. But I can see the pain in her eyes as she realizes everything she's missing out on. She holds my hand throughout the conversation, as if I'm slipping away from her permanently.

I always told myself that going into foster care would send her into a spiral, but watching her listen to someone else recap my life from the spot she should be in seems to have the opposite effect. To anyone else, even Grace, the smile Momma has is the one of a proud mother. But that's because they don't know her like I do. I've seen that smile before, when I was given Christmas gifts at the shelter that she couldn't afford, or when I'd lie to her that I'd had enough to eat so that she could have a meal. It's a smile that hides fear and embarrassment. Embarrassed because someone else was providing something she couldn't, and fear because she could only wonder if what was given to me was enough to take my love away forever. That smile is hereditary, being it's the same one I had when I told Christina to go to the dance with Ashton.

I wish I could pull her to the side and make her understand that I'll always love her, even if she relapses a thousand times. But in my haste to remedy that look on her face, I only make it worse.

"Mom," I say, voice cracking.

"Yes," they reply in unison.

The table goes silent, each of us considering the ramifications of what just happened. Momma says nothing, only grip-ping my hand so tight I can see her skin stretched over the tendons in her knuckles. Grace says nothing, and I feel for her the most, because she's done nothing wrong, her only crime has been loving me with all of her being, so I take her hand with my free one. Somehow, I'm making out the best, because for so long I've been numb to feelings of my own, content to take on the feelings and emotions of others. But right now, while soothing my birth mother's soul with one hand and assuring my foster mother that she's more than a replacement with the other, I allow myself to appreciate the silence as a moment to truly understand what unconditional love is. They both want the best for me, but one will always be a reminder to the other of her failures, forcing Momma to always look over her shoulders, knowing someone is waiting in the wings to take her place.

Our waitress comes back with our bill, and it's the final straw for Momma, who darts from the table. Grace tells me to go after her while she handles the bill. I catch up to her outside the restaurant, sitting alone on a bench, staring straight ahead and thinking Lord knows what. She pulls a small box from her purse, and hands it to me. I can't help but smile at it, because it's the one thing that lets me know it's Christmas time. My very own box of Starbucks Cranberry Bliss Bars. Whenever we'd go into Cherry Hill during the winter, we'd always stop for hot chocolate. Since we never had fancy lights or even a tree, the Starbucks decorations acted as my surrogate. Whenever I saw those bars in the pastry case, they always made me feel happy, even if I didn't have gifts at home.

"I'm surprised you remember this," I say. "Thank you."

Momma smiles and rubs my face. "Open the card after I leave; it's better that way." I can see the bus approaching and she gathers her things. "Tell Grace I said thank you for dinner. I love you with all I have to give, Percy." With a final hug she heads off to take the bus home, leaving me in front of the Olive Garden with my curiosity peaked.

Technically she's gone, so I open the card, and in the process I miss the coin that falls lightly on the ground. After picking it up, I stare in disbelief. It's her chip celebrating ninety days of sobriety. At most I'd known her to go sixty days, and even then it was giving her the benefit of the doubt by overlooking a couple of questionable days. But seeing this chip is like finding some rare currency you only hear myths about. The words she's written in the card are a simple plea:

Percy, I know I haven't done anything to deserve your trust, so I'm giving you this chip to demonstrate my actions instead of empty promises. Please don't give up on me.
    Love, Mom

She's been clean the whole time, and the thought of her finally putting her life back together makes me wanna cry tears of joy because it's all I've ever wanted. But it also makes me sad because my decision is clear now. Maybe somewhere deep down I wanted this dinner to end badly so I could stay with Grace. But it has been so long since I had seen Momma like that, alert and in tune with the world that it reminds me of how much I miss her. Our life together will never be perfect, but I owe her the chance to make up for lost time, even if it means leaving everything I love behind in the process.

It's time to go back home.

TWENTY-FIVE

EVERYONE HAS CHOICES

The first time Alex and I had a meal here was only four months ago, but so much has changed since then that it feels like it was years ago. I'm not the same Percy I was that night we walked into Donkey's, I'm more mature and trusting, with enough good memories from my time in Grace's home to balance out the bad memories from before. Thankfully, the quality of the food hasn't changed, even if my current predicament lowers my appetite for it.

I stayed up well past midnight, agonizing over what I'm gonna say to Alex, who seemed to anticipate something given how quickly his schedule cleared so we could meet. He's watching me closely, studying my every move but content to let me start the conversation. The problem with having a social worker that's been in your shoes before is that you don't have the element of surprise. Our situations as children were different, but the emotions are the same. The loyalty to our birth mothers, the feeling of never feeling like you truly belong, even the apprehension to cultivating friendships, these are emotions that anybody that's been a product of the system has felt. Having Alex is like playing chess with someone that knows your next move before you do; you can only move so far before you find yourself boxed in.

Working in my favor, something like a bargaining chip, is my knowledge of the 80/20 ratio his department strives for. It's a nice chip to have, and it's gonna be my ticket home.

Momma's sobriety chip sits in my pocket as a reminder of why I'm making the choice that I am, even though it feels like I'm taking a step back. I've told myself a million times that the relationships I've built don't have to end if I go back home, a small lie but a necessary one, because admitting to myself that one day they'll stop answering my calls is only gonna make me want to stay. Worst case, I'm two years away from being an adult, free to go where I please. Another lie because wherever Momma goes, I'm sure to follow.

Our waitress delivers our food and leaves us in peace, my cue to get this over with.

"Do you know why I asked to meet?" I start. Not the most original opening, but it gets his attention.

He finishes his bite, wipes his mouth and smirks at me. "I think I have an idea, but I'd hate to spoil the fun." Most times I enjoyed when he played coy, bringing a sense of humor to our visits, but there's too much weighing on my heart today, so I decide to put everything out there.

"When were you going to tell me about the ratio your department wants you to keep?"

I can tell this surprises him, and he tries to buy some time by taking a sip of his drink which makes me smile, because of any complaints a person would have about the food here, dry meat isn't one of them. "It's not what you think."

Usually when a person says that it's exactly what they think.

"All right," I say. "Explain it to me, because it sounds like you were gonna drop a bomb on me when I least expect it."

"It's not a mandate, so I don't want you to think I'm in the business of putting kids in harm's way for the sake of a number." He's fiddling with his wedding band, trying to find the right words to placate me and save face. "Foster homes are meant to be temporary. I mean, a good percentage of our referrals come from spurned relatives on a revenge streak."

"You know I don't have anybody else, so you're gonna have to do better than that."

He fixes his mouth to say something but his mind gets the better of him. "The goal is to find a permanent solution instead of kicking the can down the road."

"So, it's a money game?"

"Yes, but not how you would think. Take the money Grace gets for you, part of it is subsidized by your mother from the state garnishing her check."

Now it's his turn to throw haymakers out of nowhere, and this one lands flush. "You're taking Momma's money?"

"Nothing in this world is free, Percy, and as much as I would love to tell you that we have an infinite budget, the truth is that there are more kids that need a home than the state can financially accommodate."

"So, you hold us for ransom?"

"You don't think that's a little dramatic?"

I'm not sure what I expected at the start of this conversation, but it wasn't this. "No, it's not being dramatic. You're taking kids away from everything they've ever known and wagging your fingers at their parents while having your hand in their pocket. How are they supposed to make things better if you're cutting them off at every turn?"

"I told you from the beginning that I would always be honest with you. It's not the rosey picture you were expecting, but it's the truth."

I push my food away, angry not only for myself, but for

the other kids that aren't lucky enough to have someone like Grace. The kids in group homes and living in worse conditions than what they came from, those same conditions financed by their parents. If I harbored any reservations about going back home, learning that Momma is fronting this little vacation washes them away.

"I wanna go back with my mother," I say. This curveball out of left field makes Alex raise his eyebrows. "We agreed on a year, and since we're at about the halfway point, I think we should start laying the groundwork."

He leans forward. "Since we're being honest with each other, is that really what you want, or did the information I just gave you play a part?"

He knows the reservations I have, not because I've told him, but because my situation is a pretty good one to leave behind.

"You just wanna talk me out of it."

"No, I just wanna know why."

"Am I telling this to Alex the social worker, or Alex the guy that was once in my shoes?"

"You're telling this to the one you can be honest with."

"No matter how comfortable I am, that feeling of not belonging never goes away. Even on the best days, there's always that little voice in the back of my head telling me that this isn't my real life." Alex's gaze doesn't waver, and I'm sure everything I'm saying he's lived through. "At first I figured it was normal to feel that way. I mean, I'm the new kid, right? But as my life has gotten better, that feeling has gotten more intense, and it's to the point that I can't enjoy anything anymore."

"Percy, that's perfectly normal—"

"I don't want it to be," I shout, drawing glances from those within ear shot. "I should have the right to choose whether I want to be happy or miserable. Either way, I need to pick a side, because having them constantly throwing counter punches at each other feels worse. I'd rather..." I bite down on my nail, realizing that my wanting to go home is more about than it is my Mom. "...I'd rather be miserable, than have every good thing that happens to me be bittersweet."

For the next five minutes those words hang there, an awkward silence occasionally pierced by the soda machine discharging ice and the sound of new beef being slapped on the grill. Alex just strokes his beard while giving sad smiles to other patrons passing our table on the way to the restroom. I'm passing the time by staring out the window of my old neighborhood.

"If your Mom can pass every drug test and find suitable housing for you, I'll recommend that the state terminates its rights to you."

You'd think that he'd be happy at this moment, but I'm the only one smiling. His disappointment in my choice hits harder than I expected, but there's too much work to be done with Momma to really work through it. He'll eventually get over it because he cares about me, but there's a feeling gnawing at my heart that only his disappointment could bring to the forefront.

What if I'm wrong about everything?

TWENTY-SIX

WE CAN CHECK IT OFF TOGETHER

I've never understood the appeal of Valentines Day.

In the spirit of honesty I'll admit that part of it was jealousy at not having a girlfriend, but I always told myself I didn't have the money to do anything nice if I did have one. When I was a kid the only good part of Valentine's Day was hoarding candy from the parties in my class so I'd have food later. I even thought the cards given to me by girls meant they liked me, but eventually I figured out that everybody got one. Like every other holiday this year, this one feels completely different from normal, well, except the not having a date part.

Eric has some special date planned for Maria, at least I hope it's special, because he won't shut up about it. Christina is still in the awkward phase of believing something is still there with Ashton, and I don't think that'll come to an end before Saturday, so it's just me and Grace. I'm thinking that's about to fall through because she's been quite adamant that I should be out doing something on Valentine's Day. My own mother won't even be my date, if there's anything sadder than that, please step forward and show me. I would ask Randy if he wants to hang out, but the thought of being blown off by a recently-divorced, middle-aged male is a bit more than I can handle. So, it's looking like Ben & Jerry's accompanied by visions of Christina will be my plans for the evening, not a bad consolation prize considering last year I spent it around a metal garbage can burning trash to keep warm.

It's all about perspective.

But still, in spite of my feelings about Valentine's Day, the fact that I'll be alone again is affecting my mood. Why is it that when I'm miserable about the opposite sex, everyone else is in bliss. Eric and Maria can't keep their hands off each other, Randy has played the same R. Kelly *Chocolate Factory* album for the past week, even the perpetually single Grace has a pep in her step. So all of this is running through my head as I reorganize the vinyl while listening to Ignition for what feels like the millionth time.

"Hey, Randy," I yell from across the store. "We can't play Nickelback, but R.Kelly is all right? Why is that?"

He turns the music down. "Because Nickelback didn't write Bump and Grind." They also didn't pee on teenagers, but I keep that to myself. He waves me over, and as I get closer, I get the sense that he's nervous about something. "I need a favor," he asks. "If I asked you to make a mixtape for me, would you do it?"

I agree before I consider what he would need one for. "What's the goal?"

He cracks his knuckles. "There's a special person in my life, and I wanna let her know how much she means to me."

This excites me because those are the best kinds of mixtapes to make. It's like having a blank canvas with a dot on each end, and you get to use music to connect the two. Without a word I boot up the computer and create a blank Word document. "All right, first, we gotta name it. Who's it for?"

"Huh?"

"What's her name?"

This flusters him. "Gr...um, Gretchen."

"Are you sure?"

"Of course I'm sure, why wouldn't I be?"

"Because you sound like Cuba Gooding in Radio."

His moment of nervousness has evolved into frustration. "So you wanna be funny now?"

"Why are you so on edge? Is this a 'you messed up and trying to win her back' mixtape?"

Miraculously, this makes him realize how crazy he's acting. "No, it's just, well, I've never felt this way about someone before?"

This is strange to me since he's been married, but I remember how I started with Jade, and tripped right into Christina, so it makes sense. "All right, what did you have in mind?"

"I was thinking about forty five tracks—"

"Stop right there. That's a playlist, and those have their own time and place. This is about saying what you need to say and letting it marinate in her mind like a pot roast. So you gotta follow the rules."

"What are the rules?"

I've never actually shared my rules for making a mixtape, but there's a first time for everything, and I love the prospect of seeing if they make sense. "First off, the most important aspect of a mixtape is length. Say what you need to say and get the hell out of there. As a general rule, I wouldn't go longer than fifteen tracks."

"I need it to last throughout the night." He gives me a grin that makes me wanna vomit, because through the night only means one thing. I picture Randy kicking off his Air Monarchs and sliding his cargo shorts down in front of

Gretchen, my mixtape helping consummating their courtship. Maybe this isn't such a good idea. But he is paying me handsomely, so I forge ahead, nausea be damned.

The first track is the second most important part of a mixtape. They say you only get one chance to make a first impression, and viewed through the lens of a mixtape, truer words have never been spoken. It has to be something the person is familiar with, because you're trying to build trust. If you grab them with the first track, they'll follow you anywhere.

Randy likes this idea and searches furiously through the master music list to find the perfect song. With a collection so large, the task can be daunting if you aren't focused.

"What does she like?" I ask. Since the mixtape is for someone you know, making the first track an artist they like is an effective way to start. It's like an introduction from a trusted friend.

He stops searching and thinks for a second, humming different melodies to popular songs to jog his memory. "She loves Prince, but don't you think that would be too obvious?"

"With the first track, obvious is what you should be going for."

"Okay, how about Do Me, Baby?"

"Not that obvious."

"Oh." He sounds defeated, like his chances of getting laid went up in flames. We brainstorm a bit together, with me shooting down his choices for being either too erotic, or not intriguing enough.

"How about 'I Wanna be Your Lover?'" I say. "It's fun, catchy, and just nice enough to say you wanna have sex without sounding like a creep."

"That's perfect...now we gotta figure out what other

Prince songs to put on here." He starts typing in another Prince track and I slap his hand away.

"Rule number two, never put more than one song by a single artist, it comes off as lazy and makes you seem uncultured." He looks dejected again, so I have to raise his spirits. "But now that you have a killer opener, she'll be hooked by that song, which lets you be creative with the rest."

We go on for the next hour, trading songs back and forth, arguing over everything from the proper order of songs, to whether it's fair to have a John Lennon solo song on the mixtape when there's a Beatles one already selected. Each argument ends with me reminding him that he came to me for help, followed by a quip from him about my virginity, followed by a long staring contest before we dive back in. Rinse and repeat. By the end we both can only smile at the final product, and I even make a copy for myself. As the second copy is being made we chat about his plans. He booked a table at a Brazilian steakhouse, followed by a marathon movie night with her. I'm struck by how giddy he is when describing how she makes him happy, and seeing him head over heels for someone makes me happy because people like Randy deserve happiness.

"What have you got planned for Saturday?"

I'll be happy when Valentine's Day is over so I don't have to be reminded of my impending loneliness by every interaction I have with another person. "Somehow Grace managed to get a Saturday night off, but she doesn't sound too keen on hanging out with me. Maybe I'll go to the mall or something."

"How about a concert?"

It takes my brain a few extra seconds to comprehend what he just said. The closest I'd ever come to a concert was eating leftover popcorn off the ground in the parking lot of the Amphitheater in Camden. If the band had a good enough sound guy I could catch bits and pieces of their set. I make a decision to take whatever tickets he offers, I don't care if it's for a polka festival. "Who's playing in Philly?"

Without a word, he slowly opens the drawer under the register and pulls out an envelope, slapping it down on the counter for emphasis. "It's not in Philly, but I think you'll be interested."

He watches me closely as I grab the envelope, nervous excitement coursing through me at the possibilities of what's inside. But even in my wildest dreams I couldn't imagine what it held. Inside, clear as day, are two tickets for Muse at Madison Square Garden, and upon closer inspection, they're right on the floor.

"I bought those for me and Laurie, but since that went to shit I figured it would be better to give them to someone that would actually appreciate the artistry. What do you say?"

I nodded calmly as if I'm mulling his offer, but on the inside I'm screaming like a teenage fanboy. My first show isn't gonna be some run of the mill band, it's gonna be one of my top five favorites. The tickets could've been for seats on the roof of the stadium and I'd be ecstatic, being on the floor is just icing on the cake. But I don't think that Grace would wanna spend her night off doing that, so I hand him the tickets and decline his offer. This stuns him.

"You don't wanna go?" he says.

I shake my head. "It's not that I don't wanna go, it's more that Grace might not wanna go."

He laughs this off. "Who said anything about Grace? I know there's someone special you'd love to do this with."

I can't help but laugh at the suggestion. "You overestimate my social prowess, Randy."

"Okay, let me be more direct. You should take the girl that

you swear is into someone else that you stupidly keep pushing away."

"Christina?"

"Yeah."

"Why does everyone act like there's something there? Look...I get what you're saying, but part of being a friend is respecting the feelings they have for someone else."

"It's okay to be selfish with your feelings, kid." He slides the envelope back to me. "When you talk about her I see a side of you that I didn't know existed. The feelings you have for her are real, and you deserve the opportunity to give it your best shot."

"And these," I say, waving the envelope, "are my best shot?"

"Actually, that's exactly what they are, young Padawan."

"Who the hell is Padawan?"

He shoots me a look like I had just shit on the floor. "You've never seen Star...never mind. Look, if it helps don't look at it as a date—"

"I wasn't."

"But you dig this band and so does she, seeing as she just bought their most recent album. I also get the sense that her home life is in the same stratosphere as yours. So, think of it as two people that love the same band enjoying a night out together."

"You want me to take her out because her life is just as screwed up as mine? That's a terrible reason to hang out with someone."

"It's not about that, Percy. This is the last time in your life when friendships are pure, where you don't need anything from each other. Everything after this involves spouses, and hoping that your new friends have spouses that'll get along with yours. Right now, in this moment, you guys are two people that see the world in a unique way, in a way that others don't. And you've been so busy pushing her into the arms of someone else that you don't even notice the way she looks at you."

The last line makes my stomach churn. Have I really missed something that everybody else swears is so obvious? Even if I roll with this logic and assume there's something I've missed, telling her how I feel will only complicate things for both of us. Telling myself that she will find someone else is the only way I know how to save myself from the heartache of taking a chance on us and then leaving her. Both choices are devastating for me, but by helping her find happiness I can look at myself in the mirror and feel proud knowing that I did right by her. But one of the reasons I like her so much is that she comes from nothing like me, and remembering how in sync our visions of a concert were makes this too good of an opportunity to pass up.

"All right," I say. "I'll see if she wants to go."

Randy pumps his fist in celebration and tells me to finish up my duties so I can cover the register while he handles some things in the back. Now I just have to get Grace's blessing, but that looks like a cakewalk compared to what comes after.

* * *

I'M PACING my room like a carpenter measuring for new floors. This should be an easy phone call to make, but I hesitate every time I psych myself up to hit her number. Hanging out with her is normal, to the point that Grace now asks when she's coming over again. But for the last two weeks she's been in as big of a funk as me, bearing the scars of chasing someone that doesn't want her, and part of me wonders if I should leave her alone because nothing is worse than someone pestering you as you work through your emotions. I even wonder if asking her out to the concert—even as friends— is healthy for me knowing the track my court case is on.

But I also really want her to go with me, and right now that fact is overriding any and every emotion to the contrary. Over dinner, Grace could sense something was off, which reminded me that I hadn't even asked her if I could go yet. Her response was...interesting to say the least.

"You should go," she said. A bit too eager I thought.

"I don't want you to be alone on Valentine's Day; it's not fair to you."

She waved me off like secondhand smoke. "I'm a big girl, and kids your age should spend Valentine's Day with someone outside their household." I considered this by nibbling on a roll before she offered some unsolicited advice. "You should take Christina."

"Wow, you had that one in the chamber didn't you?"

She pressed her hands to her chest. "Who, me? I suspect I'm not the only person at this table with her in mind."

"What gave you that idea?"

"Percy, in the three hours since you got home, you've taken two bowel movements and practically ignored that I cooked your favorite meal. You've done everything but sacrifice a goat to the gods for good favor. Just finish the dishes, go to your room, and make the call."

"What if she says no?" That was the question hanging over my conundrum. Hearing no from her would cut deeper because of how much I liked her. I'd been replaying her idea of an experience in my head all day, swearing to any and every god that I would make it worthwhile if she agreed.

"Then you're just another teenager that got shot down. It's not the end of the world."

Her words of wisdom rang in my head like church bells

while I did the dishes, the nervousness being scraped off my consciousness like the casserole dish.

Which leads me to right now, alone in my room staring at her contact info in my phone while Morrissey plays through my stereo. I finally stop pacing long enough to hear the wood floor creak. Grace wasn't gonna miss me asking a girl out for the first time for anything, even the season premiere of Hell's Kitchen.

She picks up on the second ring. "You know, I was just thinking about how weird it was that I haven't heard from you in a couple of days," she says. I could hear the keys of Mercy by Muse playing in the background, my favorite off the album with an ironic title perfect for our conversation.

"Sorry, I just figured with everything going on you needed some space," I reply, figuring that matching her mood is the best play. "How are you doing?"

There was an awkward pause. "You called me at eight-forty-five on a Thursday night because you wanna know how I'm doing?" I can hear the smile in her voice, and I picture her wandering around her house listlessly while waiting for my phone call.

"Kind of, yeah."

"Oh, well I'm...I'm doing fine." I can hear a door close on her end with an echo behind it. She's in the bathroom taking my call. "What's up?"

Damnit, the onus is back on me, and I've almost forgotten why I called in the first place. "I was wondering if you had any plans for Valentine's Day?"

"Are you asking me on a date, Perseverance Martin," she coos, sending shivers down my spine that stop in a specific region of my body between my stomach and feet. Unfortunately it also takes the blood from my brain, leaving me sounding like an idiot.

"No, not rea...well, kinda." I shake my free hand in an attempt to reboot my brain. "I just thought that neither of us has any plans as far as I know, and I came upon something pretty awesome."

She's chuckling now, and I'm hoping it's because she finds my nervousness endearing. "What did you have in mind?"

My heart is pounding like Kanye's 808 drum machine, but my brain is working now and on a whim I decide to keep the concert as a surprise. "I kinda want you to be surprised, so I'll just say that it's something I wouldn't wanna do with anybody else, and that it's something we can check off together. Just give me one day of your time."

"A whole day?" I could hear the smile in her voice, though I wasn't sure if it was because of my request, or if she was relishing shooting me down.

"I believe that's the definition of morning until night." Someday I'd love to know where these short bursts of irrational confidence come from.

In the long silence that followed, I can't help but think of what the night could look like. What would I wear? Do the trains from New York run that late? What if everyone was right and she actually liked me? And can I keep my feelings for her in check knowing what's on the horizon?

"You're serious?"

"My foster mother is monitoring this from outside my bedroom like the NSA, do you really think I'd make this call if I didn't want to?"

She laughs at this. "All right, I'm in," she finally says. "What time do you wanna meet up?"

I never calculated how much time it would take to get to New York. "Is nine too early for you?"

"Wow, you must really have something amazing planned." She's fishing for a hint, but I'm not budging. "You're lucky I like you," she finally says. "I'll have my Mom make breakfast for us; see you at nine."

"It's a date," I say. "Well, a friend date...because we're friends and that's what friends do."

"Percy," she says. I've never heard her say my name like that, almost like a dog whistle that cuts through every part of me and demands my attention. "I'm really happy to be your Valentine."

"Me, too." I hang up before I could ramble on and embarrass myself any further. For a few seconds I just stared at the phone, wondering if I was in some alternate universe where that didn't just happen. Now I'm moonwalking, well, as much as you can on a carpet.

This is interrupted by Grace busting in like a SWAT raid and gripping me in a bear hug, telling me how happy she is for me. Long after she goes to bed, when the house has settled into the quiet I'd come to appreciate, I lay in my bed with the sounds of The Police coming through my headphones, and for the first time in my life I understand what it means to feel happiness.

I'd always thought of life as some sort of competition, with myself forever being the underdog that's constantly searching for the upset victory. But in that moment of clarity I realized that I was looking at it wrong. There are no winners or losers, just little moments you grab ahold of to sustain you when it feels like life is falling apart. If Saturday turns out to be a dud that wrecks our friendship, I'll always have the moment she said yes, when the possibilities for our relationship were as infinite as the horizon. But it won't be a dud.

Because I'm gonna seize the moment and create something that we'll both remember forever.

TWENTY-SEVEN

TOMORROW CAN WAIT FOR THE
DESIRES OF TODAY

I'm awake extra early, partially because I'm nervous, and partially because I'm scared of oversleeping. It would be just my luck that I oversleep on the biggest day of my young life.

For the past couple of days I've thought over every aspect of the day, obsessing so much that even Eric couldn't help but be intrigued enough to ask.

"A concert?" he asked when I told him.

"Yeah, I mean it's something neither of us have done and I'm sure she'll enjoy it."

He frowned and cleared his GoGurt in one shot. Instead of letting the negativity ruin my moment I flipped it back on him.

"What are you and Maria doing again?"

"We're going out to eat in Philly, then we're heading back to her house where I'll give her the gift of her first organism," he said smugly.

"You're gonna help her study for the biology final?"

He gave me a look of confusion. "No, you idiot, an organism. You know, like when you have sex." He made a sound that would be more appropriate in a documentary about the clubbing of seals.

"You sure that's what it's called?"

He caught on to my sarcasm and did a Google search, his face looking like someone told him Santa wasn't real when he realized his mistake. "Shit, well technically my penis is an organism, so I was partly right."

I patted him on the back. "I'm sure she'll see it that way, too, buddy."

Grace has been a lifesaver this week, listening to my plans over and over to the point that if she switched bodies with me, the date would go off without a hitch. I was struggling with what to do for lunch since breakfast will be covered, and she came in with the assist of a lifetime. She had me download an app that sold different experiences for travelers, telling me to pick one I thought Christina would like and it would be her treat. Most of the events involved drinking, one combined that with ax throwing, but one caught my eye. An Italian restaurant a block away from Central Park was offering a five course picnic lunch, complete with a picnic basket and blanket. That alone was enough to be my choice, but a quick Google search revealed that it's one block away from the Dakota, and the section in Central Park with a John Lennon memorial. It was perfect, and Grace agreed. She even convinced me to sign up for a free trial of Spotify and create a mixtape that mirrors Muse's setlist.

I stop in the kitchen to kiss Grace goodbye, where I'm greeted by the smell of incense and the sight of her in a silk robe that I've never seen before. When I take my normal place in front of her so she can inspect my outfit, I get a whiff of perfume that she's never worn.

"New perfume?" I ask as she brushes my shoulders off.

"Something like that," she replies, and I let it pass. "You're nervous again."

It's not a question, more like a definitive statement by a mother that knows her child inside and out.

"Yeah. I'm kinda in a weird headspace right now with everything that's going on."

"You know what's one of the worst things about getting older?"

I'm not sure how to answer that, but I know from our time together there's a reason why she's asking it. "No. What is it?"

"It's looking back on your life and regretting the moments you didn't reach for something you know you wanted. Do you like this girl?"

"More than I've ever liked anyone else."

"Then why are you treating this like you're hanging out with Eric?"

"I think I've planned a pretty good day," I shoot back. I'm not sure what she's hinting at, but I already resent whatever she's implying.

"You've planned a great day. What I mean is..." She licks her finger and wipes some crust from my eye. "...if you like this girl so much, stop pretending like you don't." I avert eye contact, but I can feel her glare. "It's about what you told Alex, isn't it?"

This isn't how I pictured my morning going. In fact, I was hoping that this day would give me the opportunity to forget about it altogether. "Yes."

"I thought so." She places both hands on my face, gently guiding my head to a point where I had no choice to look her in the eye. "Life is too short to neglect the treasures of today for the unknown of tomorrow."

"Grace," I say. "I can't lead her on and make her believe in something that might not be there."

"Do you remember what homecoming felt like? How you watched her leave for somebody else, how it burned at your soul?"

I nod.

"Then why would you put yourself through that again voluntarily?"

I don't have an answer for this, because, like usual, she's right. Having Christina as my girlfriend is something I've wanted since that first pizza we shared months ago. But like everything in my life, choosing what makes me happy carries the risk of watching it all slip away from me with one knock of the judge's gavel.

"Tonight, I want you to forget about the social worker, your Mom, hell, even me. You take that girl out, and you show her what she means to you. Leave all that other mess in Jersey and live tonight as if you'll never see her again." She plants a kiss on my forehead and after throwing an overcoat on, drives me to Christina's house.

* * *

I BOUND the rickety steps to Christina's front door after Grace's car is out of sight, stopping to check for the millionth time that I have the concert tickets. Since I'm meeting her mother, Grace took me to Walmart for flowers, a bouquet for each, saying that I should never go to someone's house empty handed. I knock three times and wait.

Her mother opens the door, where she gives me a glance up and down, followed by a smile. "You must be Percy; I've heard so much about you."

"Yes, ma'am, I am. These are for you," I say, handing her the flowers before being ushered in for a hug.

"You brought flowers for me, too? I like you already."

She's got a thick accent that I can't place, but I quickly learn where it's from by the Panamanian flag hanging over the fireplace. Christina had very specific instructions on meeting her mother. Manners were at the top of the list, which has always been easy for me, and when I'm offered food I have no choice but to accept it. Judging by the smell wafting through the house, that won't be a problem either. Salsa music is blasting from a stereo in the kitchen, and her mother dances gracefully while working three separate pans on the stove. They might not have much, but the house is tastefully decorated, and I get the sense that love was in abundance to fill whatever financial gaps they encountered.

Her energy is contagious, and soon enough I find myself pulled into a dance, much like I am with Grace, except the music is in a different language. She tells me I got moves, which is too kind of her, and sings at the top of her lungs, with her gold front tooth shining brightly. As we glide across the kitchen, I understand why I like Christina so much, she radiates joy like her mother. There's something about people that don't have much, a level of happiness you have to be poor to understand. It's also why I'm happy that my first concert is going to be with her, because we both know that stuff like this isn't normal, so we appreciate it more.

"I like you, Percy. You're different from the other kids that come by." The disdain when she says "other kids" is undeniable, and I don't have to wonder who she's talking about. "Christina told me about your situation, and I've prayed for you and your mother every night since."

This brings me a feeling that I've never had before, a mixture of gratitude and love for her. This woman only knows me from what her daughter tells her, and even if she's lying about the prayer part—which I doubt—knowing that she cared enough to even say that is the type of genuine connection that rarely happens. With one sentence she helped me accept my situation without feeling embarrassed by it. As I'm grabbing the cheese eggs off the stove, Christina says my name, and when I turn around, seeing how beautiful she is nearly makes me drop the skillet.

"Wow," I say, softly but just loud enough for them to hear me.

She's wearing a dark green sweater, fit to perfection, with blue jeans and classic Chuck Taylor's. But it's her hair, let down with her infinite curls allowed to flow as freely as they please that get me. She isn't wearing any makeup, which only accentuates her natural beauty. It's like I'm meeting her again for the first time, except we actually like each other and aren't being forced into some awkward situation. Grace's last words fire all the neurons in my brain, and any idea I had of thinking we were just two friends enjoying Valentine's Day together go out the window with the smoke from the stove.

This. Girl. Is. My. Date.

We exchange a long hug that feels like a battle of wills to see who is gonna let go first before we both let go at the same time. "You look great," she says.

"I could be wearing rags and you'd make me look great," I reply. She smiles and I pull her chair out for her at the table, drawing raised eyebrows and a smile from her mother.

As we eat breakfast my mind wanders into 'what if' territory, just like it did the night we had dinner with Eric's parents. What if by some miracle things worked out between us where I could spend more time here? Grace already made it clear that she was always welcome, and her mother hints throughout our meal that their door is always open. One bite of her food and I know that I'll never turn that down. Christina is throwing me smiles between every bite, and I return them, promising myself that I'm gonna make this the best night of her life.

Tomorrow be damned.

TWENTY-EIGHT

TWO BLOCKS TO FOREVER

The train glides smoothly through New York's underground into Penn Station.

Christina has never been to New York, and seeing her have the same look I had the first time I came here with Grace makes it feel brand new again. She stays close, walking arm in arm, which feels more intimate to me. Instead one of us pulling the other in the direction we wanna go, we lean into each other, each time her scent brings me back to the reality that she's here with me. She keeps asking what the plan is, and I continue to be coy, waiting for the perfect moment to spill the beans. Madison Square Garden is in Penn Station, and as we exit the escalator to the street, the perfect opportunity presents itself.

The marquee outside advertises the sold out show, and we stand in awe as the colors on the ad weave through all of their album covers. I'm holding the envelope with the tickets so tight, the sharp corners are poking into my hand.

"That's crazy that Muse is playing on the same night we're in the city," she says. "I wish we had the money to go, and that it wasn't sold out. I mean, this was literally what we dreamed up the first time we hung out."

"You don't know this, but that day I promised myself that I would never go see them unless we were doing it together." My heart is racing as I slowly remove the envelope, stifling my jittery hands while handing them to her. She opens it, taking an extra second to understand exactly what she's looking at, before fixing her gaze on me with a smile that makes my heart flutter. "Promise made...promise kept," I say.

"I can't let you pay for these, Percy."

"Well, that's actually perfect, because they were given to me."

"You don't have to lie."

"I swear I'm not. Randy gave them to me and made me promise I would take you."

"Oh yeah? And why would he want that?"

I don't have any experience with girls, but I know that insinuating that she looks at me with googly eyes is probably a bad move here. "He said he knows that you like Muse, so it would be a cool event for us to attend together."

She gives me a tight hug, her neck so warm and soft against my cheek that I'm surprised I didn't melt and drip down into the subway. "Wait." She looks at the tickets and checks the time on her phone. "The show doesn't start for a couple of hours, what are we gonna do until then?"

I pull my phone and ear buds out of my pocket, more than happy to share one bud with her if it means having her close to me. She sees the setlist and grins even wider. With my free hand, I walk her to a taxi and open the door for her. "Now, we make it an experience."

* * *

WE MAKE it to the restaurant right on time to pick up our order, but I'm sad because I didn't want the ride over to end. I couldn't have dreamed it up any better if I had taken a double dose of NyQuil at two in the morning.

We rode in silence, letting the playlist narrate the drive up Fifth Avenue while we held hands, with her occasionally pulling her phone out to snap a shot of some of the awesome architecture. Next to the restaurant is a used bookstore, and we killed some time walking around and talking literature, while never straying far from one another. She liked to walk to the next aisle and hide her face behind something I was looking at, the most wonderful of surprises. I lost count of how many times I almost broke down and confessed my love for her, but I know it's at least in the triple digits.

She's more loose than usual, and in a lot of ways so am I, with her being free of the shadow of Ashton and me putting my future out of my mind like I told Grace I would. We haven't even made it to the concert yet and the day was already perfect, so much so that I'm dreading the end of the night if that makes sense. At the restaurant she asks if we can eat outside and enjoy the sunshine and vibe of the city, and it takes everything in me to contain my excitement at knowing how much she'll love the picnic. She waits at the door as I walk to the bar, showing them my order on my phone before the bartender goes to the back and returns with our lunch.

When she sees me walking back with a basket she's confused, so I take her hand and lead her out of the restaurant.

"Where are we going?" Her inquisitiveness is cute.

"Do you trust me?" I ask.

"Of course."

"All right then, just follow me."

And so, she does, understanding what the plan is with

every step we take toward Central Park. We stop in Strawberry Fields, listening to passable Lennon covers and taking photos in front of the mural. She mentions how cool the pins are that one vendor has, and while she ran to the bathroom I bought the ones she pointed out, figuring I'd gift them to her after lunch. We find a quiet spot near a fountain and set up shop. As she's on all fours smoothing the blanket, I can't help but take note of how curvy she is, and work furiously to keep my thoughts pure.

Thankfully my jeans are loose fitting, because I can feel that the battle is already lost.

The spread is vast, with fancy cheese and crackers as the appetizers, truffle Mac and cheese and pesto pasta for sides, and stuffed chicken breast as the main course. As we're eating, I mentally inventory everything about her, how she hums after taking a bite, or how she covers her mouth when I tell a funny joke while she's chewing, not that I hold it against her.

"Can I ask you something?" she says.

"Anything."

"Why me? Like, why did you think of me for a day like today?" She notices my quizzical look and tries to clarify. "I know we talked about a concert and stuff, but I thought we were just dreaming out loud. I just...I just wanna know that this isn't you feeling sorry for me."

On the surface you would think that her question and feeling would come off as weird, or maybe even ungrateful. But I understand all too well the sentiment she's getting at. While kids in our financial situation might not have much, our pride is never in short supply. Instead of looking at something like concert tickets or a getaway to the city as a gift, we're constantly wondering if the gifts given to us are done for a more self serving purpose, like the videos online of people giving out food to the homeless. After meeting her mother, I can understand how she feels this way, the same way I do when Eric invites me along with his family to dinner.

I'm trying to decide how to play it. Do I give a soft answer and risk coming off as uninterested? Or do I let my feelings out in full, potentially making things awkward before the concert even starts? I decide to do a little of both, figuring I've been juggling my emotions for the past two months so I'm ready for prime time.

"Christina, I hope one day you realize how special you are to me. I've got Eric, and he'll always be the brother I never had. But you bring something to me that I can't explain...but I can feel it. Honestly, I'm not sure I could do this with anybody else."

She smiles and moves her food to the side so she can slide closer to me. In a park this large, you'd think there'd be ample space, but she's so close it feels like we're in a phone booth. She runs her fingers over my hairline, softly, back and forth across my forehead.

"Remember when we were on the dance floor at homecoming?"

How the hell could I forget that? I nod.

"Do you remember what I told you?"

Any other time I'd be able to quickly recall that moment, but right now my mind is operating like a computer running Windows 98. "Yeah...you told me that you were thankful that I pretended to be more than your friend." Now it's working again, slowly, but the memories are becoming vivid.

She gets on her knees in front of me, and I can now confirm that her eyes are in fact hazel. "Was I correct in my assumption?" She takes a bite of the last cracker, head cocked to the side and fully aware of her powers in this moment.

As nerve wracking as this is, I kind of like this game. "No, you had it pretty wrong."

"Hmm." She finishes the cracker and moves her face closer, so close that if a colony of ants needed to migrate, they could find a perfectly suitable bridge on the tips of our noses, close enough that I can smell the tangerine Pelegríno on her breath. "I believe I also asked you what you wanted, and told you not to be scared to reach for it. So...can you tell me what you want?"

If my mind was a plane, the damn engine just cut off mid flight. I'm not sure what she wants; okay, maybe I am, but I'm not completely sure, and to do what I want requires absolute certainty. "Um...I..." Fading fast I remember the John Lennon pins, and I pull them from my pocket like a Wild Card in UNO. "...I want...to give you these," I say, dropping them into her palms.

She seems almost disappointed, and by the time I recognize that we were thinking the same thing, the moment has passed. "Oh my God, these are perfect. What do I owe you?"

I'll take a rewind of, say, forty five seconds. "Dude, you don't owe me anything for today."

We're starting to cut it close with the concert, so she cleans up while I order us a Lyft to the arena. I tell myself that I made the right choice, and on the ride to the Garden she seems to have forgotten about it, holding my hand for so long that I could put hers down as my forwarding address.

TWENTY-NINE

ETERNAL THOUGHTS OF A SPOTLESS MIND

I've waited my whole life for this.

This is what I'm thinking on the exhilarating ride up the escalator at the most famous arena in the world: Madison Square Garden. What I've been waiting for specifically, well, that's a bit more complicated.

Could it be my first concert? Or maybe it's that I'm seeing the band that has been the soundtrack to the best year of my life, and that I'm accompanied by a female that is neither my guardian nor the person that carried me for nine months. Ah, yes, I can't forget the girl, so beautiful and one of a kind, like she was the first one made and her creator died before he could make copies of her blueprints. It's a combination of all of these, and the ride up the escalator gives me a few moments of clarity to think about everything that's led to this point. Christina is one step ahead of me, looking back every few seconds to make sure I'm still here, unaware that I'm doing the same to her.

Neither of us has been to a concert, so we just follow the crowd, reading signs for our tickets until we find the right concourse. The walls are adorned with memorabilia and photos from famous events held here over the years, giving it the feeling of walking through a museum. I can hear the sound of the openers playing their set, but I'm in no rush because I'm not here to see them. On our concourse Christina tries to steer me towards our entrance but I pull back.

"You're right, we probably should use the bathroom before we head down," she says, looking around for directions.

"You've already forgotten part of the experience?"

She's puzzled by this, so I point to give her a hint, watching her eyes follow my hand to the merchandise stand. "No way, I can't let you do that. You've already done so much."

"Part of what makes this great for me is experiencing it with you, and merch is part of the deal." We've taken turns guiding each other throughout the day, and since it's my turn, I take her arm and we head to the back of the line. She doesn't say much as we work our way to the front of the line, and I wish I knew the right words to say so that she won't be embarrassed. The stand has pretty much anything you could want with Muse's name on it, each piece having a number that you give to the attendant along with your size. Since I work in a music shop, the vinyl and discs hold no value for me, and after careful consideration I choose a gray sweatshirt with the album cover on it, along with a matching shirt. Christina compliments my taste and tries to slink away, but I catch her and she stays put. There's one sweatshirt that she's had her eye on the entire time we've been in line. It's got every one of their albums arranged on the front, with every tour date in the back.

"I'll take number forty five in a large," I say, probably off on her size but giving it room to shrink over time. She smiles at me. "I'm doing this for me since you have a bad habit of not bringing a jacket anywhere," I say.

She laughs at this and the night returns to normal.

The crowd starts to thin out, which I assume means that Muse will be coming on soon, so we both use the restroom to stop anything from interrupting the show for us. Walking down the stairs to the main floor is surreal for both of us. Their stage setup is hidden behind a curtain, but from what I can tell it's three huge pillars, each one standing out like a tower, even more so once we're on the floor itself. We shimmy up as far as we can, so close to the stage that even a below average arm could land a baseball in the middle of the stage. We're two people in a sea of thousands, hearing everyone's conversations but picking up nothing at the same time.

All of a sudden the lights go out, and the sea of individuals become one, bringing the decibel level to one I've never experienced before. On stage I can see a light from behind the curtain, the screen on lead singer Matt Bellamy's guitar rising higher as he's lifted to the top of his pillar. Christina shakes my arm, and it dawns on me that I really pulled it off. Before I can consider the thought, all three curtains are dropped and they start playing the opening chords to Uprising. Bellamy encourages us to clap to the beat, and we oblige as we watch all three members descend to the stage.

Their musicianship is something to behold. Every note is played, from horns to obscure bass patterns, each getting their moment to shine throughout the show. I'll never forget the roar of the crowd when the first few chords are played and we recognize the song. She holds my hand through every song, jumping in rhythm with me to the music and collapsing into my arms when each one ends. We sneak glances at each other every so often, the neon lights of the stage magnifying her beauty. When parts come for the crowd to sing the lyrics, we join in with everyone else, just a crowd full of people forgetting about life for the night. After playing Resistance, they exit the stage, and while I loved the show, I'm a little disappointed that they didn't play the one song that made me love them in the first place.

But I realize that the crowd isn't heading for the exits, in fact the faint hints of a chant start low before engulfing the arena.

Encore.

Encore.

Encore.

We join along for a minute, then, as if God himself demanded it, the band emerges from the right side of the stage and picks their instruments up again. They play three more of their most popular songs.

And then it happens.

The bass line comes in just like it did the first time I heard it. Slow and steady, holding our attention long enough for the keys to come in, but this time the neon lights come with them. The moment I thought I'd never see is upon me, when I could sing the chorus with everyone else like I'd heard on the live album during the quiet hours in the house. I'm singing every lyric as if my life depends on it, my eyes meeting hers towards the end of the first verse.

I'm singing the words while never breaking eye contact, hoping that she can feel my sincerity as the lyrics spell out my feelings for her in a way I struggle to verbalize. The song bursts into the chorus, and the moment I've dreamed of is upon me.

I'll never let you go
Almost there.
If you promise not fade away
Closer.
Never fade away
Here we go, I'm ready.

My part comes, but I don't join in; not because I forgot the words or they stopped playing, but because Christina has pulled me into a kiss, effectively muting the music and making it feel as if we were in an empty arena. The cherry red chapstick that she carried everywhere now dances across my lips, expertly applied by her. I don't have the faintest clue of what I'm doing, but I've ruined enough moments for the day and this for damn sure isn't gonna be another one. We separate as the song ends, our friendship in an entirely different dimension than it was when the song began. She goes to kiss me again and I stop her.

"Why are you doing this?" I ask. Not that I don't want her to, but I can't comprehend how someone so beautiful could settle for me.

"I saw something I wanted," she pecks my lips again, "and I took it. The question I have is, what do you want?"

I'm tempted to go with my standard answer, the one that takes into account my complicated life, but it fails me. The adrenaline from the concert and finally kissing the lips I've dreamed about won't allow it. As the lights come on, I hear Grace's words about not worrying about the unknown play in my head on a loop, spliced in with the memories of Ashton pulling her away at the door of the dance and the heartache I felt. My situation may be unknown, but right now I can ensure that I never have to feel that kind of pain again, and I take it.

"I want you to be my girlfriend," I say. "Like...for real this time."

She says nothing, holding out with her response so long that I almost pass out. Instead of agreeing, she pulls me in for another kiss, somehow managing to say nothing and everything at the same time.

The answer is yes.

THIRTY

ONLY PETER PARKER COULD UNDERSTAND ME

There's a scene in the first Spiderman movie, right after Peter Parker discovers his powers, in which he takes a leap of faith and seemingly falls before figuring out how to shoot his web and taking off into the city.

That's what it's been like having my first girlfriend. An ever evolving lesson of learning that great power comes with great responsibility.

On the surface not much has changed: a credit to the friendship we had as a foundation, except now we're a lot more handsy than we were before, not that I'm complaining about that part. But what I've come to like the most is the subtle changes, the ones that are more mental than physical. When I hold her hand now, it's because I want to and that it's expected of me as her boyfriend, instead of how I used to hold it whenever I was comforting her about someone else. She's brought a sense of routine to my life that wasn't there before. She'll come over to do homework, we eat and complete said homework, then make out until it's time for her to go, leaving me harder than my calculus homework. Rinse and repeat.

On Saturday mornings she comes over for breakfast,

joining in my dance parties with Grace, and I return the favor on Sunday having dinner at her house. But my favorite moments with her are the ones nobody sees. Like when she balances her history book on my back while I'm laying down knocking out equations, or how she won't look me in the eye when she's verbalizing her affection for me, probably scared that I won't feel the same way. I'll lift her head up to confirm that I feel the same way, and next thing you know our text-books are all over the floor and we're wrestling again.

With every new person that's come into my life, they've each brought something with them, and Christina is no differ-ent. With her I've had to learn how to be vulnerable and share more of myself, letting her in on my insecurities and fears.

Like Grace, Christina has unlocked something in my heart that I didn't know was there, coaxing out smiles that come a little easier than they did before, and even getting me to laugh at myself.

Somewhere around our first month of dating, we were sitting in my room doing homework. She'd taken a liking to my CD collection and had fallen head over heels for The Smiths. After she had devoured their discography, I mentioned that Morrissey's early solo work sounded close to what she was used to. The first album she found was *Bona Drag*, which I thought nothing of, telling her to play it while focusing on my homework.

"Woah," she said.

I chuckled, still not looking up. "It's a great cover, huh?"

"Uh huh, but not as good as what's inside." I looked up to find her holding the porno that Eric left me awhile ago. When I hid it there, the intention was to stop Grace from prying, and the idea of a girlfriend was laughable. But here I was, about to take the fall for a movie I never even got off on.

"Okay," I said, sounding like someone with a gun to his head. "It's not what you think."

She shook her head, the blank look on her face giving no indication of how she was feeling. "Oh, really? It's not what I think? At all?"

I've done so well pointing out the pros of having a girl-friend that I'm due for a con, and this was the biggest. Being questioned by your girlfriend is like being a criminal in the last fifteen minutes of a Law and Order episode. They know you're caught, but you still decide to go down with the ship instead of hopping on a lifeboat.

"That's actually Eric's...well, it's his dad's." Still no sign of emotion from her, so I decided to embarrass myself in an effort to stop the bleeding. "We were talking about how I've never jerked off and he gave me that to help. In my defense, I turned it off before it they started having sex, so its kinda like I really never watched it."

Nothing.

"Can you say something?"

Still nothing. She just stood there, spinning the movie in the case like some twisted game of spin the bottle. Finally, she smiled. "At least I know you'll never cheat on me." She tosses me the movie and I smash it into pieces, guaranteeing it was the only time it would make an appearance in our relationship.

Later that night, we were laying on the floor listening to music when my curiosity finally got the best of me.

"Why me?" I asked. We were so in tune with each other's thoughts and feelings that no context was needed for the question. She often caught me staring at her, and when she inquired, I would always tell her I couldn't believe how lucky I was. Part of it was my way of doing everything Ashton never did, but on a selfish note I still couldn't understand how I ended up so lucky.

She sat up quickly, and for a second I thought she would leave. "If I tell you something, you have to promise me you won't get mad and break up with me."

That left me with more questions, but I agreed. "I promise."

Satisfied with my answer, she continued. "I knew how you felt, and the more I hung out with you, I realized that I liked you, too, in some ways more than you liked me."

I wracked my brain trying to figure out where I gave myself away, not that it mattered because she ended up being my girlfriend, but I still had to know. "Would it be weird to ask how you knew?"

"You told me." My face must've given away my confusion because she kept going. "Do you remember what you did after homecoming?"

That night was etched in my brain like Egyptian hiero-glyphics. The mere mention of the word homecoming brought the night rushing back into my brain like a tidal wave. "I came home and listened to music, analyzing your every word on the dance floor. Man, I beat myself up so bad that night. My mom called me, it was like she knew I was strug-gling, so I dumped all my feelings about you onto her until I fell asleep." Wondering if she felt the same way, I lobbed the question back, and her response would change our relation-ship forever.

"You weren't the only one beating yourself up that night."

"How? You were practically asleep when we dropped you off."

She sighed deeply and started flipping through my CD collection, the telltale signs that something had been on her heart. "When I got home, I couldn't fall asleep. I just sat on my bed, still in my dress, wondering if I had just made a huge mistake. I knew I liked you since we spent the day together in Haddonfield, when you told me about your mom as a way of making sure I didn't feel alone. That was the nicest thing anybody had ever done for me."

I started to talk, but her fingers found my lips.

"Just listen." She buried her head in my chest and went on. "So, I'm in my room angry because the guy I wanted all along saved me when it felt like everything was crumbling around me, and I made a vow that if the opportunity arose again I wouldn't let it pass. But even then, I couldn't stop thinking about you, so I called you from a blocked number. I don't know if I was gonna tell you how I felt, but I needed to hear your voice."

My mind drifted to Olive Garden, and the look of confusion on Momma's face when I mentioned talking to her that night, and I'm angry at myself for questioning her sobriety.

"You picked up, and I heard you talk about your feelings for me, but I could also hear the pain in your voice because your mom was getting clean and even though we were only friends you were scared to leave me."

"Christina...I don't know what you want me to say." And I really didn't. That black cloud over my life had appeared again, this time with a vengeance, threatening the one thing that meant the most to me. So, I just held her tightly in my arms, afraid that if I let go she'd walk out of my life forever.

We'd talked enough about my relationship with my mother, that she knew I'd have to go back, and if the shoe was on the other foot I would do the same. Laying with her in my arms and knowing that our relationship was on borrowed time was the hardest thing I've ever done in my life.

But I was also thankful.

Thankful that she didn't ask if I would leave, sparing us

both the heartache of me acknowledging the obvious. Thankful that she was willing to play the game with me, even though we knew the final score was rigged. Thankful that she was willing to watch me walk out of her life, instead of making me watch her walk out of mine.

"When's the date?" she asked.

We both knew what date she was talking about.

"May twenty-ninth," I replied.

The timer had started, and knowing what was coming made time feel as if it were moving twice as fast.

"My mom is working the overnight shift tonight. I was thinking maybe I could stay awhile, you know...make the most of the time we have left."

I didn't say anything, because that would take up time and I wanted every moment with her to matter. So we just laid there, with the occasional kiss and hum of a lyric from our mixtape, determined to focus on the present instead of the future.

THIRTY-ONE

THE EXPENSIVE TICKET HOME

People always wonder why I prefer to consume music on a CD player instead of my phone. Up until a couple of months ago, it was due to not having a phone, but these days it's because I paid upfront for three months of Spotify to make the Muse setlist for Valentine's Day. I'll concede that it's far more convenient to search for a song and have it playing within seconds, but having your music fade out at the best part because someone is calling makes me count the days until my subscription expires.

The shop is slow when my phone rings, a Camden area code but an unfamiliar number. Area codes go by county as a whole instead of city, so I pick up assuming it's something important.

"Percy, it's me, Mom," she says.

Dumbstruck, I check to verify she's actually calling from a real number. "Is this your cell phone?"

"Pretty cool, huh?" she says, impressed with herself.

It is pretty cool, because having a real phone I can call is a small but significant step toward stability. Hearing her sound happy and full of life again raises my spirits a bit, making me forget about the inevitable implosion of my relationship with Christina.

"I'm so happy to hear your voice, Momma. What's up?"

"Your social worker called me last week."

"Alex."

"Right, Alex. Anyway, he told me that if I find a place and pass all my drug tests, you can come home after our next court date." Her excitement is contagious, and my respect for Alex grows knowing that he's kept his word despite his personal feelings about my decision.

"I know, Mom. So have you found a place?" A small part of me hopes she hasn't found one yet, and I'm wondering if there will ever be a day when I'm totally comfortable with going back home.

"I have found a place," she says, her voice squeaking at the end. "But...well, it's complicated."

I say nothing as a way of making her explain just how complicated it really is.

"The state, they...well, they garnish my check and I'm short on the down payment for an apartment."

The word apartment is about as synonymous with my mother as sobriety, but I can tell she's found something that she's proud of by the passion in her voice. "How short?"

I can hear her clicking her tongue, and I imagine she's staring at the ground, her feet drawing different imaginary shapes into the ground as she searches for the right words for her request. "About four hundred."

The number is high, but I needed it to be. Anything lower would make me think she's gonna buy drugs and set off all kinds of alarms in my head. Momma has never asked me for money—granted, when we lived together I never had any—but building a new life together requires me to go all-in, and we're rapidly approaching now or never territory. "All right, Mom. I'll go in with you."

"Really?" she says. I'm not sure if she's shocked that I said yes, or that I have the money in the first place.

"If you're really serious, I'm in." I have about half on hand since I've been putting everything into savings. It has to be in cash because Momma doesn't have a bank account and withdrawing that kind of money would alert Grace. The trick is having her come to the store when I'm working alone so I don't arouse suspicion in Randy. He usually heads out around four on Fridays, so that's the move. "Can you be at my job at six on Friday?" I ask, thinking a later time will give me a buffer in case Randy starts going on one of his rants.

"I get off at five, but I think I can make it by that time."

I'm still not used to her having stable employment, but I guess this whole situation is gonna be an exercise in learning a new normal. "Even if you're late, that's all right." I remember that Christina and I are going to the movies that night. "Just try to get here before we close. I've got plans that night."

"Oh yeah, I forgot about your girlfriend. Will I get to meet her one day?"

"We're not gonna talk about that, Mom."

She sighs deeply like I disappointed her. "Fine, but I'd like to meet the girl that's got you head over heels in love. I'll see you Friday."

"All right, Mom." I start to hang up when she calls me through the speaker.

"Hey, Percy."

"Yeah."

"It's gonna be different this time, I promise."

She waits for a response, but I don't have one because my choices and actions should be enough. I'm wagering everything I love, every relationship and comfort, on her being sober for the first time in my life. I'm keeping everyone at arm's length, hoping that she'll fill the gap that's left in between. No, I don't think I owe her anything anymore, in fact, she's in my debt. "I love you, Mom," I say, meaning it, but ignoring her promise as a subtle way to demonstrate that from this point forward she'll be judged by her actions.

"I love you, too, Percy."

* * *

AT FIFTEEN MINUTES past six on Friday the door chimes, making my heart flutter because it's Christina. Flutter is accompanied by fear because Momma still hasn't arrived yet and of all the ways for her to meet my mother this wasn't one of them. If I'm being honest I liked her knowing that Grace is my mom better than the truth.

"Hey, babe," she says, giving me a kiss before handing me a Tupperware filled to the brim with my share of her mother's cooking. We've gotten so good at sensing the mood of each other that she notices something is amiss. "What's wrong?"

The food provides a convenient distraction to figure out how to play this, unfortunately, she must've cooked it in the parking lot because the rice almost burns the roof of my mouth off. "Damnit," I say, jumping up and down while fanning my mouth. "Nothing is wrong, why do you ask?"

She shakes her head and hands me a bottle of water. "You know my mom makes me bring every plate fresh so it'll taste like it's supposed to." She opens her own serving and drizzles homemade pepper sauce on it. "You're giving me 'porno in the CD case' vibes."

Ever since that night when we talked about me going back home, we've done everything in our power to ignore the obvious and maximize our time together. But we're starting to show cracks from the pressure, because even though we agreed to stay together, knowing that the end was coming has changed the foundation of our relationship. Watching it dissolve slowly has given me the same feeling I had watching my mother kill herself over the years with drugs, and while watching it hurts enough, the feeling of being powerless to stop it makes the pain unbearable at times.

Part of being in a relationship is talking about the future, but that's been stripped away from us, so we settle for retelling stories about the night we met, so much so that we could finish each other's sentences. I used to enjoy staring into her eyes, except now I stare into them for longer than usual, trying to sear them into my brain for the days ahead when they'll be just a memory. Part of me wants to end it now and be thankful for the run we had together.

But I've given enough to everyone else, enough that I feel like I've earned the right to be selfish.

"My mom is coming to pick up some money," I say.

Christina lights up at this. "Awesome, I love Grace."

I run my fingers over my mouth, and she gets that Grace isn't who I'm talking about.

"Oh...Well, it'll probably be the only time I meet her so—" She stops, cupping her hands to her face in embarrassment of having broken our cardinal rule of mentioning anything related to me leaving. "I'm sorry—"

"Don't be...I mean, it's gonna come one way or another, right?" I smile sadly as she grabs my hand, pulling me in for a kiss.

"I wanna ask you something, and you don't have to give me an answer right now." Whatever it is must be important, because she looks down for an extra second to summon the courage. "Have you ever thought about losing your virginity?"

The headlights of a car driving through the parking lot

shine in my peripheral, and I can make out the pink hue of the Lyft logo on the dashboard as it gets closer, stopping in front of the store. It's ironic because her question gives me the same look of a deer in headlights.

"Um, hold that thought," I say. My mom had to show up now, when our relationship was taking a turn into a new and exciting place.

"Don't worry about it, just...think on it, and when the time is right, we'll come back to it."

I agree to her terms, wondering exactly when the hell the time would be right.

But it's a moot point as the door chimes when Momma opens the door. She's in awe of the place, and any other night I'd give her a grand tour and pull a stool up to the counter so we could listen to records together.

"My baby," she coos, and I break into a smile because seeing her clean is the lift that my spirit didn't know it needed.

Christina looks on as we hug, with a smile on her face that would look normal to everyone else, but I knew her well enough to know that behind that smile her heart was breaking because this is the first time that the prospect of me leaving feels real.

It was easy to put off the thought of me going home when we're hanging out in my bedroom or grabbing a bite to eat, but it was another thing entirely for her to meet the person responsible for taking me away from her.

If she held any resentment it was hidden well, because she hugs my mother after I introduce her, complimenting her sweater and thanking her for raising such an awesome son.

"Well, I would have to raise an awesome son to be good enough for someone beautiful as you," Momma says. It would be a beautiful moment if she wasn't here for a particular reason.

"Can you give us a second?" I say to Christina. Since Momma has a ride waiting for her I walk her out, not wanting Christina to see me giving her the money that'll ultimately end our relationship.

"I like her," Momma says outside.

"Yeah, she's pretty great, huh?" This isn't a conversation I want to have with her so I get straight to business. "Where's the place at?"

"Pennsauken, just outside of Camden. It's nicer than anything we've had before. My boss at the warehouse owns it and gave me a great deal."

I'm listening, but in my head I'm calculating the distance from Stratford, trying to figure out if it's close enough to convince Christina that we can stay together. "That's um...that's great, Mom." I pull the bank envelope from my back pocket, and handing it to her is the most bittersweet moment of my life. Bitter because this is the beginning of a long goodbye, but sweet because it feels like things are different this time.

I open the car door for her and kiss her on the forehead.

"Thank you, Percy..." She steps into the car, looking back one more time before closing the door. "...For everything." I close the door and watch the car pull away, leaving me in a heap of emotions that only Dashboard Confessional's discography can help me sift through.

For some reason, seeing her outside everyone connected to the State has put me at ease. It was gonna be us against the world again, and this time I like our odds.

THIRTY-TWO

A IS FOR ANXIETY

Men's Warehouse is surprisingly empty for this time of year.

Eric and I are here with his dad, getting fitted for tuxedos and having a guy's getaway for the day. Our respective girl-friends have done their research, giving us the exact shades of their respective colors to ensure that we don't screw it up, but as of right now I'm the only one that's being successful on that front.

"Oh yeah, this is the one," Eric says in the mirror. He's in a bright orange dress shirt, which is the color Maria wanted, the problem is that she's expecting a tie that's orange, and he seems hell bent on talking himself into this shirt. "I mean, the shirt makes my chest hairs itchy, but I'm gonna kill prom in this."

I look over at him from my own mirror. "You've lived with that Teen Wolf look long enough, you'll be all right."

"Indeed I will. Maria is taking me to her waxing lady."

Jot that one down as conversations best friends should never have inside of a Men's Warehouse.

"You're gonna wax your chest?" I say slowly, thinking that

hearing them that way would alert him to how weird that sounds.

He smirks and nods his head. "Also my back, among...other places."

"I really could've gone the rest of my life without that last part, Eric." The thought of it makes me rub my chest. "Why?"

"She doesn't like cuddling with me," he says. "She said, 'It's not normal to have that much hair, Eric,'" he says in a brutal but spot-on impersonation of his girlfriend that'll never leave this store.

"I'm with her on this one. I wouldn't wanna lay my head on that patch of Easter basket grass you have on your chest either."

"You, sir, are an asshole."

I shrug and carry on with choosing my own vest. Christina has chosen dark red to be our color for the dance, chosen after seeing Grace pour a glass of wine one night while having dinner. A regular tie was a struggle for me at home-coming, so I axed the idea of a bow tie, instead going with a vest and a sleek tie to match. Taken as a whole, I think I look pretty good.

"I look like a million bucks," I say into the mirror.

"You look like 'The Help,'" he says with a laugh.

"Who's the asshole now?"

He blushes. "We all have our crosses to carry, Percy."

I take a picture and send it to Christina. My court date is two days after prom, and since it'll be our last night together I wanna do everything in my power to make it perfect. I'm living in a weird space right now, with everyone around me making plans for the future while I'm stuck in my own head, bitter that I won't be around for any of it. I would've thought that living most of my life focused on only the immediate future would make this transition an easy one, but those were the days when I had no friends, when it was easy to ignore the future because I assumed there wasn't one. My phone chimes with her response.

"There's my stud muffin" she replies, adding an emoji with the heart eyes that always makes me smile.

"Can you believe we're about to be seniors next year?" Eric says. "Man, we're going in with girlfriends already, so we're two steps—"

"Could you stop talking about the fucking future for once?" I reply.

He's taken aback by this. "All right, man, jeez." He looks over at me and his face goes from being annoyed to alarmed. "Percy, are you all right?"

But I don't reply, because I'm trying to figure out what's going on myself. My legs are shaking uncontrollably as if I'm walking on stilts for the first time, and my heart is pounding at an alarming rate as I try to breathe through my nose to bring it back down. I reach for a coat rack to steady myself, but I miss and collapse onto the floor.

"Dad," Eric shrieks. There's a fear that I've never heard in his voice before. "Dad, something's wrong with Percy."

Seconds later his dad comes running into the dressing room, quickly deducing the situation and dropping to his knees and putting my head into his hands. "Percy? Percy, can you hear me?" he says.

I can hear him, but I don't have a response as saliva dribbles out of my mouth and down into his hands.

"What happened?" he yells at Eric, who tries to come up with an explanation, parsing out pieces of our conversation that led to this.

"Breathe, Percy," he says, taking slow breaths himself for me to catch on to. "That's it, slow and steady." We repeat this exercise, with me occasionally falling behind before he guides me back on track. He mumbles something about an anxiety attack to Eric, who looks like he's about to pass out himself. "Okay, close your eyes, Percy. Try to focus on something that makes you happy."

This seems to help, with me focusing on the events of the past year playing like a montage inside my head. All of them, even the bad moments playing on a loop highlighting the best year of my life, one that would soon be taken away from me. I start to cry as my breaths become more steady, because I took all of it for granted when I should've been holding onto them for dear life.

Louis pulls me into his embrace, rubbing my back as everything is starting to settle. I'd spent so many nights at their home, sharing meals and jokes, becoming almost like a third son, that they know about my court date as well.

"You're not going anywhere, Percy," he whispers. "Pennsauken isn't that far away, and if it was, we'd make the drive for you." Soothing words from a man that's been the closest thing to a father I've ever known.

One of the employees asks if he should call an ambulance, but Louis waves him off. "Nothing to see here," he says.

I finally make it to my feet, apologizing profusely while Louis grabs our clothes and heads off to finalize our transaction. Eric rubs my back while shaking his head.

"If you didn't like the shirt, you could've just said so," he says. "You didn't have to go all Shakespeare and die on me."

THIRTY-THREE

A LIFE TOLD IN SECONDS

"You'd think I'd know how to put this damn tie on by now," I say in frustration.

"Language, Percy," Grace snaps back. She takes what's become her usual position in front of me, making sure I look presentable. "Someone is nervous again," she says in a sing-songy tune. "You've got a date this time, so you're covered there. You need dancing lessons again?"

"No."

She's puzzled by all of this, and as she forms the perfect knot on my tie I know that she's also forming a hypothesis for why I seem so down. Suddenly she smiles. "I get it now, you and Christina are planning on having sex and you're nervous."

"No...NO."

"My goodness, Percy, why are you acting like it's so taboo? You know I was your age once."

"It's not that, I swear. Besides, that's really not a conversation I wanna have with my mother."

"Well then, spit it out."

I pull away once she's finished and plop down on the bed,

fiddling around on my phone as a way of avoiding the conversation.

She waits in silence for a while before shaking her head and heading for the door. "Suit yourself."

"Why are you so cavalier about all this?" I'm not sure if it's the question that stops her or my tone. "I'm leaving soon and it feels like you don't even care about everything that's going on."

"Is that what you really think, Percy?" she asks, back still turned to me. The coldness of her tone when she says this makes my stomach churn.

"Sort of." My teeth chatter as I say this, but it's not cold in the house right now. We've ignored the elephant in the room for so long that I can't take it anymore.

"Well, you couldn't be more wrong." She lets out a sniffle and I rush to comfort her, laying my hand softly on her shoulder. She wipes her eyes with her sleeves before she turns around, and I'm wrecked with the guilt of knowing that I'm the one causing this.

"I'm sorry, Mom, I didn't—" She holds up a hand that silences me.

Apparently my tie isn't right, because she's fooling around with it again, but I think it's because she's got nothing else to do with her hands.

"I do cry, Percy. I cry every night, just not in front of you. But since you're so convinced that this is easy for me, let me break down the things you don't see. Every night for the past month, I come in here when I get off work and sit in that chair right over there." She points to the chair in front of my desk. "I sit there every night, and I watch you sleep, because I know there's gonna be a day when I come home and you won't be sleeping there anymore." Her tears are creating a trail through her mascara as they slide down her face, but she's focused, her tone working in defiance of whatever is going on inside of her right now.

"I make sure I'm gone before you wake, and I try to carry on everyday like it's normal because if I think about you leaving, even for a second..." She bites her fist and inhales through her nose, summoning everything she's been holding under the surface. "...then I'll lose it, because my son that I love with all my heart is going back to a world I can't protect him from, and it scares me. So, I may not cry in front of you, but don't think for a second that any of this is easy for me, because it's not." It's quiet for a while as we compose ourselves, the faint beep of the smoke detector she's been on me about beeping periodically in the background. "You remember when I took you to New York for your birthday? When you told me you were scared that I would forget about you."

I nod. "I remember it like it was yesterday."

"Well, I was scared, too, because you've been the final piece of my heart that I was missing, and I'm gonna have to learn to live without it again." She wipes her tears and claps her hands. "So, I'm gonna run my errand to Rite Aid while you clean up, and if your friends get here before I'm back, you wait so I can get my pictures."

"Are you gonna be alright?"

"As long as you keep me in your life I will be." She kisses me on the cheek and runs off to her errand, leaving me to think on all of that before Eric and Christina arrive.

I'd spent so much time and energy making sure Christina and I were good that I neglected to consider what Grace was feeling. Knowing that I'll still be on her phone plan gave me a sense of security that the only change would be where I sleep every night.

But our relationship is deeper than that.

There's a level of comfort between us that I've never had

with anyone else, a product of each of us being exactly what the other needed. I see it everyday when we interact, sometimes needing no words at all, like when we're both in a rush every morning and perform our well choreographed routine of maneuvering around each other, close enough to feel connected, but with enough distance so that we don't run into each other. At the end of my day, I'm always excited to go home, not because I finally have one, but because she's in it.

My thoughts are interrupted by two car doors slamming and the sound of Eric and Maria arguing as they come into my house.

"I need to talk to my best friend...alone," he says to her from the living room. He knocks on my door a few seconds later, coming in before I can answer.

"What's up, dude?" He takes a closer look at my face. "Have you been crying?"

"No."

"You sure, because you look like you've been crying."

"Whatever, dude." I go for our normal hug handshake, but he only holds out a fist. "Eric, everyone else in my life is acting weird and on the verge of a mental meltdown, I could really use my best friend holding it together."

Now he feels bad and acquiesces, but I notice how stiff he is as we go through the motions. I offer him a seat—the same one he sits in every time he's here—but he declines. "I'd rather stand," he says. Something about him isn't sitting right with me.

Eyeing him suspiciously, I decide to go with my gut. "You went and got waxed didn't you?"

He doesn't say anything, only dropping his head and frowning like a child being scolded for being caught with his hand in the cookie jar. This is just the distraction I needed to take my mind off of Grace, and I take full advantage, laughing until I'm in tears. "Stop laughing dude, I'm in serious pain."

Like throwing whisky on an open flame, this admission has the opposite effect of how it was intended. "Where'd you get waxed?" I ask.

"Back, chest, and scrotum. When she did my chest and back, the pain was manageable, but I didn't realize how bad of an idea it was until she started spreading wax on my bal—"

"Okay, I get your point," I say, stopping him before I can get the full visual.

"I'm serious, Percy." He shifts his weight and puts his thigh on my dresser, earning some well needed ventilation. "I didn't have a choice; she practically forced me to do it."

This just gets better and better. "Do tell."

"We were in my room, getting hot and heavy like usual, and when I pulled my pants down she looked like she was gonna puke. Whenever I touched her she'd get skittish. Turns out she'd been feeling that way for awhile but was too scared to tell me." Not getting the air he was looking for he takes his leg down and rocks from side to side with his legs spread apart. "Anyway, she said no more sex until I did something about it."

"So you went with the nuclear option?"

"I went with the option that assured me future rolls in the hay." He opens the door to check that Maria isn't outside listening. "Anyway, I'm scared something is wrong down there, and I...uh...need you to take a look and reassure me."

"Absolutely not."

"Percy, you're my best friend, and the only person I trust in this situation."

"Being a best friend entitles you to my fists in a fight, unlimited storage in my mind for your secrets, and telling the occasional lie to get you out of a jam with Maria. This, well, this isn't in any part of the package, no pun intended."

He tries to get on his knees to beg but the pain makes him rethink that approach. "Just one peek, that's it. I just need to know if it looks normal to you."

Eric is one of the most stubborn people I've ever met, and also incredibly neurotic. Telling him no is only going to ruin his night, which will then trickle down to my own evening in a stunning example of Reaganomics working as intended. "I'm not gonna touch it," I say.

"Not asking you to," he says, unzipping his pants and taking our friendship to a whole new level. "How does it look?"

"It looks normal."

He's not convinced. "You're sure? Nothing looks wrong at all?"

I hold back a laugh and decide to have a little fun at his expense. "Well, it looks like a hairless anteater that drowned in a hot tub."

"Dude, you're such a dick."

"At least I have hair on mine and can move horizontally without any discomfort."

The front door closes and I grab my jacket while Eric zips his pants up and tries to pull himself together.

Grace comes in, showing no signs of how I last saw her, which puts me at ease. After hugging Eric, she turns to me. "There's a surprise waiting for you in the living room."

She's got a genuine grin on her face, making me wonder what she's done this time. I put my coat on and head to the living room, where I'm greeted by the shock of a lifetime. Randy is here, invited this time, followed by Maria, Christina, and the most shocking of all.

Momma.

It takes me a second to comprehend it, and part of me doesn't believe it's real, but she pulls me into her arms,' removing any doubts. We hold each other for a while, and over her shoulder I see Grace, beaming with joy. I have no words for her at the moment, because there aren't enough in the dictionary to describe her. In a move befitting her name, she put her feelings aside and made sure my birth mother could see her only son off to prom.

It's hands down the nicest thing anyone has ever done for me.

"I can't believe you're here, Mom," I whisper to her, unable to let go in case she faded away.

"Grace wouldn't let me miss it for the world, baby."

The rest of the parents arrive: Eric's mom and dad, and a carpool of Christina's mom riding with Maria's parents.

With over an hour until prom we spend the time hanging out, telling jokes, giving tours of the house to everyone, and making sure each of us have everything we need for the evening. Everyone here, with the exception of Maria's parents, knows what's gonna happen in two days, but nobody says a word about it, and because of that I'm not thinking about it anymore. Grace is the unofficial timekeeper for the evening, and as the sun starts to go down we gather on the front lawn for photos.

It's crazy to think that eight months ago every person here was a stranger. I'm including Momma because she's clean now, which to me means she's a new person. We get pictures with every possible combination, but my favorite one is the last one I take. Momma is on one side and Grace is on the other, with both of them wearing blouses that match with my colors. For the final shot Christina says that they both should kiss me at the same time, and when they do I smile. It's the best picture I've ever taken, a living example of the power of forgiveness. Christina is driving us to the dance in her Mom's car, but before I can get in Grace pulls me to the side.

"Monday is gonna come when it comes, so leave it alone for the night," she says. Looking at Christina, she offers one final piece of advice. "Focus on her tonight, Percy. The poor girl is barely holding it together."

THIRTY-FOUR

HEADPHONES AND HEARTACHES

Drake's newest single is reverberating through the gym as we're patted down at the door, and I say a silent prayer that there's a holdup at the front of the line so it's finished by the time we walk in.

I laugh watching Eric get searched, since the three areas they focus on happen to be the places on his body that are now hairless and fragile. What's not funny is watching the female security guard search my girlfriend. As I watch closely, I can't help but observe that she's getting farther with her than I have in the time we've been dating.

Just inside the door is Mr. Jones, looking casual in jeans and a blazer, yet still the best dressed person in the place. "Aight, Percy, I see you," he yells, hyping me up as if I'm king of the world. We share a hug, the culmination of a relation-ship that goes beyond teacher and student. "You look flyer than a five dollar Spirit flight to Miami," he says to Christina.

"What does that mean?" she asks, her confusion speaking for the both of us.

"It means you look good enough to start a fight," he says, and sensing that we were still confused, pulls out his phone to show us a video of people fighting on an airplane. "Y'all just getting here?"

"Yup." I can see the gym, but I don't have a clear line of sight to the DJ booth. "Is Marlon spinning tonight?"

Mr. Jones looks at me like I've lost my mind. "I don't think the administration would let anybody else DJ at this point."

"Sweet. It's prom, so I know his mix is gonna be fire tonight."

Christina is surprised by my reaction. "You do more than just slow dance?"

"Last time we were at a dance, you were on the friend package, which entitled you to one dance and a picture. Now, you've been upgraded to the girlfriend package, which includes dances in different genres."

She squeezes my hand tighter but says nothing.

"You guys should take pictures before dancing," Mr. Jones says. "This is the best you'll look all night."

I look to Christina and we agree that it makes sense before saying goodbye and nabbing a spot in the line.

"It was here," she says suddenly. I'm looking around for anything that'll give me a clue to what she's talking about.

"You gotta help me out because I'm lost."

"Homecoming, this was the spot where you found me. That was the moment I knew I wanted us to be something more."

The words send chills down my spine, because I remember that moment vividly. Replaying it in my mind, remembering how my heart jumped when I'd finally found her, and the anger I felt as she cried on my shoulder, a sense of regret washes over me. If I had told her how I felt that night on the dance floor, we'd have had more time together. "I should've told you sooner."

She shakes her head vehemently. "That would've made

tonight unbearable."

The photographer finishes with Eric and Maria, and after a group shot with us they disappear into the crowd of students near the food line. At this point neither of us is holding it together very well, but we make it through our own pictures with genuine smiles. As we're walking to the coat check she stops. "If I asked you to do something crazy with me, would you do it?" she asks.

I'm not sure how to answer the question, but I'd be lying if I said the question itself isn't intriguing. "Anything, you name it."

"Since I upgraded to the girlfriend package, I believe there's a clause that entitles me to having you all to myself on our last night together." She heads to the exit and holds the door open. "If you can think of a place for us to go, I'd like to exercise that clause right now."

For the first time tonight, I'm seeing the girl that I've been dating for the last month, and the thought of one last adventure together is too exciting to pass up. I check the time on my phone, formulating a plan for the night on the fly before locking arms with her and walking to the parking lot.

School dances are overrated anyway.

* * *

CHRISTINA HOLDS the food while I unlock the door and key in the alarm code at my job.

I hatched the idea that we should have our own prom, where we have control over the music, and there's no better place for such an event then a record store. We grabbed dinner from the pizza shop in Haddonfield where we hung out for the first time, except this time she admitted up front that she was hungry.

The back office is about the size of my bedroom, with only a desk and a dusty couch from Randy's time living here during his divorce. After setting up the food and moving some clutter to create an impromptu dance floor, we spend ten minutes finding our soundtrack for the evening, walking hand in hand through each section of the store, with a rule that we have to agree on every choice. Unsurprisingly, most of our choices are in the same arena, and we end up with a huge stack of records that lean heavily towards 80's pop.

"All right, cowboy," she says. "Let's see what kind of moves you got."

Since we're not in a gymnasium full of students we detest, our shoes come off and we spend the next couple of hours dancing as if the night would last forever, with only the occasional interruption to eat or load a disc into the stereo. At one point she heads to the car and comes back with one of her mother's salsa mixes. Though I was apprehensive at first, I quickly got over that when I realized it required our bodies to stay close to one another. Within two songs I'd found the right rhythm in my hips, and she took our lessons to the next level, guiding me through spins before pulling me close to grind our bodies together into the end of the song.

There were certain songs where we couldn't catch the beat of, so instead we held hands and sang the lyrics at the top of our lungs, just like we did at the concert. I let slip that House Party is one of my favorite movies, so we looked up the Kid and Play dance on YouTube, learning it on the fly, and after a couple of false starts we had a passable routine. In another highlight, we had a spirited dance battle to Bell Biv Devoe's 'Poison,' which I lost, but it didn't matter because it wasn't about winners and losers.

It's just before midnight and we're sitting on the couch, with my head in her lap as she runs her nails through my hair as we share a bag of kettle corn. There should be music playing, but we're both too tired to get up and hit play on something new. The weight of what's been left unsaid is crushing, but she seems as determined as I am to delay the inevitable until the last possible moment.

"Tell me a secret, Percy," she says to break the silence. "Make it good, something that you've never told anybody else." She drops a kernel into my mouth and while I'm chewing I try to think of something that would fit the criteria.

"All right, it's gonna be weird," I say, unsure if what I have in mind will be too weird. "But trust me."

"Go for it."

I take a deep breath and start. "When I was in kindergarten, we were super poor, I'm talking splitting off the dollar menu poor. One day Momma came home with a VCR, which now that I think about it, was probably given to her by one of the men she was sleeping with. But I swear Christina, it felt like we'd won the lottery." She's smiling at me in a way that I've never seen, and I can feel a love for her growing by the second, so I focus on the ceiling instead. "Only problem was that by this time VHS was a thing of the past."

"My mom still has one," she says with a laugh.

"On Sundays, Momma liked to shop the tag sales at the Salvation Army for new work clothes, and I remember always seeing the VHS tapes next to the music, so the change that I usually spent on a toy would go towards my first movie. But all the good stuff like the Disney movies were out of my price range, and I knew I couldn't ask her to kick in."

"So what happened?"

"There was one movie I could afford that looked interesting, and it came with two tapes, so I really felt like it was a steal."

She's chuckling like she's expecting a punchline. "What was the movie?"

"It was Titanic."

Her eyebrows raise at the revelation.

"I know, super random. But I watched that movie every day, and even now I can remember the exact moment when the first tape ends. But in Jack Dawson, I found a kindred spirit. I mean, he had nothing more than a bag of clothes but was the happiest guy in the movie."

"There was room on that door for him to get on," she says in disgust.

"Dude, there totally was. But my favorite part is the dinner scene, when he talks about being content with what little he has, and the adventure of living each day without knowing what was gonna happen. That sense of contentment has guided me my whole life."

"You really are special, Percy. In spite of everything...you still find a way to be an amazing person."

"Don't get sappy on me like it's gonna get you out of telling me a secret of yours." I hold up a single kernel and she takes it off my fingertips with her mouth. "The floor is yours, Madam Christina."

With her free hand, she turns my face toward hers. Staring into my eyes, she asks if I'm sure that I wanna hear it, and though that scares me, my gut feeling says roll with it so I nod.

"I love you."

Up until now, the thought of court on Monday has felt like an illusion, but hearing those words roll off her tongue flips a switch inside me that makes it all feel real for the first time. I'd found everything I was looking for in life, and now I'm going to walk away from all of it. I love Christina in a way that I've never loved anybody else.

But I can't bring myself to return the words. No matter how I feel, I'd be a fraud of a person to tell her I love her and then waltz out of her life. She deserves better than that.

I watch her face slowly change into hurt as she realizes the words she's waiting to hear aren't coming. But just like that moment on the dance floor, she doesn't know the why behind it. I look away for a second, and I feel her tear drop onto my forehead, followed by sobs that I know are gonna haunt me on the loneliest nights.

"Don't say that, please."

"Why not?" She shoots back. "Are you gonna honestly tell me that all of this means nothing to you?"

The anxiety is just under the surface, biding its time to join the show. "You mean everything to me, Christina."

"If I mean so much, then why are you leaving? Or maybe I'm the idiot for dating you and knowing that you were gonna leave."

If our relationship was a plane, the engine has just gone out and we're descending rapidly. "I can't stay; my mom needs me."

"She had her chance," she yells. "She had her chance, and it's not fair that she fucked it up and we all have to suffer because she managed to stay clean for a couple of months."

"We?"

"Me, Grace, Eric. We love you just as much as she does, and we actually show it instead of showing up for a handout when times get rough."

Her points are valid, but she doesn't have the same investment in my mother that I do. I was stupid enough to believe that everything would end peacefully, but if I hadn't been so damn naive I could've seen that this was the only way for it to end. "It's not that simple."

"It really is, Percy." She grabs her keys and bends down in

front of me. "It's not your job to save her, even if you think it is. I watched you chase Jade and I kept my mouth shut, because I knew that I'd still see you everyday, and that was enough. But now I'm in love with you, and you expect me to smile while holding the door open for you to walk out of my life. So either you stay, or you watch me walk out of yours."

For a second I consider telling her what she wants to hear, if only to stop her from leaving. But I made a deal with Momma, and it's my turn to hold up my end. "I owe her the chance to make it right."

She gives me a sad smile, the kind you give the cashier after your card has been declined and they're taking your stuff back. It's a smile of bittersweet acceptance, and the final nail in the coffin of our night and our relationship. "You're always putting everyone else's needs before your own...it's actually one of the reasons I fell so hard for you." She's running her hand across my face, slower than usual, like she's taking a mental image one last time. "But I hope you figure out that it's alright to let someone else be the hero of your mother's story." She gives me one final kiss on the lips before walking out of my life.

I don't move for a long time, hoping that she'd cool off and come back to me.

But I know she won't.

It's a weird pain that I've never felt before, the kind that even crying can't make go away. I've watched my mother convulse while suffering from an overdose, literally laying on death's doorstep, but the pain of that doesn't come close to what I'm feeling right now. Going home is out the question, knowing that Grace is going to want a full status report. So, I do the only thing I know to do when the world becomes unbearable.

I put my headphones on and lose myself in an album.

THIRTY-FIVE

MAY 29

From the moment I agreed to go with Alex, I pictured what this day would be like, adding little details every day until I could repeat them verbatim if anyone asked me to.

I'd stride confidently into the courtroom with a Vince McMahon like strut, stopping to give Alex a pound and blowing kisses to Grace, even giving the judge a hug after she slammed her gavel down one last time to end my case. After that, Momma and I would walk out of the county building to start our new life together.

But that's the funny thing about being at the beginning of a journey, you only focus on the end instead of accounting for the people you'll meet along the way, the people that make you believe in things that you thought were only a myth. As I walk into the courtroom, it doesn't take long for me to realize that something is amiss.

Alex's cheery disposition is gone, replaced with a business-like nod of the head as I take my seat in front of the bench.

Momma seems oblivious to my presence, lifting her head to acknowledge me only after I've called her name several times. It feels like everyone is in on some big joke, with me standing to the side trying to figure out the punchline.

A bailiff emerges from the back and orders us to rise for Judge Martinez, who comes from the back and takes her seat on the bench, rapping her gavel and getting right down to business.

As she starts reading Alex's report, it quickly becomes apparent why everyone is so down.

That apartment in Pennsauken? A run down dump with no electricity or running water. The job that she called me from? A come as you please commission based gig selling overpriced skincare products. And yet, knowing all of that, I still had hope for her because she was clean. But even the most skilled batters know what's likely to happen when they're facing an 0-2 count.

She'd failed her two most recent drug tests, sealing my fate in foster care for the foreseeable future.

"Ms. Martin," Judge Martinez says. "I don't think you understand the gravity of your situation. You have a son that's making the most of a terrible situation, one that you put him in, and in the most important time of his young life, you continually choose to make the wrong decisions."

Momma doesn't acknowledge Judge Martinez, keeping her head down while taking her tongue lashing.

"I'm ordering a hearing to determine whether or not your parental rights will be terminated."

I get the feeling that she's sprucing the language up because she's in a professional environment, and if these words were being said during an intervention, the language would be much more colorful.

But I'm not thinking about that right now, because all I can see is Christina kneeling in front of me on Saturday night, telling me a truth I refused to acknowledge before she broke up with me, followed by Grace, on the edge of tears because she thought I was leaving. And what about the money I gave Momma? I imagine it's the feeling a degenerate gambler feels after losing his life savings on what he thought was a sure bet. Anger consumes me more and more by the second as I rock back and forth in my seat, trying to hold it all together.

"Percy," Judge Martinez says, with a softness that was absent when addressing my mom. "Would you like a visit with your mother after I adjourn us?"

I nod.

I can tell by the look in her eyes that she doesn't enjoy this part of her job, and her tone when she spoke about me makes me wonder if she's a mother herself. For the first time in my life, I realize how underreported the numbers of the opioid epidemic are, because they only account for the addict. They don't account for the children, or on a deeper level, the Judge Martinez's, Grace's, and Christina's of the world, everyday people that find themselves entangled in that world because they chose to love someone like me.

Momma always told me to never let anyone do something for me that I could do myself. So, while I appreciate the judge's attempt to terminate Momma's parental rights, in my mind I respectfully decline her offer.

Because in the after-court visit, I'm gonna do it myself.

* * *

MOMMA IS PACING the room as I enter, munching on her finger nails and trying to come up with the right words that'll fix the situation.

But there are none. For the first time in my life I've taken the blinders off, allowing me to see her as an addict instead of my mother, and all the anger I had for the world turns inward, because I should've known better. There was sixteen years of evidence—from broken promises to false starts—that should've told me that this was an illusion.

She beckons me to the couch, but I shake my head.

"I'd rather stand."

She tries to speak several times, but the words get caught in her throat.

"Relax, Mom, I'm not even angry." Her eyes widen, as if something went off in her head telling her that maybe it won't be that bad, so I move quickly to extinguish whatever hope she has. "Let me rephrase that. I'm not angry with you because I knew all along how this would end, and I still wagered every relationship in my life because I wanted to believe in you."

I'm surprisingly calm, like a person sitting in a packed theater watching a horror movie, except I'm the only one that's seen it before. Momma doesn't know how this movie is going to end, and the sick delight I get in knowing that I'm cutting her off is the only thing that'll make us close to being even.

"If you knew I was using again, why'd you give me the money?"

The question starts to dissolve the calmness. It's the classic move of an addict that takes the blame off themselves and places it on others. Instead of apologizing, she's chastising me for believing in her, forgetting the fact that it was her that called me for help in the first place.

"I gave you the money because I'm the reason we're in this position in the first place, and I felt guilty." I take a seat directly across from her, leaning on my elbows to get as close to her as possible, not wanting to miss the moment when she puts it all together. But that same misplaced feeling of loyalty starts to form in my throat.

Her eyes are moving left to right like she's reading the morning paper, only stopping to look up at me. "You were the person that called social services?" she whispers. She doesn't give me time to confirm it. "Why?"

I've grappled with the question for the last nine months, constantly putting it off because I didn't have a good enough answer for myself. Living how we did taught me to rely on my instincts, to trust that the first feeling in my gut was the right one. My anger would tell me that I called because I was tired of living in her nightmare. But the truth, a truth that I didn't wanna admit until right now, is a lot more sentimental.

"I'd tried my whole life to help you, hoping that one day you'd wake up and realize that my love was enough, and that I'd be there until the very end." I lick my lips and taste the salt of my tears, and after a deep breath to compose myself, I continue. "Watching you almost die made me realize that my love wasn't enough, that you'd never change because you knew I'd always be there to pick up the pieces."

"You were enough, Percy—"

"No, I wasn't." I let out a sigh of frustration because she just doesn't get it. "We are what we are, Mom. So we don't have to lie to each other anymore. The only card I had left to play was myself, so I made the call, hoping that losing me would be the final straw. But today I learned that it wasn't."

I always thought watching her learn the truth would bring me some sense of happiness, but she's still my mother, and I vow to myself that I won't say anything mean spirited on my way out, even if I want to.

"Just give me a few months to fix this," she pleads, and I almost believe her.

"Christina told me that I couldn't save you, crazy, right? She literally got down on her knees and begged me to stay, because she could see what I couldn't. She told me to choose between you two, so I chose you, and she broke up with me."

"Is that what this is about?" She rubs her hands together, forever plotting some half-assed solution. "Okay, so now you can go back to her while I—"

In a flash, all the compassion I have dissolves into a white hot anger. "It. Doesn't...WORK THAT WAY," I scream, startling Momma and bringing the chaperone into the room. "You can't just walk in and out of someone's life," I sob. "Maybe, I don't know...maybe because I let you do that to me you think it's alright. But it's not, especially to the people that love you."

"Maybe we should end the visit," my chaperone says.

I turn to her. "Just a minute longer; I promise it won't take long." I fix my gaze back on Momma, who won't even look at me. "Where's the money, Mom? Did you put it in your arm, because, really, it's okay if you did."

Still nothing as she stares at the floor, unwilling to speak.

"You know what, don't worry about it."

Something sparks her because suddenly she starts furiously rummaging through her purse before she emerges with a fistful of cash. There's only one problem: I gave her four one hundred dollar bills, and what she's holding is a clumsy mess of random amounts. That tells me everything I'll ever need to know.

Rising from my seat, I look down on her, her face almost a mirror image of mine, just a bit more scarred. "I'd tell you to keep that as your last memory of me, but we both know it won't last through the weekend." I turn to follow my chaperone out when Momma grabs my arm.

"Percy, you're all I have in this world. Please, just give me one more chance to make it right."

We all have our favorite songs, the ones that you recognize as soon as you hear the opening chords, that make you turn your radio up and lose yourself within them. Great songs, classics even, but at some point they just don't hit the same anymore, and this one is number one on my playlist.

"Mom, I love you more than anything I've ever known in my life." I can feel the end coming, and I force myself to keep my gaze on her so that I leave no doubt. "But I'd rather never see you again and know that you're all right, then to see you like this every day." I watch the hope drain out of her face, as her grip on my arms loosens. "If you really wanna make it right, you can start by staying out of my life."

With that, I pull myself away as she collapses into the seat. The door closes behind me, where I stand to gather myself before heading to the elevators. About halfway down I feel myself breaking down, and as soon as the door opens, I rush to the nearest restroom, locking myself in the handicap stall and giving myself a moment to mourn in peace.

I came here today with two mothers, expecting to lose one of them, and ultimately I did lose one.

Just not the one I expected.

* * *

IN A PERFECT WORLD, I get home from court, kiss Grace on the cheek, then head to Christina's doorstep with my heart in my hands hoping that she'd take me back.

But I don't live in a perfect world.

When I got home, Grace was on the porch waiting for me, having been filled in by Alex about what happened at court. But she didn't know about my visit with Momma after court had adjourned, and we cried together as I gave her the play by play. What I'll always remember is the way she held me as I sobbed, carrying my pain as her own and never giving me the sense that she turned out victorious in the battle for my love.

In this situation nobody wins; we've all lost, with the only difference being that Grace and I have each other to lean on, while I don't wanna think about what Momma will lean on to get through this.

I feel like one of those prisoners that gets convicted of a crime they didn't commit, and is later exonerated by DNA. I'm happy to have my freedom, but I didn't really win because I lost time that I can't get back. Maybe one day she'll figure things out and come find me, but if that day never comes, I'm at peace with it. Grace is the silver lining in all of this, giving me the peace of mind knowing that I'll have a mother at my graduation, or on my wedding day. She'll be the reason that Mother's Day doesn't hurt anymore.

It's just after nine and the song fades out into my ringtone. I check the number, declining it in disgust when I recognize that it's from Momma. She calls back again, and I do the same thing. Picking up the phone is out of the question, so as she keeps calling, she's met with my voicemail. Finally, after what feels like the hundredth call, she blocks her number as if I'm too stupid to realize what's going on. Annoyed by the constant interruption from my music, I switch to my Sony Discman, once again proving that the technology of yesterday is superior in certain ways.

I'm listening to an album that Mr. Jones recommended, Kendrick Lamar's Good Kid M.A.A.D City, and one song in I understand why he was adamant that I listen to it. The theme of the album centers around a kid living in poverty but not quite fitting in. He isn't tough enough to be a gang member, but he wants to be down. He's intelligent, but is boxed in by the treacherous environment he lives in, lacking the resources to help him achieve his potential. There's humorous freestyle sessions with friends, reminding me of the laughs Eric and I share daily. These kinds of albums are the best, the ones that feel in your soul, speaking to you in a way that makes you feel that all the pain you've been through was worth it, just so you could understand the record in a way that others can't. As the album ends, I check my phone, shocked because Momma seems to have gotten the point.

The only notification I have is a voicemail from her last call, which I save without listening to it. Once I've had time to process everything I'll listen to it, but for now I'm content with loving Grace like I never have before.

Because she's my mother.

THIRTY-SIX

ALL BILLS COME DUE

"Have you ever shaved your calves?" Eric asks. He's smiling like he's in on a big secret, a stock broker with a tip of the month.

"No, Eric, I haven't," I whisper back. "Because my calves are fine the way they are." Curiosity gets the best of me though. "Do I even wanna know why you asked?"

He gives me the same grin he did before handing me the porno. "Feast your eyes on these," he says, lifting his pant leg proudly to show off his freshly shaved calf muscles. "What do you think?"

"I think they look like frost bitten chicken breasts."

"Wow, that's my best friend everyone." He pulls his pants leg back down. "I know it seems weird, but when you rub them together after putting lotion on, it's like getting a massage from Jesus himself."

"Really could've gone without that visual."

Our teacher tells us to pack up our stuff and talk amongst ourselves until class is over. Now that we've gotten past finals, the teachers seem to care less than we do.

"In all seriousness, you need to get back with Christina.

You aren't going home anymore, so you have no reason to keep ignoring each other."

"You sound a little too chipper about my relationship with my mother falling apart."

He frowns. "Look, I'm sad that things didn't work out for you, but I love you, dude, and knowing that you're staying means we can really do some damage together this summer. Also, Christina talks to Maria all the time about you, to the point where I haven't gotten laid in a week."

"My heart bleeds for you."

The classroom door opens and one of the student assistants to the main office comes in with a summons. Her name is Alexia if I remember correctly, and the word around school is that she gets rid of tardies for the popular kids. I watch her hand it to the teacher, who reads it and looks up right at me, nodding that it's for me. Since class is over in ten minutes, I grab my stuff.

"I know you want to get laid again, but I gotta figure some stuff out before her and I can even consider getting back together."

"And what am I supposed to do in the meantime?"

I laugh. "Rub your calves together and jerk off like the rest of us peasants."

He flips me off before I head for the office.

As I walk through the hallway, Eric's words buzz around in my head. Since prom, I've made it a point to go anywhere on campus that would allow me to avoid her. She was right about everything, but there's a bitterness toward her for making me choose between her and my mother, then leaving in a huff knowing how hard I was taking everything. If there was one person I needed at that moment, it was her.

But then I think about all the special moments we shared together, like seeing our first concert together, and I wonder if it would really be the worst thing to put my pride to the side.

I open the door to the main office to find Alex and Grace, both with a look on their face that makes my stomach turn. In the back I can see Mr. Jones making copies during his off period. I'm uneasy because there's only one person that connects me to both of them.

"Hey," I say cautiously. "We're doing our visits in public now?"

Nothing from either of them, not even a smile. Grace has a frown on her face, like she did on prom night in my room.

"Percy," Alex says. "Can you sit down for a second?" His voice is shaking like I'm holding a gun to his head. "Please."

I look back and forth at the two of them, knowing something bad is coming, but I take a seat anyway. "You guys are scaring me."

"They did a homeless sweep in North Camden yesterday," he says.

"Momma is in jail, isn't she?"

He shakes his head and swallows hard. "In one of the tents they found a body...and..." he trails off.

"She overdosed again," I say, but the feeling of relief vanishes when I notice Grace holding her hand over her mouth, her tears seeping through her fingers. "Is she at Cooper again?"

They say nothing.

On Wheel of Fortune there's always one guy that keeps asking for letters even though it's clear to everyone else what the answer is. I feel like that guy right now, because in my heart I know the answer, I'm just hoping that it's the wrong one.

"I'm sorry, Percy, but your mother has passed away."

The words land, but I don't quite comprehend them. I

smile at them, hoping that they both just have a really dark sense of humor they've been keeping from me. I shake my head. "No, n-n-no, that isn't possible. She just called me on the phone and left me a message." I furiously search for my phone in my hoodie before looking at the date of that last voicemail. "See? Right here," I point the voicemail out to them. "She called me on May twenty-ninth, right after court."

"Percy," Grace says. "That was almost two weeks ago."

"I know, but she was giving me time to calm down. I'll prove it to you." I dial her number, but it goes straight to voice-mail. So, I end the call and try again, but it's the same thing. The reality sinks in with each call, and after the fifteenth consecutive call, the truth finally hits.

Momma is gone.

In my heart I always knew this day would come, such is the life when you're the child of an addict. But I always thought she was different, that she would live forever.

Alex puts his hand on my shoulder but I slap it away. "If you'd have just let me go home, she'd still be alive." This hurts him, which brings me peace because knowing someone else hurts makes me feel comfort in a world that just grew lonely. "Why couldn't you just let me go home, man? I could've protected her."

I can see in his eyes that he wants to say something, but knows that it won't come out right. But all I'm seeing is red, and he's the closest target for my fury.

"I told you she needed me," I scream, bringing all four principals out of their respective offices. "You knew she was using again and you strung me along. This one is on YOU." I jab my finger into his chest.

"Percy...please," he says.

"Please isn't gonna bring my mother back. You guys took all of her money and left her to die alone on a street corner.

Fuck you and your please." I start to raise a fist when Mr. Jones grabs me from behind, lifting me off my feet while Alex makes a getaway.

"Come back, Alex," I yell after him. "If you needed to hit your ratio you could've just said so."

Mr. Jones lets me down and pulls me into his embrace, whispering in my ear while I sob into his shoulder. "It's okay, Percy," he says. Over and over, his deep baritone calming me down before he hands me off to Grace.

I really did want her to be my mom, but not at this cost.

THIRTY-SEVEN

MISSED CALLS

"Percy, its Momma. You've ignored all my calls and I don't blame you. I know I let you down like I always do, but I want you to know that I understand why you never wanna see me again. I'm not asking to see you again, but I really just wanted to hear my baby's voice one more time, but I'll settle for your voicemail. If I ever call, you don't have to pick up anymore, just send me to voicemail so I know that you're still out there striving to be something I could never be. I love you so much, Percy, and I know you're gonna go on to do great things. Just know that Momma is always rooting for you, and one day I'll earn my spot in your life again. I'll always love you more."

I play the voicemail over and over, connecting it through my headphones and listening with the lights off so that it feels like she's here in the room with me.

Why couldn't I just pick up the phone?

That question will haunt me for the rest of my life, even though it's not the worst part. If I had taken the money from her, she wouldn't have had the means to buy the amount of dope that she did. Grace is handling the funeral arrangements, but there won't be one because I'm all that she had in the world.

Sleep evades me, because every time I close my eyes all I can see is Momma, walking the streets of Camden by herself, knowing that her only son wanted nothing to do with her.

Grace told me that she'd been dead for a week, and when I think about my activities for the past week it makes me sick to my stomach. Here I was living carefree, going out to lunch with Eric, dancing with Grace, even typing messages to Christina that I was too scared to send, all while my mother laid dead in a tent less than 15 minutes away from me.

As I sit in the darkness, I'm angry because there's no album I can listen to that'll make the pain go away, no chorus to make me feel like things will get better. I killed my only mother because I was too stupid to forgive her for being human.

So, no, I don't deserve an album.

I deserve to sit in the darkness and feel every shred of pain that's owed to me, with my deceased mother serving as the narrator for the evening, and hopefully by the time my phone battery dies it'll hurt a little less.

THIRTY-EIGHT

CHOICES AND THE CONSEQUENCES THEY CARRY

You would think that a life of disappointment and poverty would leave me somewhat prepared for the grieving process, or at least give me a bucket of emotions to pull from.

But it doesn't.

I've never felt as alone as I do right now, knowing that the one person I could always count on to be there is gone. When I close my eyes all I can see is the last image I have of her from court, scrounging for every dollar she had to prove that she was still worthy of a place in my life. It haunts me because now that she's gone I realize that in spite of her relapse, in the grand scheme of things I would've eventually forgiven her and started anew. That's just how things went between us.

I'm left in a basket case of emotions, alternating between wanting to talk about it, and wanting to be left alone completely. Everyone that's still left in my life have been more inclined to believe the latter, though they each approach it in different ways.

Grace gives me ample space, bringing meals to my bedroom door and quickly making herself scarce so as not to intrude. At night I can hear her weeping in her bedroom, unsure of how to broach the subject but still carrying my grief as if it were her own. Every time I try to express my feelings I start bawling again, sobbing in her arms until I can collect myself and retreat to my room.

Eric calls everyday, but on a good day he's not the most emotional guy, and consoling your best friend about losing his mother is more than he can handle. He knows I've been eating lunch in the staff bathroom, and everyday he slides a pack of Skittles underneath the stall as his way of trying to cheer me up. I also suspect that Christina is having him keep close tabs on me to make sure I don't do anything crazy.

Speaking of Christina, not having her around is the second most hurtful part of this situation. I'm still angry with how she ended things, but late at night I long for her presence, wishing that things could go back to how they were. At school we pass each other as if we're strangers, except our eyes meet for a second, and in that moment I can see that she still loves me. Sometimes our breakup hurts worse than losing my mother, but I quickly extinguish those thoughts by convincing myself that we would've broken up anyway.

The most curious reaction has been Randy's. He told me to take whatever time I needed, and even continued paying me for the days I've been out. On top of that, he knows I've been sneaking in the shop to listen to music at night, at least that's my suspicion because there's a whole pizza waiting for me in the office every night when I get there.

Today is the first day I've felt somewhat normal, so I decided to come back to work. After making sure I was ready to handle the store, Randy left to run an urgent errand. I quickly find my groove, organizing inventory that Randy felt was a chore because it wouldn't sell anyway. Bill Withers comes up on the store playlist and I smile as I shuffle to one of Momma's favorite songs. Whenever our benefits card got reloaded she'd sing this song as we walked to the grocery store.

As I'm finishing up the last of the inventory, the bell on the door chimes to let me know I have a customer. When I make it up front my jaw almost drops when I see who it is. Standing at the register with a card is the girl who went from being the apple of my eye to the bane of my existence in record time.

Jade.

"Hey," she says.

Thanks to a combination of Bill Withers, and my newfound regard for letting things go, I give her a genuine smile. "Hey," I reply. "What can I help you with?"

"I'm actually not here to buy anything." She hands me the card and pulls me into an embrace, which I accept. "I heard about your Mom, and I...well I thought with our shared history of rotten family dynamics..." she trails off, trying to find the right words. "...I just thought that maybe you could use a friend right now."

"That's really nice of you, but I'm not really in the mood to talk."

She nods and gives me a sad smile. "Well, my number hasn't changed if you need an ear. I know I haven't been the best friend to you, but I really do care about you, Percy." She turns for the door and I feel a surge of guilt because all I've wanted is someone to listen, and though Jade isn't who I had in mind, the fact that she came with a card means a lot to me.

"Hey, Jade," I call as she gets to the door. "I can't promise that I'll be the most forthcoming, but it would be cool if you stayed for awhile. After locking the door and putting up the 'out to lunch' sign on the window, we head to the back of the store.

"You want anything? Soda, bottled water, leftover pizza?" I offer, waving at my pathetic spread of comfort food.

"No thanks," she says. "Did you go to a Muse concert?"

"Huh?" I look down at my shirt, not realizing I'm wearing the one I bought at the concert. "Yeah, Christina and I saw them in New York City on Valentines Day."

"That's so cool, speaking of her, where is she?"

I can't be mad at her for being unaware of our break-up, but blocking it out completely has been a sound strategy for me up until this point. Now it's brought back to the forefront, in the place she broke up with me no less.

This is some bullshit.

"Um, she actually broke up with me." I say, bringing the pain of that moment roaring back. "It was on prom night," I add, making it clear that it was before Momma's death. I wonder if every guy is willing to protect their ex girlfriend's reputation.

Jade raises her eyebrows at this. "I'm so sorry, I didn't mean to reopen that wound."

I join her on the sofa and pat her on the back. "It's alright, I mean... that's life right?" This conversation is depressing, even for my current state of mind, so I change the subject. "How are you and Casey doing?"

She smiles and shrugs her shoulders. "We're...going."

That isn't exactly a ringing endorsement, and though I tell myself that I don't care, I'd be lying if I said this didn't bring me some sense of satisfaction. This must also be a sore subject for her because she quickly lobs the ball back into my court.

"How are you feeling?" She asks.

The question catches me off guard. Nobody has asked me that yet, everyone has assumed that my life was pretty shitty and moved accordingly. This is the first time someone has looked me in the eyes and asked how I truly feel.

"I feel like I can't win, Jade," I start. "My Mom killed herself because I cut her out of my life, for doing the same shit she's been doing since I was in kindergarten. The worst part is she tried to make it right with me, but I was too selfish to pick the phone up."

She slides closer to me on the sofa. "We can't blame ourselves for the trauma that people put us through. Even though you loved your mom, you have the right to your own feelings. Believe me, I know what it feels like to carry the burden of a parent's addiction." She lays her head on my shoulder, and my mind goes to a different universe, one where Casey doesn't exist and everything worked out between us.

"This whole foster care shit is rigged, Jade," I say. There's no winners in our situation. I mean, if we go back to our parents, all we'll remember is the love we experienced, while our parents will strive for a bar that's unreachable. But if we stay, we'll always feel like we don't belong, no matter how much our foster parents try to make it feel normal."

"You have a great home, Percy."

"I know...I know I do, but why do I still feel so alone?"

She raises her head up to look me in the eye. "You're not alone." She places her hand on my face. "You'll always have me."

In spite of everything that's happened between us, I know that she means it. I'm trying to think up the words to say when she leans in and kisses me.

My mind stalls like a teenager learning to drive stick for the first time. Thankfully, my hormones—which have been dormant beneath the wreckage of my breakup and my mother's death—take the lead as we skip past first base like a RedSox hitter that sent a line drive off the Green Monster. For the first time since Momma's death I feel alive, throwing caution to the wind and acting on instinct. Our shirts come off as we jockey for position on the couch. And yet, though I'm doing something I've dreamed about, something feels...off.

Not that I'm doing anything wrong, in fact, judging by her moans I'm doing pretty well in that department. But even though I've dreamed of doing this a thousand times, I stopped dreaming about doing it with *her* a long time ago.

I pull away.

"I can't do this," I say. I'm not sure whose more surprised between the two of us.

"It's alright, I promise Casey will never know," she says, before going for another kiss.

Once again, I pull away.

"It's not that." My heart is pounding inside my chest as I try to find the right words.

There was once a time when I would've walked over hot coals for her if it meant I could soothe my feet in her bath water. But losing my virginity feels like something reserved for Christina, which is a weird thought given how we're no longer together. If I've learned anything from the last week, its that the bill will always come due when I choose to be selfish. Christina helped me get over her, and no matter how much I resent her, I can honestly say I'd only enjoy sex with Jade because of that resentment.

"You really love her, don't you?" Jade asks. A long uncomfortable silence follows her question. After what feels like an eternity she reaches for her shirt. "You know, I've always dreamed of someone loving me the way you love Christina, and I guess at one point you did...but I was too blind to see it."

"I'm so sorry Jade, I—"

"You don't have to apologize." She finally gets her shirt on and grabs her bag before joining me on the couch again. "Just tell me that it's not because of what I did to you, because that night has haunted me ever since."

I shake my head. "Its not that at all, I just..." I take her hands in mine, looking into the same eyes that made me comfortable with being a foster kid. "...I love you, Jade. From the moment I met you I've loved you. But I'm in love with Christina."

She nods her head at this, both of us realizing that the timing was never gonna be right, just two foster kids sent on another search to find somewhere to fit in. "You're one of the good guys, Percy. Don't ever let our circumstances make you feel that you're not." We share one more kiss and she heads for the door.

"Jade," I call out. She turns and locks eyes with me. "We can still be friends right?"

She smiles at this. "Always."

After she's gone I sit for awhile, in the same spot Christina left me in, chuckling at how I've had two chances at losing my virginity in the same room and failed. But once the chuckling subsides I'm sad again, because my mother is still dead, and though I made the right decision to turn down Jade, I'm no closer to getting back with the girl I actually love.

Emotionally, I'm at my breaking point for the day, so I write Randy a note saying that I was overwhelmed, lock the store up and head home for the day.

Nice guys really do finish last.

* * *

WHY IS Randy's car in my driveway?

While I'm thankful for the distraction from the grieving process, the anxiety it gives me is no better. He said his errand was urgent, but him being at my house gives me a sinking feeling in the pit of my stomach.

As I collect the mail before going inside, I notice an envelope that's different from the others. There's no return address, but I recognize the handwriting as Christina's. We haven't talked since the night she walked out, and dealing with everything that's happened since without having her to lean on has made me wish the school year would end immediately, which mercifully is tomorrow. I'm not sure how much longer I could stomach eating lunch in the bathroom.

I toss it in my backpack so I can read it when I'm in the right mind space.

As I open the door, I almost trip over Randy's shoes, but somehow I still refuse to believe what's going on. But when I think of all the signs, the Muse tickets on Valentine's Day, the flowers on the night of homecoming, and Grace's recent affinity for silk robes and bedding, I can only chuckle at the irony of them pushing me to get laid so they could lay with each other.

And then I hear it, and nothing is funny anymore.

Coming from Grace's room, I hear the sounds of their lovemaking, freaking me out because it reminds me of when I used to come home and Momma would have one of her 'clients' in the house. I sit on the couch and feel the anger throbbing inside me, just under the surface like an impacted wisdom tooth.

I'm thankful that they're middle aged, because the sounds don't last long. As I hear them giggling and talking about things to do together, I realize that this is the first step on the long road to me becoming homeless again. There's a new man in her life that's gonna replace me, and with Momma laying in the mortuary down the street, I don't have anywhere else to go.

I have no girlfriend.

I have no mother.

I have no job.

I have no home.

And on top of that, I gave Momma the money that she killed herself with, basically assisting in her own suicide. No, I'm not good for people, and they damn sure aren't good for me. I hear Randy ask Grace to call his phone, and the house goes quiet as they listen for a ringtone, but they don't hear it because it's on silent, vibrating in his pants pocket next to the shoes by the door.

It's showtime.

I catch it before it stops ringing.

"Hello," I say.

"Percy?" Grace asks, shocked to hear my voice. "Randy, you can stop worrying, you left it at the shop," she says to him.

"No, actually, he left it in his pants next to his shoes down here."

The line goes dead as I hear them scramble above me to get dressed and come downstairs. My anger crescendos as they come down the stairs, and I'm practically foaming at the mouth once they're within my eyesight, each of them wearing one of Grace's robes.

"What gives you the right?" I whisper, barely controlling my rage.

Grace says nothing, so Randy takes the lead. "Percy, I can explain." He starts moving slowly toward me but notices my free hand is curled into a fist. "It's not what it looks like."

"You sure? Because it looks like you've been sneaking off to fuck my mother." He and Grace exchange nervous glances. They know the jig is up. "Wow, Randy, I thought you were different. You thought because you gave the poor, little foster kid a job it would give you a clear conscience."

Now it's Grace's turn to take a shot. "Percy, I swear on my life we were gonna tell you."

"When? On Mother's Day?" I toss him his phone, if only to make sure I have two fists. "You knew I was struggling, Randy, and you snuck over here for a roll in the sack with the only person I got left that cares about me."

"Percy, I love her."

And just like that, the dam holding every emotion I've been carrying breaks. "She's all I got left," I scream. "She's all I got and you're trying to take her away from me." I bring my fists up. "Let's do this. If you win, I swear I'll leave and never come back. C'mon, I'm older now, so Momma doesn't have to worry about me getting hurt by a John."

Randy has no idea what I'm talking about, looking to Grace for help, which she provides by stepping between us. "You should go," she says, kicking his pants into her hand before shoving him towards the back door.

I head to my room and slam the door behind me.

Soon after, Grace comes knocking, letting herself in and taking a seat in my desk chair. This makes me smile, because she said that one day she'd come home and I wouldn't be here, but she doesn't know that the day is tomorrow. "I'm sorry, Percy. I didn't want you to find out like this."

I scoff at this. The same rules I had for Momma in our visit after court apply here. Under no circumstances will I say anything disrespectful. "Can you just give me a couple of days?"

She comes to kiss my cheek but I turn away. "Sure," she says before closing the door on her way out.

I pull out my phone and load up the list of shelters in New York City that I never thought I would use. I check my bank account, seeing that I have just over six grand to take with me, which is more than enough to live off of.

I love Grace more than anything, but I'm not gonna stick around for her to cast me aside when Randy decides that kids aren't his thing. With tears in my eyes, I turn the music up, throw some Skittles in my mouth, and start packing my things.

THIRTY-NINE

THE WRENCH THAT WOBBLED THE JENGA TOWER

I always hated the last day of school.

Walking the halls and hearing the other students compare plans for the summer—plans that I wouldn't be a part of—made the last day of school feel like one big reminder of the home life I craved. On top of that, I knew it was the last day I would be assured at least two meals a day, along with a distraction from the hell I was living in, so my feelings were warranted.

But in a year that everything in my life has changed, I'm actually sad about today being the last day of school, because once the school bell rings I'm saying goodbye for good. After agonizing all last night, I made the decision to not tell any of my friends. Telling Christina I was leaving last time had only made things worse, so I figure just disappearing would save us all the heartache of having to look each other in the eye and say goodbye. I packed light, with only two outfits, my phone and phone charger, CD collection, and Discman. Since I'm technically homeless again, I don't have the storage for any extra baggage.

All that aside, my plan is pretty simple.

Grace works at four, so once school is out I can kill an hour until she leaves for work, allowing me to stop by the bank and withdraw my savings. I told her that I was hanging with Eric to head off any suspicions, and by the time she gets the notification that I withdrew the money, she'll be at work and unable to stop me. After leaving the bank, I'm stopping at the funeral home to say goodbye to Momma. It's the last night that her body is available for viewing since we made plans to cremate her, and I can only hope that Grace keeps her ashes even though I'll be gone.

The good thing about the last day of school is that nobody cares about attendance anymore, so I'm spending my last period in the corner bleachers of the football field, reliving memories of the past year and coming to grips with it being the last time I'll see this school. Occasionally my mind drifts into what-if territory, with thoughts of what senior year would look like for Eric and I. My teachers were convinced that I could get into a really good college with my grades and test scores, building me up to the point where I believed it myself. Once I get my GED, the plan is to do just that.

I see a figure emerge from the bottom of the bleachers, a well-dressed man with his back to me. He seems to be looking for something, and once he turns around I can see that it's Mr. Jones. He makes a beeline for me, making it up the bleachers with impressive quickness for someone wearing dress shoes.

"Just the man I was looking for," he says. "Mind if I take a seat here?"

I'm not really in the mood for a lecture, or for the company of people in general, but I'm not a jerk either. "You taught us that we have free will as Americans, so I can't really stop you."

He chuckles at this and takes a seat next to me, and for a while we just stare out at the football field.

"Can I ask why you were looking for me, Mr. Jones?"

"Desmond...or Des for short."

"Oh, so we're on a first name basis now?"

"I've given you music recommendations, introduced you to my personal DJ, and had to restrain you during the worst moment of your life. I'd say we've earned enough to justify that."

"That's fair, but I'm not in the mood for a lecture right now. No offense."

He strokes his beard at this. "Well, that's perfect, because I'm not in the mood to give one. I went looking for you because I felt that maybe you needed someone to sit and just listen to you."

Knowing that I'm leaving is making it easy to open up, and I don't want my last memory with him to be terrible, so I give in a little. "I feel like I'm living in a Billy Mays infomercial. Like, every time I think life has handed me enough shit, it pops up like, 'But wait, there's more.'"

For some reason this makes him laugh hysterically. "How do you know about Billy Mays?"

"When I was a kid we couldn't afford cable, and I guess the television companies got tired of poor people free loading quality programming, so after eleven it was all infomercials until the morning news at six."

We laugh together at this. A couple comes to the bleachers and he tells them to clear out. "You ain't coming over here to get your rocks off," he yells at them before they scatter like roaches. "Sorry about that," he says to me. "So why do you feel like you're in an infomercial?"

"My mother is sleeping with my boss, my birth mother died of a heroin overdose, and the only girl I've ever loved walked out on me because I was too stupid to see that she was right." He only knows that my mother died, so I bring him up to speed on my life as a whole until he understands the whole picture. This is followed by more silence as he considers all of it.

"Have you ever considered why your mother dating someone bothers you?" he finally asks.

I blow a raspberry out of my mouth at the question. Des takes this as a sign to approach it from another angle.

"Your boss, would you say that he's a good guy?"

"When he's not sleeping with my mother, sure."

He shakes his head. "Take that out of the equation for a second. Just as a person, would you consider him a solid dude?"

I nod begrudgingly at this. Randy has been nothing short of awesome to me. When the store exceeded his expectations, I was gifted with a generous bonus, and he worked around my school schedule and accompanying social life. Taking him and Grace out of the equation—and it's a very big part of it—I don't have a bad word to say about the guy.

"If you love your mother and want to see her happy, shouldn't you be ecstatic that she found a good man?" He studies my reaction to his question, noticing how I clench my fists in anger. "Unless there's something deeper going on with you."

His little addendum makes me relax a bit, and I wonder for a second if he was put into my life for a purpose. "My whole life my birth mother was a prostitute," I say. "When I was really young, she tried to hide it, just like she did with the drugs, but as I got older she stopped caring and would bring guys into our home. Sometimes I'd sit outside and hear them hitting her if they didn't wanna pay, and I felt so useless because she always told me that it was part of the job. When I saw Randy at my house the other day, I felt so violated because all those memories came rushing back."

"Did Grace know about your mother's line of work? Because if she did, I'd like to think that she would've had a conversation with you to make you feel at ease with her dating."

I shake my head. "There's more, though. After I found them the other day, he told me that he loved her, and it scared me because I was being replaced by someone else. I finally found something in my life that I could have to myself and someone was taking it away from me."

He slides closer to me, so close that I can make out that his shoes are made of some sort of reptile. "Did Grace know your birth mother?"

I nod.

"You ever consider that she was waiting for you and someone else was trying to take you away from her?"

Damn, this guy is good. "It's not the same thing," I say, sounding like a stubborn guy that doesn't wanna admit it's the same thing.

Des starts sniffing. "You smell that?"

I sniff as well, unsure of what he's smelling. "No."

"You don't smell the bullshit?" This makes me laugh before I can remember that it's at my expense. "So, what are you going to do?"

That stops my laughter in an instant. I was enjoying our conversation so much that I forgot about my plan to leave. "I'm not sure I can trust you with that."

"What's said in these bleachers, stays in these bleachers, unless you're planning on killing yourself."

"I'm not." I consider the ramifications of letting someone else in on my runaway plans, but in my heart I know he's a solid guy. "I found a couple shelters in New York. I mean, homelessness isn't anything new to me. I'll get my GED, and hopefully find a college that'll accept me." Now it's my turn to gauge his reaction, and I grip my backpack just in case he gives off a hint that he's gonna tell. But he's calm about it, just nodding his head before coming to terms with it.

"Let me see your phone," he finally says. Without thinking I unlock it and hand it to him. He goes to my contacts and starts typing his number in. "If you need anything, I don't care if it's food, clothing, or a place to stay, you give me a call, Percy. I got people in Brooklyn where I'm from...actually, Marlon stays up there, so you'll always have a place to go."

"You're not gonna try and talk me out of it?"

He hands me my phone. "I told you on the first day of school that it's not my job to convince you to do anything. Part of the fun in life is figuring out stuff like this. Plus, I know in my heart that you'll make the right decisions and eventually fulfill your potential." He smiles at me, and I know in this moment that I've found someone that really understands me. "But if something changes and you do stay, I think with your grades and your story a college scholarship is definitely on the table."

We both stand and embrace one final time before he descends down the stairs.

"Yo, Des," I shout.

He turns around.

"That Kendrick Lamar album spoke to my soul. I don't know if we'll ever see each other again, but I wanna say thank you...for everything."

"I knew it would, and if you stick around, I got some more in the stash. Take care of yourself."

Once he's gone, I start gathering my things since the final bell is ten minutes away As I'm putting my headphones in the bottom pocket of my backpack, I find an envelope addressed to me. It's the note Christina left at my house, but since I walked in on Randy and Grace I forgot to open it. It's far too formal for her, but when I open the envelope I notice that the real letter is inside.

I can tell how much work she put into it, with every curve of the origami paper folded with the precision of a surgeon. Every letter on the front is a different color, and I laugh at how she managed to turn a heart into the first letter of my name. Though I don't want to open the letter because I'm scared of its contents, I know she wrote it after hearing about Momma dying, so I know it's from the heart. Pulling softly at the corner tab, the note opens and I start reading.

Dear Percy,

Maria told me about your Mom passing, so I'll start by giving you my condolences. I know how much she meant to you, and my heart broke for you when I heard. I'm sorry about the things I said after prom, so I'm writing this to explain myself, and I hope you'll forgive me after you read this.

I broke up with you like that because I knew you wouldn't do it. Yes, I was angry about losing you, but if I didn't do it, I knew you would run yourself ragged trying to keep us together when your focus should've been on helping her stay clean. I guess I thought if I broke up with you, you'd hate me and forget about me, making it easier for you to move on. You'd already been through enough and I didn't wanna see your face as you broke up with me, knowing that it wasn't your choice.

I miss you, Percy, and seeing you at school while knowing what you're going through just kills me, but I walked out on you, so I have no right to blame you for ignoring me. You were so honest with me about everything, respecting my boundaries when most guys would've tried to

*use your situation to have sex with me. I'm not sure where
we go from here, but I want you to know that I love you and
I'm here to talk if you find it in your heart to forgive me.*

   Your First Love,
   Christina

I have to say goodbye.

This is my first thought after reading her letter. I know it'll
hurt, but knowing her reasoning makes it impossible to disappear without letting her know that we're ok. The final school
bell is two minutes away, so there's no hope of finding her on
campus. I pick up my phone and dial her cellphone.

She picks up on the second ring. Of course, given all that's
happened between us, I have no idea where to start.

"Hey," I say, as if we don't have a mountain of shit to work
through.

"I was beginning to think you actually hated me." She
always did know what to say to lighten the mood.

"Never. I actually got your letter awhile ago, but five
minutes later I walked in on Randy and Grace having sex. I
just read it a couple of minutes ago."

Pure silence on her end.

"I'm leaving tonight, Christina."

"Grace taking you on another trip?"

"Not exactly. This is more of a solo kind of trip, one that
I'm never coming back from. I just..." Words fail me because it
feels like we're breaking up again. "...I just want you to know
how much I love you."

The final bell of the school year goes off, and I hear it on
my end as well as hers. "Are you on campus?" she asks.

"Bleachers, but I gotta make the bank before I head over
to the funeral home, so I'm taking off."

"I got my Mom's car; meet me in the student lot."

"That's only gonna make this harder for both of us."

"You're not even gonna give me a kiss goodbye?"

She knows damn well I'm not gonna turn that down.

"That's not fair."

She finds this hilarious. "Nothing about us is fair, now meet me in five minutes."

FORTY

SEE YA LATER DOESN'T HURT AS MUCH AS GOODBYE

My mouth goes dry as we pull into the parking lot of the funeral home.

I knew it wouldn't be as simple as kissing her goodbye and heading on my way, and honestly, I didn't want it to be. But we talked, which turned into laughs, that ended with her giving me a ride to the bank, and now we're outside the mortuary because she refused to let me deal with this on my own.

Up until this moment, I didn't believe Momma was really gone, but seeing a hearse parked under the shade near the front door crushes any fantasy I had of thinking this was all a really bad joke. Christina held my hand the whole way over, and if you left out the destination it didn't feel like anything had changed between us.

"Are you prepared for this?" she asks. Being the product of a single parent home gives her insight into what I'm feeling.

"Not really. But I'm the reason why she's laying in there right now, and I won't be able to live with myself if I leave without saying goodbye."

"Percy, what happened to her isn't your fault."

"She called me," I say. "That night after court she called me, over and over, but I was so angry at her that I couldn't stand to hear her voice." The doors of the funeral home are becoming blurry from my eyes welling up with tears. "She needed me at that moment, and I turned my back on her."

She lets out a sniffle and I feel worse because we were trying to end on a happier note.

"Every time I close my eyes, I see her in that tent, abandoned by everyone and having nothing to live for. And then I think about what I could've done different and it makes me feel like I killed her all over again."

She squeezes my hand. "Stop saying that, all right? You didn't kill her..." She wants so badly to shift the blame, but knows that if it's not on me, then it's going on Momma. If she can convince me otherwise without putting it on Momma she'd have my recommendation for a Nobel Peace prize for science.

"She used the money I gave her. After court, she tried to give it back but I told her it wouldn't last through the weekend." I lay my head on her shoulder and wail into her jacket, letting out everything I've been ignoring since she walked out of the record store.

Christina doesn't say anything, holding me as I sob while silently weeping herself. As the tears start to subside, she unbuckles her seatbelt. "Let's go," she says, opening the car door.

"I can't force you to go through this with me."

She's having none of it. "Since we met, you've always shown up during the moments when my life was crashing down on me. I wasn't able to the first time around, but I'm not gonna miss the chance before you leave."

* * *

THE FUNERAL DIRECTOR greets us in a weird way, but after explaining who I am, he offers his condolences and takes us to the room Momma is in. After making sure I don't need anything, he heads off to attend to other families.

The casket is placed in the back of the room, and Christina holds me up for support as we approach it. Momma is laid out nicely, dressed in a white gown with her hair trimmed to perfection. It's almost like she's sleeping, with a peace on her face that evaded her in life.

The tears start to fall again as soon as I touch her face. "I'm sorry, Momma," I whisper. "I should've been a better son."

I fall to my knees and sob, angry with myself for all the mistakes I made. Everything I hated her for seems so trivial right now because I can't make things right. If I could, I'd give up all the money in my pocket for her to sit up for a couple of minutes, just so I could see her face and know that she didn't go to heaven with any bitterness between us. What hurts even more is knowing she's been laying in this room with no visitors, as lonely in death as I left her in life. Christina holds me in her arms, whispering that it's alright to let it out.

"I've got an idea," she says. "I see a pulpit and a microphone. Why don't you give her a proper send off?"

"There's nobody here that cares about her outside of me."

"I do." She looks me dead in the eye. "Maybe I didn't know her like others did, but she raised one of the best things that ever happened to me, and for that, I love her."

"What do I even say?"

"It's just you and me here, so say what's on your heart, as if nobody is listening." She helps me off the floor and points to the microphone, making sure I go up there before taking a seat in the first row. "You ready?"

Not really, but I nod anyway. She points to her heart, and after giving her a smile, I turn my attention to the casket and start to speak."I used to be scared when you'd go off for work, but that fear was nothing compared to how I felt the morning I woke up and you weren't here anymore. The one person I could always count on was gone, and it hurts, because in spite of everything, you kept loving me until the very end."

As I speak, I feel a calmness come over me, and I swear it's Momma calming my soul so she can hear what I have to say. "You've always been there, Momma, propping me up on your shoulders, high above the hell we were living in, making sure my dreams were always within my sight. I swear I'll reach those dreams Momma, but each milestone is gonna come with pain, because all those years you taught me to guard those dreams, and now you won't be able to see them come to fruition."

Christina is smiling through her own tears, and they give me the strength to finish.

"You weren't a perfect mother, but you were perfect for me. I can't take back the things I said, but I can make you a promise. I promise to never let the bad memories overtake the good ones. If I do that, maybe you can find it in your heart to forgive me letting you go. Some people believe in reincarnation, and if that's really a thing, then I'm jealous, because there's a kid somewhere that's gonna luck his way into an awesome mother. You used to tell me that there's no such thing as goodbye, and since I'm not ready for life without you I'll roll with that, hoping that one day I'll see you again, and I swear I won't take you for granted next time. I love you."

I walk down to the casket and kiss her forehead, remembering all the times she would do the same to me. Christina slides in next to me, rubbing my back.

"That was beautiful," she says.

"Thank you for staying." I kiss her forehead as well,

because we're just friends now. "Could you just stay a little longer? I don't really wanna be alone right now."

"Don't worry about it, Christina," a familiar voice says. "I got it from here."

We both turn to find Grace, work apron in hand, followed closely by the director. If I had a million dollars, I'd bet that Grace called and said to be on the lookout for me. Either that or his customer service skills are terrible.

Christina kisses me on the cheek, whispering in my ear to text her when I get where I'm going, before the director shows her out.

Another person leaving my life before I could tell them how I felt.

* * *

GRACE and I sit in silence, watching Momma's casket as the weight of everything unspoken between us makes it impossible to start the conversation.

"How'd you know I was here?" I start.

Neither of our eyes leave the casket.

"Well, I got a notification that you withdrew everything from your savings...that was the first clue. Nice touch by the way, waiting until I was at work before making your move. Anyway, I knew you'd want to see your mother one last time, so I came over here and gave old Larry out there a picture of you and told him to call me if you showed up."

I wanna be angry, but I can only smile. "He gave it away when I got here, but it didn't register until you showed up."

"Not gonna lie, it hurt knowing that you were gonna leave without at least saying goodbye to me."

I suck my teeth at this. "Now you know how I felt to find

out you were dating my boss. Not so fun when the runner has the gun, is it?'

She frowns. "It's a rabbit. Not so fun when the rabbit has the gun. Jesus, Eric really rubbed off on you."

Someone in another room lets out a shriek, the agony all too familiar to me because it's the same one I had the first time I saw Momma in her casket. Knowing that someone you love has passed on hurts, but you don't believe it until you see it yourself.

Grace rises from her seat and walks over to Momma's casket, dwelling over her for a second before placing her work apron inside of it. "How are you dealing with it?"

"It hurts...but I guess it's supposed to because I'm the one that killed her."

Grace doesn't move when I say this, instead she holds Momma's hand one last time before sitting next to me again. "She came to see me," she says. "One night, a couple of days after court, she came into the diner during a slow period and asked if we could talk. I assumed she meant you, but she was adamant about honoring your request of her to stay away."

"I'll always regret that."

"I'm not so sure about that," she replies, with an air of authority. "We sat down for two hours and talked about you, and I sensed that she had something to get off her chest, but I didn't know what it was. I had wondered why you reacted the way you did when you found out about Randy and I, but after she told me about the things you'd seen growing up it all made sense. You were everything to her, Percy."

And here come the tears. "I wish she'd shown me that while she was here."

"She did, you just didn't know it." She pulls a familiar looking pink envelope from her pocket. It's from the shelter we used to stay at, given to residents that needed to send outgoing mail. "She told me that she was willing to give up parental rights on two conditions. I had to promise that I wouldn't let anything happen to you, and whenever she got herself together she wanted to know that she could be a part of your life again." She hands me the envelope. "She said I'd know when to give this to you, and now seems as good a time as any."

I open the envelope and notice Momma's handwriting immediately, admiring the neatness of it like I always did. I look at the casket again, shaken to know I'm reading a letter from her while her body lies in front of me. But I get over it and read it anyway.

Percy,

I know the value of my words are at an all-time low, so I'll keep this short.

If you're reading this, then you know what I've done. I'll never know what I did to deserve a son like you, which is why giving you up is so hard for me. You are the flower that bloomed in the midst of the darkness, and seeing you on your prom night helped me understand how selfish I was being.

My greatest gift to the world is you, so I'm letting go and watching you fly high without the baggage I've put on you your whole life. I'll never be far away, and if you need me, just wrap yourself in a hug like I taught you when you were younger, and I promise I'll be there. It's time for me to put actions to my words, so consider what's in this envelope as a deposit. I don't know when I'll be back, but I promise that I'm never far away. I'll always love you more.

Mom

As I close the letter I notice the 'deposit' she alluded to. Tucked into the envelope are four crisp hundred dollar bills.

"She was trying to fix her life, Percy," Grace says. "It's not on you, so there's no need for you to carry that kind of grief."

The words bring me peace, but I have a bit more cleansing to do. "I'm sorry I ruined your relationship with Randy."

"You didn't, but I should've been honest with you upfront."

I walk up to the casket for the final time, looking down at the woman that I feel I just met for the first time. I smile at her, because in my heart I know that we're alright with one another. "If you're gonna take me to the county building, tell me so I can split now."

Grace joins me at the casket, looking as confused as a Klansman at a Wu-Tang concert. 'What are you talking about?"

"I broke rule number one, right? I stole from you at the bank earlier today." I pull out the bank envelope from earlier, but she won't accept it.

"That was your money," she replies. "Look at me." Our eyes meet. "I don't care about a judge or a social worker. You are my son, Perseverance, and you always will be." She plants a kiss on my forehead, and after promising Momma that she'll hold up her end, grabs my backpack and starts walking out.

"I'm not calling him, Dad," I say as I follow her out.

"Wouldn't expect you to, that's my job."

"Awkward. And if he's gonna be around all the time, he can help with the damn dishes."

"Language, Percy."

"Sorry, but my point is still valid."

At the door I look back one more time, blowing her one more kiss before following Grace to the car.

FORTY-ONE

RENEWAL NOTICE

Grace stops the car in front of Christina's house and throws it in park.

"What are you doing?" I ask.

She rolls her eyes at me. "Like you weren't gonna scurry your scrawny ass over here first thing in the morning."

A very valid point. "I thought you'd wanna hang out since things have been so weird between us."

She throws her hands up in frustration. "What's the point of having a girl love you if you're just gonna curl up with your mother on a Friday night?" I eye her closely and she breaks. "All right, Randy invited me to this Halal place that just opened up in Center City."

"You're just relishing having someone other than me fawn over you."

She laughs at this. "Hey, Momma's gotta have a life, too." She unlocks the door from her side. "Have fun, be safe, and don't do anything that I wouldn't do. I love you."

She pulls away once I'm on the porch, and my heart is pounding furiously as I knock on the door. I can hear her mom's accent as she gets closer to the door. It swings open and

I'm teased immediately by the smell of her cooking. She smiles at me like she always does, giving me a hug and telling me that dinner is waiting for us whenever we come down. Some things never change.

I quietly open the door to her room and find her laying in the shirt we bought at the concert, headphones on and oblivious to my presence. She jumps when I sit down on the bed.

"Oh my God, bab...I mean Percy, you scared me."

I shrug my shoulders and her face turns to one of panic.

"Did you miss your train? Let me get dressed and I can give you a ride."

"No, the trains are running fine." She looks puzzled, so I decide to have a little fun. "I was just wondering...what you thought of the girlfriend package?"

Her face lights up, but she quickly settles down into a more serious tone. "You know, I thought it was a solid bargain with plenty of perks. I felt like it expired a bit too quick for my enjoyment, but overall, I'd give it five stars."

"So, you're saying you'd do it again?"

"I mean, if it lasted longer, I'd be down, but my salesman is on his way out of—"

"How about forever?"

The business facade fades into the smile that I get to spend everyday with this summer. Without a word, she walks over to her stereo and loads a CD into the disc changer, fumbling around for the right button before she hits play. The bass line of Starlight starts to play, and by the time the piano kicks in, the lights are off as we navigate each other in the darkness. She never gave me an answer, but I know we're in agreement on the package of her choice.

We can work out the details later.

A MESSAGE FROM THE AUTHOR

If you enjoyed this book, it would make a huge difference if you leave a review for me on Amazon and Goodreads. Being an independent author means reviews are a vital part of getting our work out to the world. Also, if you want to drop me a line about the book, I'm always more than happy to chat with readers.

On top of that, half of every copy of this book that is sold will be going to Camp To Belong River Valley. It's a 100% volunteer organization that hosts events for siblings separated by foster care. You can learn more about their cause at www.ctbrivervalley.org

ACKNOWLEDGMENTS

Just over a year ago, I stumbled upon a book called 'The Idyllic Chaos of My So-Called Life" by Amy Noelle Smith. It's a great book that I recommend to anyone, but I'd be a jerk to not mention how that book helped me find my voice to write this story.

Outside of that, the list of people I have to thanks vast. To Matthew Hanover, thank you for always helping make sure my brand is on point, doing so out of the kindness of your heart. Lord knows what my stuff would be like without your help and friendship.

Lauren H. Mae, put simply, this book doesn't get finished without you. Knowing that we had a schedule kept me accountable, and it was so much fun getting to know you better during our critiquing process.

To Jennifer Kitchens, Kelly Coppola, Leighann Hart, Laura Baird, and Kelly Maurica, you guys read every word as it was being written, taking the time to talk me off the ledge and keep me going when I'd get frustrated. I can't thank you two enough.

Thank you to Kaitlyn Keller and Jennifer Hellenschmidt for helping me polish everything and giving wonderful input.

Maryann Tippett, thank you for volunteering to make sure everything looked smooth before proceeding to publishing.

To the beta readers: Andie Hartz, Sarah Neofield, Ian Shane, Ashlyne, Allison Coleman, Nicole Bates, Chris Brosseau, and Nikki Lamers, thank you for taking time out of your lives to read this book early.

To Tamara Wyandot and Deidre Evans, you were the best social workers I could've asked for growing up. Thank you for refusing to let me give up and become another statistic.

And finally, to anybody thats ever been in foster care, this book is for you. While our stories and circumstances are different, the feeling of not fitting in and searching for a place to call home is universal.

ABOUT THE AUTHOR

Wesley Parker has enjoyed reading his entire life. When not writing he can either be found making a mixtape, engaging his fandom of Philadelphia sports, or hanging with his wife and three children.

Visit his website at weswritesforfun.com. He can also be reached on Instagram @weswritesforfun and on Twitter @weswritesforfun.

.

Printed in Great Britain
by Amazon